THE ASSOCIATE

KANSAS CITY LEGAL THRILLER #6

RACHEL SINCLAIR

ONE

HARPER

Erik Gregorian was currently my client. Against my will, of course. It turned out that Sargis Gregorian, Erik's father, was not as good as his word. Who knew that a gangster and a thug would be somebody who wasn't a man of honor? I had to laugh a little when I asked myself that question. Of course Sargis would go back on his word. His son was in trouble. He also was a cheapskate because he apparently didn't want to pay for an attorney to represent the kid. No, he wanted his legal representation for free. Since I was intimidated by his threats to my girls, I would do what he asked. I wouldn't try to cross him. I might never be rid of him. I knew that for a fact. I might have stepped into a mess of quicksand, and I couldn't get out of it.

"Erik is coming in," Pearl informed me. "At 2 PM."

I sighed. My little interlude in Los Angeles somewhat helped me in that I finally got a break and got my alcoholism under control. Hopefully for good. I came home and found an AA sponsor. Her name was Katie Wright, and she had been on the wagon for 20 years. She talked me off the ledge more than once in the past few weeks, and I was finally working through my 12 Steps.

So, I was in a better place, mentally, than I was before I went out to LA. I was more relaxed because I finally had an associate, Damien Harrington, helping me out. Liam McNeil, the associate I hired before I went to Los Angeles, returned to his large firm. That was my fault, of course – I threw him into the deep end and didn't give him a life raft. Since he worked for a large firm, he knew very little about the nuts and bolts of practicing law. He thought he wanted to get right in the courtroom but had little stomach for the clients he had to deal with. I thought Liam was the right person, but if he wanted to stay in his ivory tower and not get his hands dirty, he wasn't the right person for my firm.

Damien, on the other hand, was perfect for what I needed. He had experience in criminal defense because he had worked for the Public Defender's Office. He was used to trying cases. I was lucky he was willing to become an associate instead of a partner, although he and I had discussed the possibility that he would become my partner in the future. I wanted to make sure he had what it took before I made him a full partner.

So far, he was doing stellar. He was bringing in cases. I told him he could eat what he killed, meaning the cases he brought were his. He could work them, and he could keep the fees brought in. In addition to those cases he brought in, I had him help me out with my cases. So, I had somebody who could cover for me in court when needed, and I had somebody who could second-chair me in trials. In short, I had somebody who could back me up when I really needed it.

I was much more relaxed because of Damien, and I was also more relaxed because I finally hired an investigator. I had one before, but I have been doing my own investigation for the past few years. That put additional pressure on me and it seemed there needed to be more hours in the day. But Damien convinced me I needed somebody to do the shoe-leather work, and he and I worked together to find Tom Garrett. Garrett was an ex-con who became a private investigator once he got out of the joint. He was very good at what he did because he was a part of the criminal underground, so he knew many players in that world. He could bring me information because his buddies from the streets knew he was working for a criminal defense attorney and they were eager to help their friends.

Damien would help me with Erik's case, too, as would Garrett. It would have to be all hands on deck to figure out exactly how to win the case for this kid. He was accused of killing a journalist. Her name was Shelly McMason, and she was working in the field, covering the kidnapping of a young girl sold into white slavery. Shelly was a brave reporter, not afraid to get her hands dirty, meaning she befriended many of Erik's gang members. The gang was a subset of the Armenian mafia, which controlled them from the headquarters in Los Angeles. Erik was the leader of that particular gang, so it was up to him to control his turf. As such, he decided Shelly was dangerous because she was getting too close to his operations. She threatened to expose him and his men, so he decided Shelly had to go.

This was a problem because, as Sargis found, the police tend to turn a blind eye when hits were turned onto thugs. Sargis had apparently killed many members of different gangs infringing on Sargis' turf. Since the people he killed were other criminals, he never got into trouble for these hits. The "victims" in these cases were vermin the cops wanted off the streets anyhow, so it was safe to say the cops were happy to be rid of these men.

It was the same in Kansas City. As Sargis explained, Erik ran his turf as a general might run his troops. He took care of threats swiftly and violently. Yet, he had never been charged with any of these murders. But Shelly was a different thing. She was a pretty young girl, only 23, a graduate of the University of Missouri's journalism school. She was a Delta Gamma alumnus, one of the best sorority houses at MU, and she had ambitions to work for a national presidential campaign. Her family was wealthy and considered to be old money. They owned a mansion in the Mission Hills area, where many old money people lived.

In short, Shelly was the kind of girl people cared about. She was the kind of girl whose murder would be a national story in ordinary times. She was the girl who might get an entire Dateline episode devoted to her killing. She wasn't just some low-profile victim who would get a small story in the *Kansas City Star* and nothing else.

The fact she was the victim in this case was a problem. Not just because she was a pretty young girl with a good family but also because she was a journalist. She was murdered doing her job, and because she was one of the press, the press took her killing very personally.

The upshot was I was stuck representing Erik, knowing he was good for the murder, with the spotlight of the media glare trained upon me. And I wasn't allowed to plead him out. Sargis made that extremely clear. I would have to try this guy's case and have to find a way to win it. As impossible as that seemed.

Damien came into my office and sat down across from me. Damien was my age, 35, and I knew little about his personal background. He kept to himself about those issues. I knew he was married, although I didn't know how happily. I had heard him on the phone several times, talking in hushed tones, as if he didn't want anyone to hear what he was saying. I noticed he seemed slightly agitated and distracted after he got off the phone during those times. I didn't pry, however. I didn't know him well enough to ask about what was happening. It wasn't my business.

I also understood that he had two children – a son, Nathaniel, and a daughter, Amelia. He talked about them and had pictures of them in his office. Nathaniel looked a lot like Damien – dark curly hair cut short on the sides and slightly longer on top, green eyes, olive skin, lean. He was 8. His sister, Amelia, age 6, was the opposite of Nathaniel and Damien – she was small, blonde and pale. She had the same blue eyes as her brother and father, however. I could see she was a Harrington by looking at her eyes. Other than that, however, I would have never guessed she was kin to Damien.

"So," Damien said. "You got that kid coming in, huh? The Armenian thug?"

"I do," I said. "The Armenian thug. I have no idea how I'm

supposed to win this case. But I have to. Of course, I always give my clients my all, but on this one, I'll have to give him even more than usual. If I don't..." I sliced my hand across my neck. "Seriously, that Sargis guy scares the shit out of me. He's so strange. You meet him and you almost feel like you should hear classical music piping in through his walls. You can imagine him going to the opera and appreciating every note. You can see him reading Dostoyevsky and Proust in his spare time. He probably plays chess with his men. You get the idea. Yet, he's a thug, as sure as his son is. He personally killed people when he was coming up through the ranks, and even now, he personally kills people. Mostly he has his henchmen do it, but occasionally carries out the murders himself. I still have a hard time trying to square the outward image with the monster within."

Damien shook his head. "I don't know how you got roped into this bullshit, Harper. How do you get stuck with representing a guy for free? And forced into finding a way to win the case or else your girls will end up kidnapped?" He crossed his arms in front of him. "Personally, I think you should call his bluff. You can't give in to terrorists like that. That's common knowledge. You give in to terrorists and blackmail and it just never ends. Before you know it, you're representing the entire Gregorian clan and not earning a dime. That's not fair to you. You got a firm to run here." He smiled. "And now you got an associate to pay too. Don't forget that."

"It's okay," I said. "I mean, as far as the firm balance goes, I'm pretty flush. I've had some major cases lately. I'm not too worried about the money thing."

"You will be once this jackass starts monopolizing your time with his freebie cases. I'm telling you, this Erik case is only the beginning. You let Sargis get away with this and you open the door to being completely manipulated. Lucky for you I just brought in a wrongful death case that will give your bottom line a huge boost." He nodded his head. "It's a good one, too. I'm really lucky I found it."

"Tell me about it," I said. "And I'm assuming you're going to share it?"

"Of course I'll share it. I can't work it on my own. But it's a case I found yesterday afternoon while visiting my daughter Amelia in the hospital." He looked sad all of a sudden. "So, yeah, I was visiting Amelia in the hospital when I got to talking with this woman. She told me her son was in surgery. Amelia was also in surgery and other people weren't in the waiting room, so we talked and bonded."

I wanted to ask him where his wife was while his daughter was in surgery but didn't want to pry. "Go on."

"Her son was in the middle of a routine hernia surgery. She didn't seem all that concerned about it. It was in the oncology ward, though, where her son was having his surgery, so I figured the hernia probably wasn't all that was going on with her son. And it wasn't. He was also suffering from leukemia. But the mom, her name is Betsy Ward, said that her son, Austin was his name, was in remission. The hernia was being repaired by her kid's usual cancer doctors because the doctors thought the hernia might have resulted from an earlier surgery the doctors did on Austin, a bone-marrow transplant."

I wrote down what he was saying and wrote a question mark by my notes. I would have to come back to the questions I had for Damien. "So, Austin, the son, was involved in routine hernia surgery, and what happened?"

"Well, as I sat there, the doctor came out and talked to Betsy. I could tell by the way the doctor talked to her that it wasn't good news. Then Betsy started to cry and wail and she collapsed on the seat. The doctor didn't even try to put his arm around her. He just walked out of the room. So, I went over to her. She told me the doctor had just come out to tell her her son was dead. He died on the operating table." He shook his head. "The kid died during a hernia surgery. That kind of thing shouldn't happen. So, I got the mom's permission to get the kid's medical records, and I had an independent doctor review them. According to that other doctor, Austin apparently died because he was given Propofol in a high dose. Plus, according to this other doctor, Dr. Peter Wagner, Austin wasn't in remission at the time he had that hernia surgery. In fact, it looked like Austin's leukemia had advanced to the point where he was near death at the time he had his surgery."

"What's wrong with Propofol?" I asked Damien. "That drug has been commonly used in general anesthesia for quite some time."

"Nothing is wrong with Propofol *per se*," Damien said. "Except Austin was allergic to the drug. They used Propofol in his earlier surgery for the bone marrow transplant and he had an allergic reaction to the drug. They almost lost him during that surgery, and it was determined that Austin was allergic to Propofol. Yet the anesthesiologist used it on him again. That makes this whole thing a pretty open-and-shut case if you ask me."

I shook my head. "Yeah, but it's kinda a dog of a case. After all, according to Dr. Wagner, Austin was not long for this world no matter what happened in that surgery. That would mean the damages would be extremely limited." The way actual damages are calculated in wrongful death cases depends heavily upon what the lifetime earnings of the dead person would have been throughout an average life. Economists and actuaries are employed in the courtroom to testify about the earnings potential of the person in question. That was a complicated formula as it was – it was dependent upon the person's age, education, profession and income at the time of death. It sounded like Austin not only didn't have much income if he was a minor, but he also didn't have much potential income if he was dying.

"It's not that much of a dog case," Damien protested. "Austin might have only been 18, but he had been accepted at Harvard and MIT and was a mathematical genius. He was carrying a 4.4 GPA at Pembroke Hill, which, as you probably know, is the most exclusive private school in the Kansas City area. He had a lot of potential. His vision in life was to work for NASA. He had the grades and the drive to do it. Not only that, but his mother had enrolled him in a clinical trial that hopefully would have helped him. His bone marrow transplant apparently didn't put him in remission, but this clinical trial sounded good. If we can convince the jury there was a chance Austin could have lived and gone on to fulfill his potential, then there's a chance this case might be a good one."

I sighed. I knew what he was saying, but I hated wrongful death cases. Especially wrongful death cases that involved medical malpractice. They were expensive to try – when you get all your experts lined up and paid, you typically pay $100,000 out of your pocket. That meant you better win the case. It wasn't like a criminal case where the expenses were nominal – you might have to get expert witnesses involved. You often had to do depositions, which cost some money. Still, you could try a criminal case with almost no money out of pocket if you do all the investigation yourself.

But medical malpractice cases were a different beast. You had to get actuaries, economists, and a team of doctors to testify. I tried to stay away from the usual suspect doctors – the hired guns that have built a cottage industry out of testifying for every medical malpractice case that comes along. They were way too easy for the other side to pick off and show the jury how biased they were. That meant I had to find other doctors to testify, doctors who aren't hired guns for anyone and everyone with a medical malpractice case. These doctors typically charged even more than the hired guns because they were going out of their way to give testimony.

"Okay," I said. "I won't talk you out of your wrongful death case. If you believe in it, then, by all means, pursue it. I hope you know what you're doing on it, though. I'll help you as much as possible, but medical malpractice cases aren't my forte. I guess what I'm saying is you killed this. You can eat it. I don't really want to get too much involved."

He raised an eyebrow. "Your loss," he said.

"In the meantime," I said, "you'll have to have actual income. Contingency cases like medical malpractice won't pay off at least until you settle or it goes to trial, and if it goes to trial, it'll be nothing but a money sink for up to a year. The attorneys for the hospital will bury you with discovery requests, ask you to pay their attorney's fees if they win and do everything they can think of to make you quit this case. The only exception to that rule is if, somehow, someway, you find something that makes this case stand out. You find something that makes it likely a jury will hand the hospital its ass in trial. Then you can settle. But if this case is marginal, and the hospital knows it, then good luck."

"Giving the kid a drug he was allergic to – that's not good enough to make them settle?"

"No. Not if the kid would probably die anyway. I admit that it helps that he was so bright and had been accepted to Harvard and MIT. That he had ambitions to work for NASA. That shows his earning potential. But we have to understand that he wasn't in remission for his leukemia and would likely die before he could fulfill his potential. You find a way around that and we have a chance. But, from the facts, this case seems marginal enough that the hospital will turn the big guns on you to make you quit. It's not like you have one of the big medical malpractice names in the city."

Some attorneys in the city tried lots of personal injury and medical malpractice cases and won more cases than they lost. If Damien had a name like Cullan and Cullan, who were licensed physicians and medical malpractice attorneys, or Fowler and Pickett, a large firm that tried lots of these cases, the hospital would probably back down. But Damien Harrington was a nobody. He just got the case because he was in the waiting room with Austin's mother.

Damien shrugged. "Okay. Well, I guess if you're not in on this case, you're not in. I'll need a partner to help me out, though. I'll see if I can't find an attorney in town interested in trying this case with me." He looked disappointed, and I felt guilty.

"I'll think about it," I said. "Get some more discovery done on this case, find out what the weak spots will be, and I'll think about getting in on this case with you. But I can't help but think the two of us on this case will be blind leading the blind. I have little experience with medical malpractice, and you've been working with the Public Defender's Office since you left school. You have trial work, but it's all been criminal trial work. You have a steep learning curve on this case, and the hospital attorneys will eat you alive if they know you're a newbie."

"Think about it," Damien said. "That's all I can really ask. In the meantime, what do we know about Erik Gregorian's case?"

"I looked at the file the prosecutor gave me. According to the Statement of Information, Erik knew Shelly McMason personally. Shelly had successfully infiltrated Erik's organization. She had essentially become one of them. She was working as an undercover journalist for the *Kansas City Star* and was getting ready to publish a five-part story on Erik's organization and the practice of white slavery in the Kansas City area. Shelly died in a car accident but it turned out her brake lines were cut. Erik definitely had motive to kill Shelly. He also had the means and the opportunity, as he was friendly with her and often rode with her in her car several times. Obviously, the best way to try this case would be a SODDI defense – show somebody else could have killed her. Somebody else had motive to kill her. I will have to find out who that somebody else might be."

"I don't get it," Damien said. "Why does the prosecutor's office have such a hard-on for Erik? Yeah, he was the head of the organization Shelly would report on. That doesn't mean he killed her."

"Well, it doesn't exactly look good, either. Even if he got one of his men to cut her brake line, it still means Erik himself will get busted as a conspirator or as the instigator. As the leader of the local Armenian Power controlling the East Side of Kansas City, any violent end met by somebody in the Power will implicate Erik. That's the problem we'll have with this case. We have to show the jury that the person who killed Shelly wasn't involved in the Armenian Power at all. That will be tricky."

"Tricky but not impossible," Damien said. "We'll just get Tom Garrett to do a thorough background investigation on Shelly, including all the other people she was investigating, and show it could be any number of people who might have wanted her dead. If she was an undercover journalist, it stands to reason she probably pissed off many people along the way. Seriously, we have to find a way to throw the jury off. Even if Erik did it. Which he probably did."

"I know. That's the problem. I think Erik is good for this case all day long. I hate I have to get stuck with trying it. I really hate I could be in danger if I can't win this case. So will my girls. This Sargis guy has way too much power. I wish I never met him."

"That's what happens when you get tied up with these mafia types. You can't just quit them. If you let him, he will intimidate you for the rest of your career. So don't let him. Hire a bodyguard and stand up to him. Show him you can't be pushed around."

I sighed. "Easier said than done."

Indeed.

TWO

DAMIEN

I was grateful for the chance to join Harper's firm. After the fucked-up life I had before I went to college and law school, I pretty much have woken up every day grateful. Not that any of what happened was my fault. Well, that's not exactly true – it was my fault and it wasn't. It wasn't my fault I was born into a wretched situation – my mom never actually knew my dad. I think he was one of her johns. Why she wasn't using birth control during her street-walker days, I'll never know. Or maybe she was, but it didn't take. Whatever. All I knew was my mom was a prostitute and then had me. I didn't exactly fit into her plans. To say the least. She couldn't work the streets anymore because she had a squalling infant in her trailer home, so she got on welfare and depended upon a variety of men to support us.

One of those men, Steven Harrington, actually stuck around for long enough that my mother gave me his last name. She married him and he adopted me. But he was an abusive bastard. He beat on my mother and me on the regular, and it got so bad I ended up running away. I ended up in a home for wayward boys, just like my idol, Steve McQueen. The Ozanam school was the place for troubled kids like me. It provided therapy and schooling and got me out of the house. It also introduced me to the kids who became my lifelong friends until all of us ended up in prison.

Actually, I didn't belong in prison. I truly didn't. It was guilt by association at its finest. The others – Tommy Arcola, Nick Savante, Jack O'Brien and his brother Connor – actually belonged in prison. They were all involved in a robbery that went very wrong. Connor - at 16, he was the youngest out of the bunch – got trigger-happy with an armed security guard who happened to be at that liquor store getting cigarettes. The security guard pulled his gun on Connor, who panicked and shot him in the leg. That wasn't a kill shot, and Connor didn't know much about firearms. He didn't mean to kill the guy, of course – if he meant to kill him, he would have shot him in the head or chest. And the security guard should have just been injured, but it was Connor's luck that the guard, whose name was Emilio Garza, contracted the MRSA virus while he was in the hospital and died a month later from his infection.

What that meant was that all four of the boys, who were my best friends from Ozanam, were put on trial for felony murder. Then, somehow, I got roped into the whole mess. I wasn't anywhere near that liquor store, and the boys told their attorneys that as well. Yet, I was put into a lineup, and an eyewitness fingered me as the one driving the getaway car. Tommy was actually the one driving that getaway car. He does somewhat look like me – we both have dark curly hair, and, at the time, we both were wearing our hair long. To our shoulders.

The five of us were tried separately, and we all were convicted for the murder of Emilio Garza. Connor was still only 16 when we were put on trial, but was tried as an adult because of the nature of the crime. I was only 18, and so were Nick, Tommy and Jack. We were lucky we didn't get the death penalty. The jury opted for life in prison with the chance of parole for all of us, mainly because of our age and the fact that all of us came from really messed-up homes. We

all were in the same school for troubled kids, and all of us had basically the same stories to tell the jury - chaotic and abusive parents,
drug abuse and alcoholism in the home, etc. The same basic story that
a lot of kids can tell. The same basic story that all of the kids in our
school could tell. Most of them came from homes that never gave
them a chance to have a normal life.

So, the upshot was I was 18 and in prison for a murder I had
nothing to do with. For that matter, Tommy, Nick and Jack didn't
really have anything to do with that murder, either. Especially
Tommy – all he did was drive the getaway car. I personally have
always thought that what happened was unfair to all of us. Yes,
Connor was young and probably shouldn't have been given a gun to
start with, but he never meant to kill Emilio. And, really, in a
different situation, Connor could've claimed self-defense. After all,
Emilio was the first person to draw his weapon and he pointed it right
at Connor. It was basically kill or be killed in that situation. But the
felony murder rule is very explicit – any killing done in the commis-
sion of a felony is murder. Period, end of story. Even if Connor would
have gotten really stupid and accidentally shot one of the guys
involved in the hold-up, the result would have been the same. Felony
murder. And all the guys involved in the holdup would get the exact
same charge, as they all were acting in concert. That was how it
worked.

But, with me...that was a different thing altogether. I had done
some jacked-up shit in my youth – I used to steal cars and, more than
once, I helped the guys burglarize businesses after they closed. I
never got caught for those things except one of the cars I stole. That
theft was what landed me in Ozanam to begin with. That and the
fact my mother decided she couldn't control me and told the judge in
my car theft case she was afraid of me. Whatever that meant. My
mother's testimony in my car theft case combined with the fact I stole
the car in the first place meant I would be put into a special school
where I could receive therapy for my anger issues, in addition to
getting a decent education.

I belonged in Ozanam. I'll be the first to admit to that. But I didn't belong in prison.

Still, I tried to make the best of it. For five years, I made the best of it. I felt like my appellate attorney wasn't doing anything for me and I wanted a new trial. So, I went to the legal books in the prison library and studied them. I found some sample appellate briefs and some sample writs of habeas corpuses, and I worked on writing them. I only had a certain amount of time to file my appellate brief and I missed it. The notice of appeal could only be filed within 10 days of the judgment becoming final, and that judgment in my case became final when my motion for a new trial was overruled and my sentence was imposed. I missed that window of time. Or, rather, my lawyer missed that window. I then sought leave of court to file the notice of appeal late, but that was denied by the courts. I was out of luck as far as getting an appeal going. But I could file writs, and I did. I filed writ after writ, all of which were ignored by the courts.

At some point, I gave up filing writs, but, by then, I knew the law backwards and forwards. I became a jailhouse lawyer. All the other inmates came to me for legal help and help with writing their own appellate briefs and writs and other documents to try to get them out of prison. I was always very careful about timing issues, especially with the appellate briefs. I was always preparing motions for new trials and notice of appeals, and I often wrote entire appellate briefs for some of the inmates who couldn't afford an appellate attorney. Which was all of them. Some of the guys inside got lucky and got a court-appointed appellate attorney, but most of them weren't entitled to a special attorney and all of them wanted to try to get some kind of post-conviction relief. I wrote the briefs for them, they would get their chance for oral argument, and argued on their own behalf. Once in awhile, one of my "clients" would win the argument and get a new trial, and that was always a cause to celebrate.

When I was 23 years old I had given up hope I ever would see the outside of a prison cell. As unjust as it was for me to be in prison, and as angry as I was about being wrongly convicted, I had made peace by that time. I had come to understand I probably would spend the rest of my life in prison for something I didn't do, mainly because I happened to look like the guy driving the getaway car and the "eyewitness" couldn't distinguish me from Tommy and decided both of us were involved in the robbery. Tommy felt awful about the mix-up, and he apologized to me every time we met in the prison yard, but I always told him he had nothing to apologize for. All the guys swore up and down I wasn't involved, and nobody would believe them. I knew the guys weren't at fault for what happened to me – that stupid eyewitness was at fault. Not the guys. For that matter, the defense attorneys and the cops were also at fault, because they never listened to the guys when they protested I was nowhere near the crime scene.

Then, one day, I got a notice that the Innocence Project had taken up my case. As I understood it, the Innocence Project was dedicated to freeing the wrongly imprisoned. They specialized in using DNA evidence to get convictions overturned. They found out about my case when the *Kansas City Star* ran a story about my work behind bars helping other inmates get new trials and get cases overturned on appeal. I was interviewed for that article, and I emphasized I was innocent of the crime for which I was convicted. I told the reporter for the *Star* all about what happened – how my buddies were convicted for an armed robbery, how I wasn't anywhere near the scene, how I was still put into a lineup and an eyewitness identified me, and how the guys told anyone who would listen I wasn't involved in the crime.

There was a saving grace, one I never even thought about – I was never in the car used in the robbery. That was a car the guys had stolen and used specifically for the robbery. And the car was still available for DNA testing. That was one of the things the reporter had asked me – if I had ever been in that car. I told her I hadn't. I had never been to that liquor store, either – I hadn't been there before the robbery and I hadn't been there afterwards. That was the starting point for the Innocence Project. They managed to find the car used in the robbery – after we were convicted, the car was released as evidence and sold at auction. My lawyer on the Innocence Project, Chuck Riegel, tracked down that car, got a court order, and tested it for DNA. The DNA for all the guys was all over that car. Mine wasn't. They also went to the liquor store and tested the entire store for DNA. It was the same as the car – my DNA wasn't anywhere on the premises.

Chuck worked his ass off for little money and managed to get me a new trial. I was assigned a Public Defender for my new trial, and I couldn't have been more impressed by my new attorney's dedication. Her name was Colleen Sutton, and she looked like she had just walked off the boat from Ireland. Red curly hair, freckles, pale skin and big blue eyes. She was the first woman I had seen in awhile, and I thought she was the most beautiful female I had ever laid eyes on. She was a workhorse, and I found out she wasn't unusual in the Kansas City Public Defender's Office. She turned over every stone and made sure my case was adequately worked up. She tried the case and won it – the jury came back in less than an hour.

I felt ashamed I didn't have faith in the Public Defender's Office when I was a teenager. I didn't want a Public Defender for my case because I had the impression they were poor attorneys and only got a job with the PD's office because they couldn't get a better job. That they were the attorneys who graduated at the bottom of their class. That they were overworked, underpaid and would give my case short shrift.

I couldn't have been more wrong. The attorneys at that office were some of the most dedicated I had ever seen. They were passionate and intelligent and were working there because they were true believers in the Sixth Amendment – that everybody is entitled to representation, no matter what they did and no matter how little money they had. They were, in short, true believers. Many of the attorneys at the PD's office went on to become judges. Others went on to work for the federal government, defending people accused of federal crimes. Still others ended up making the big bucks for large defense firms in the KC area. But there were some who remained right where they were – representing indigent clients, making a fraction of what they could make in the private sector, all because they truly believed in what they were doing.

I fell a bit in love with Colleen, especially since she worked so hard to get my case overturned. I never pursued it, however. I was too embarrassed. She was an attorney and I was an inmate who didn't even have a college degree. I knew I was smart and, if I put my mind to it, I could also become an attorney. But I didn't have anything to offer her at that time, so, even though I thought she might also be into me, I didn't pursue her.

What I did do was go to college. My SAT scores were high enough to get into UMKC, and my Ozanam high school grades were excellent as well. I never got the chance to graduate from high school because I was convicted for that robbery before I could walk down that aisle to get my diploma. I got my GED and then went to UMKC and got my BA in Criminal Justice. Then I took my LSAT and scored in the top 2% in the country – a 172. That score, combined with my 4.0 undergraduate average, combined with my essay where I wrote about my experiences in prison and my work on behalf of other inmates, combined with letters of recommendation from my Innocence Project attorney and Colleen, got me into the University of Chicago Law School. UChicago is the fourth rated law school in the country, right below Yale, Stanford and Harvard. It's the school where Barack Obama taught Constitutional Law. I was shocked I got in and then had to figure out how to get the money together to go. I managed that with a combination of scholarships, grants and a lot of student loans.

When I got out of school, I went right to work for the Public Defender's Office in Kansas City. I never forgot the dedication and work ethic of the attorneys in that office. How hard they worked on my case, how tireless they were...I never forgot that. And Colleen was still in the office. She was married, but we became great friends. I was also married to Sarah by the time I got out of law school. She was also a student at UChicago, but was in grad school, working on her Master's Degree in Art History. We fell in love, got married my first year in law school, and quickly had our two kids – Nate and Amelia.

That was then. This is now. And things were very different.

THREE

Harper came into the office as I was sitting behind my desk. I was looking at the picture of me, Sarah and our two kids. Looking at this picture, taken of us on a float trip in the Ozarks three years before, always made me sad. It always astounded me about how pictures take a snapshot in a moment in time, and, somehow, I was always able to feel how I felt at the moment the picture was taken. This picture, like all the pictures of us as a happy family, felt like a lie to me. It wasn't a lie then. At least, I didn't think it was a lie then. But it certainly turned out to be a lie.

Harper sat down across from me. In a way, she reminded me of Colleen. Same red hair, same blue eyes, same freckles. Tall and lean like Colleen. Yet she was different. She was harder than Colleen, somehow. Like she had been around the block a time or two. Colleen, even though she represented some of the hardest criminals there are– serial killers, gang-bangers, low-level mafia guys, rapists, you name it – had a certain innocence about her. A certain sweetness. That drew me to her even more than the way she looked.

"I've given it some thought," she said. "I think I'll tentatively go in with you on your Med Mal case. I've been reviewing the file, and it does seem there might be a case there."

I smiled. I knew Harper would come around. I had great instincts for cases and knew this case was a winner. Yes, it was an uphill battle. Austin Ward was only a kid who hadn't established earnings potential just yet, and, yes, his prognosis was grim to start with. But I knew there was an X Factor with this case. There was something that felt off to me about it. It didn't strike me as just another medical malpractice case where there was a tragic mistake made in the administration of a common anesthetic. I didn't quite know what I would find once our investigator, Tom Garrett, started talking to witnesses. I just had a feeling there was something major underlying this case, right below the surface.

"I knew you would want in on this case," I said to Harper, lightly chiding her. "I think it'll be a good one. Like it's going to be the case that will keep this firm afloat for the next year or two, at the very least. I don't know why, but I just have that hunch."

Harper grinned. "I wouldn't go that far, unless we can somehow get punitives. But, I'm sorry, this case doesn't seem like a punitive damages case just yet."

Punitive damages in medical malpractice cases were rare. You pretty much had to show some kind of intentional wrongful conduct to even ask a jury to consider punitive damages. At the very least, the conduct had to be wanton and willful disregard for the safety of others. Harper was right – on the surface, this case didn't seem to warrant an award of punitive damages. There wasn't anything in the records that would show that what happened to Austin was anything but a tragic mistake. Perhaps the anesthesiologist didn't look at Austin's records thoroughly enough, or maybe there was some kind of mix-up where the anesthesiologist ordered a different drug, but ended up getting Propofol instead. I knew I would get to the bottom of exactly what happened in this case, but I doubted there was any kind of intentionality or wanton and willful disregard for Austin's safety.

In the State of Missouri, punitive damages were originally statutorily limited to $500,000 or five times the total amount of the award. However, the Supreme Court of Missouri unanimously decided that a limitations on punitive damages were deemed to be unconstitutional, because juries have the right to decide the amount of damages. Putting a cap on punitive damages takes that right out of their hands.

"Okay," Harper said. "Let's put that med mal case on the backburner for now. Erik's case is a four-alarm fire. Or, at the very least, it has the potential to get that way. I have a list of questions I need to ask him when he comes in, but why don't you take the lead on this?"

Harper was testing me, of course. I was new to her. She was feeling me out, seeing what kind of instincts I had. She handed me a list of the questions she had for Erik, and I looked at them. I wasn't necessarily going to go by them, however. I would go in any direction I felt needed to be explored, even if these questions didn't cover that particular direction. That was how I worked.

"Of course I will," I said. "But I have to warn you I tend to get pretty aggressive with my clients. Especially if I think they're lying. And, let's face it, most of them are lying right to our face. My first few trials, I took my clients' word about anything and everything. Then I get to trial and find out exactly how much they were lying to me, and that was that. I now go into just about every case assuming the worst about the clients but hoping for the best. And, for this kid, I will definitely be on my guard. He's a mafia kid, raised by a criminal and surrounded by thugs his whole life. I can assure you that lying will be his MO. I hope you don't mind my cynicism and my skepticism."

Harper smiled. "Not at all. It's refreshing, really. I've been a criminal defense attorney for 10 years, and I've tried some really messed-up cases. Yet I've always retained my rose-colored glasses. It hasn't always served me well, because you're right – most of our clients are lying. And I've had my ass handed to me on more than one occasion because I believed their stories. So, it's good you're here. You can balance out my Pollyannaish view of the world."

I didn't tell her exactly why I was so cynical. That was a story for

another day. Maybe Harper and I could share some shots at the bar
and I could tell her what kind of life I've had. Maybe she wouldn't
ever believe me when I told her all I had seen and all I had gone
through. Prison wasn't a walk in the park, of course. I made it work
for me, though, because of my crack legal abilities. When word got
around I was actually getting guys out of prison, I was revered. Guys
didn't mess with me. My brain became my best protection inside.
While other guys were running protection rackets inside and messing
with scared newcomers, I was basically sitting on a throne, protected
by some of the baddest guys in some of the roughest prison gangs.
What's more, I made sure the guys enjoyed that same protection.

I worried about Tommy, Nick, Jack and Connor constantly.
When I got sprung from prison, their protection ceased. I still kept in
touch with them, tried to visit them whenever I could and wrote
letters to them every week. Thus far, they were doing okay, but it was
only a matter of time before they would be subjected to the laws of
the jungle. That scared me.

I looked up and saw Erik was coming into the office suite. At
least, I assumed it was Erik. He was about 25, not tall and not short –
he probably stood about 5'9" – and was wearing a three-piece suit
that was slightly too big. He had a baby face – fine featured and olive
skin. Pale green eyes, dark hair worn in a buzz cut. His watch was a
Rolex and his shoes were custom made in Italy. That was one thing I
knew – men's shoes. His were extremely expensive.

Pearl came into our office. "Erik Gregorian is here," she said.
"Can I send him in?"

Harper drew a breath and her eyes got wide. I saw fear in those
eyes and I immediately wanted to calm her down. I knew why she
was afraid – she was under so much pressure to make sure this kid
walked.

I nodded my head. "Let's take this down in the conference room,
okay?"

I gathered up Erik's file and then followed Harper down the
hall to the conference room. It was a typical conference room,

nothing special – long wooden table, tall bookcases lined with every kind of treatise imaginable. I was impressed with Harper's collection of legal books, even if I never used them. I always preferred to do my legal research on-line. It was faster that way, and much, much easier.

Harper had summoned Erik and he followed both of us into the conference room.

Erik sat down and Pearl came in and poured him a glass of water. He looked out the window, which overlooked The Country Club Plaza down below. "Nice view," he said, with a smile. He sipped his water as he swiveled his chair restlessly. "So, are we going to get right down to it then?"

Harper looked at me uncertainly and I sat up straighter in my chair. I glanced down at the questions and then looked up at Erik. "Yeah," I say to him. "By the way, my name is Damien Harrington. I'm Harper's new associate and I'll be conducting this interview."

Erik shrugged his shoulders. "Go ahead. I don't really care. As long as I walk down this bullshit charge, I'm good." He looked me up and down. "You look like a street fighter. I like that." He smiled his approval.

I didn't quite know what he meant by "looking like a street fighter." I *was* a street fighter. I had been in more hand to hand combat situations than I cared to remember. But I wondered what gave me away. I had always tried to look professional – tailored suit and tie, sharp shoes, hair cut short. My hands weren't calloused. I knew, when I got out of prison, that having rough hands would give me away. Rough hands were always the sign of a guy who labored or a guy who had been on the inside. Steven Harrington, my ersatz father, had rough hands. He worked construction when he worked at all. He was what I considered to be trailer trash. Not because he worked construction – I considered that to be an honest day's work. No, to me, "trailer trash" was a state of mind. He had the mind of a victim. Whenever something went wrong, it was always somebody else's fault. I resolved to never be like him in any way, shape or form, so that was another reason why I always chose to have my hands and nails manicured.

I raised an eyebrow and looked Erik right in the eye. He stared back, two alpha males trying to establish dominance. He finally looked away and I nodded my head and looked down at my questions. "Yes, so, we'll get down to it," I said. "Now, let me get this straight. I'm just going to nutshell this whole thing to you, just to make sure I have the basic facts right, and then I'll drill down. You're the leader of the Armenian stronghold in the territory that spans from Troost on the west side, Brooklyn on the East Side, 25th Street on the South Side and 18th Street on the North Side. Is that correct? Is that the territory you control for your organization?"

"Yeah, that's the territory. See, we have this pact with the other families and organizations in the area. The Italians, the Russians, the Albanians and the Armenians. We've had a friendly arrangement where each of the organizations get to control a certain amount of real estate." He nodded. "So, yes, you have that right. That's the part of the city I control."

I nodded my head. "And the activities you are involved in, that your particular hierarchy is involved in, are white slavery, sex slavery, prostitution, drugs and cyber crime. But the emphasis is on white slavery and sex slavery. Do I have that right?"

"Yeah, that's right." Erik nodded. "We find girls, high-end girls, to sell on the open market to people living overseas. Mainly Sheiks in the Middle East, but we sometimes find girls for businessmen looking for somebody to service them long-term. And the prostitution is a very lucrative part of our business, too. We service some of the best call girls in the city to traveling businessmen. Very high quality – educated, sophisticated, beautiful, talented. They're very pre-screened."

"By pre-screened, you mean?"

"Well, we screen them for STDs, of course. Every time a girl visits one of our clients, she has to have an STD test when she gets back. We're very on top of that. But we also screen them for education level. No joke, our girls have to pass an IQ and vocabulary test, and we make sure they speak properly. If a girl opens her mouth and sounds like she has little education, she doesn't pass our screening test. Our clients demand a certain level of sophistication and discretion, and that's what we provide. Now, I'm not saying that all our girls have their PhD from Yale or anything like that, but most of them have at least a bachelor's degree, sometimes even a master's. They work for us while they're paying for their higher education, so many of them are working on their PhDs. Of course, once they actually receive their PhDs, they quit working for us. They find better jobs and age out."

"Age out." I nod my head. "What's the high end as far as age goes?"

"25, generally. Our clients like the girls to be young and nubile. No cellulite, perky breasts, fresh face. Some of our girls are a bit older, but they look much younger, and I pass them off as being in their early 20s. But, by and large, our girls are 25 and under."

I looked over at Harper and wondered what she was thinking. She was a woman over the age of 25, probably was around her mid thirties. She obviously took good care of herself – she was lean, like a runner. She ate a lot of kale salads for lunch and I never really saw her eat anything junky. Her face was fresh, hardly any wrinkles. Yet, here was this guy pretty much saying a woman her age wasn't sexually desirable to his clients. I wondered if that bothered her. Her face was impassive, so I had to figure she probably wasn't that offended, but I wondered if I was right about that.

I went back to Erik. "Let's talk about Shelly. How long was she with your organization? And how did she come to be in your organization?"

Erik looked uncomfortable. He looked out the window, and then back at me. He steepled his fingers and swiveled in his chair. "I should have known she was up to no good," he said. "I should have known. But no. The other guys in my clan told me to trust her. She was an amazing hacker. She wanted to work for us because she wanted to put her hacking skills to use. That was the story I got about her. My father even vetted her and told me I needed to hire her. So I did. I hired her. She was on our cyber team. Her role was to break into bank networks around the world and steal five cents out of every account, every month. Since she could hack into millions of bank networks and steal a nickel out of 100s of millions of accounts, it came up to be a pretty penny for us. I'll admit it, I was thrilled to have found her."

That was a new piece of information. There was nothing in the prosecutor's discovery file that indicated our vic was a computer genius. But, apparently, she was. I wondered if that was an angle for us to look at. "She was a computer whiz?"

"Yeah. She taught herself how to hack when she was 8 years old. She claimed she had been an underground hacker for various organizations around the city since she was 13. Her references checked out. What I should have done was check out her references more thoroughly though. If I did, I would have found they didn't really exist. I figured out she had several of her friends and people she worked with at the newspaper claim to be her past employers, but, in reality, she was a hobbyist and an amateur. A very talented amateur, I'll give her that, but it turned out she had never done any serious hacking for pay until she met up with us."

"So, she told you she had been a hacker for money before you, but that wasn't true?"

"Yeah, that wasn't true." He shrugged. "How was I to know? The girl was good. Spectacularly good. She had some major skills. I took her at her word she had done this professionally for years. I really should have figured that a girl like her wasn't somebody to court trouble. I should have figured out she was trying to infiltrate us. Man, all I had to do was look at her Facebook Page and I would have seen what she really was – a rich sorority girl who graduated from the best journalism school in the nation and was working for *The Star*. It was all on her Facebook page for the world to see. Somehow, I didn't even think to look at it, and neither did anybody else in my clan. That was our mistake, and it's a mistake I'll never make again."

I wrote that down and circled it. Not looking at her Facebook page seemed like a rookie mistake, to say the very least. I immediately put a question mark by that and wrote down the words *is he already lying?*

"So," I said. "You're trying to tell me your organization doesn't do even a cursory background check on your new hires? It would seem you didn't do your due diligence, to say the very least."

I noticed that Erik's left cheek started to tic slightly when I called him out. "No, that's not right. We always do a thorough background check on anybody who comes to work for us, but this one was different. She came so highly recommended I figured she was clean."

"Highly recommended? What kind of recommendation would be so trusted you wouldn't bother to do even the slightest amount of due diligence on Shelly?"

"My father sent her to us." He crossed his arms in front of him. "Is that a high enough recommendation for you?"

FOUR

I cocked my head, wondering exactly what kind of game was being run here. Sargis Gregorian, the man I had never met, but Harper assured me was intimidatingly intelligent, apparently set his own son up. Unless one would believe that Sargis also didn't do his due diligence with this girl, but that beggared belief. From what Harper told me, the man was meticulous.

"Your father sent her to you," I said, hoping my voice didn't belie my disbelief. "Are you telling me your father didn't know what Shelly was either? That your father didn't do his due diligence on her? Is that what you want me to believe?" I shook my head and glared at him. Either this rat wasn't being truthful or Sargis Gregorian was up to no good. That pissed me off when I thought about it. Here Sargis was, apparently setting his own son up for a murder and then pressing Harper into getting him out of it. For free. What kind of a man would do that?

A gangster. A thug. A man who had no morals, no scruples and no sense of family pride. That surprised me in a way. I had done my share of research on criminal families. I had known quite a few guys who were a part of these families. I met them in my prison stint.

What I got from them was that there was quite a bit of familial loyalty that was the glue that held everything together. They spoke of their fathers, sisters and brothers fondly. They usually got letters from their family and visits from their parents and siblings. From my talks with some of these guys, I understood that loyalty was the only way their organizations could function. The family members who weren't loyal were usually the first ones on the chopping block, and they didn't always go down pretty.

Yet here was a father who apparently was setting his own son up. Why would he do something like that? I looked over at Harper, quietly sitting next to me, absorbing everything this kid had to say and writing down notes. She shook her head and looked perplexed, and I knew she and I would have to have some talks about all of this later.

"Yes, my father sent her to me." Then he shook his head. "No, that's not exactly how it all went down. Actually, she came to us and asked for a job and I did my background check and ran it through my father. He called back to tell me she was perfectly clean and I should hire her. So, I didn't pursue her background any further. That was my mistake, I'll admit. I should have kept on doing my background check, but if my father tells me she's clean, then she's clean."

I stood up. "Get your story straight," I said. "Now, did your father send her to you or didn't he? And if he didn't, then how did she come to know about your organization in the first place? Did you ever ask her that?"

He put his hands out in front of him. "Easy, easy." He swiveled in his chair some more and ran his hands through his short hair. "I told you, she came to us, I called my father, and he told me she was clean. I can't be any clearer than that."

"Then how did she come to your organization? To your clan? She didn't just waltz in off the street, did she? You didn't do a job posting on Zip Recruiter, did you?" I had to smile at that one. I imagined what kind of job posting Erik would post on that website – *computer hacker needed. Must be able to illegally tap into worldwide bank networks. Relevant experience would include hacking into govern-*

mental databases, planting malicious code on user networks throughout the globe, and stealing. Must be ethically blind and not mind having to serve 10 years to life if caught. Apply within.

He nodded his head. "Vardan Dorian, one of my closest friends in our clan, referred her to us. He told me she was a friend of a friend and was interested in working with us. That was another reason why I didn't do my due diligence on her background. Vardan is like a brother to me. Needless to say, when I found out what she was and who she was really working for, I cut Vardan completely out." He shook his head. "I had to take care of him. I didn't want to do it. That was the last thing I wanted to do. I might as well have killed my own brother, but it had to be done. I figured Vardan was a complete rat."

I looked over at Harper, who was chewing on her pen and making notes. "So, let me get this straight. A close friend of yours brought Shelly into the organization and your own father vouched for her. That's what you're telling me?"

"Yes. That's what I'm telling you."

"Well, it looks like you trusted the word of not one rat, but two. One of the rats being your own father. What do you have to say about that?"

He shrugged. "What am I supposed to say about that? I trusted them and they both screwed me over. Vardan I took care of. My father, of course, I haven't done anything about. Listen, I have this job just because my father put me in this position. That's the only reason why. Now, I don't know why my own father was so careless as to vouch for Shelly. I try not to think about that particular angle."

"It's my job to think about that angle," I said. "To think about who might have set you up and why. Now, I'm not going to ask you if you actually killed Shelly or if you were behind it. I don't want to know the answer to that question. If I know the answer to that question, and you tell me you did it, then that limits my trial strategy. Basically, it means you cannot testify on your own behalf. So please don't tell me if you killed her or not. I have to look at your circle and figure out if I can pin the murder on anybody else. That's my job. Your job is to tell me the absolute truth. The absolute truth up to the point where you tell me you killed her, because, I reiterate, I don't want to know that."

Erik sat back in his chair and stared at me. He had a bit of an eerie look about him. His eyes were light, a pale color I rarely saw on anybody. The sun was shining through the window, so his eyes were illuminated by the rays dancing on his face. The way he was carefully studying me unnerved me in a way that hardened criminals I knew inside didn't. With those criminals, with most of them anyhow, what you saw was what you got. There were the guys with the personality disorders who had delusions of grandeur. They would say things like "I was a bassist with Nirvana in the early days," or "I'm the love child of Elvis Presley and Marilyn Monroe" – which usually was impossible, because this would come out of the mouth of a guy who wasn't 30 years old and Marilyn has been dead since 1962. I usually was friends with them just because they were so entertaining. Then there were many, many guys who literally thought they were Jesus. I took them all with a grain of salt. Then there were the violent and delusional guys – I tried to steer clear of them. If they were in the throes of their violent delusions, they could cut you down because they thought you stole a cheese sandwich from them. Then there were the garden-variety thugs. Those were the guys I bonded with, because they were usually the ones who had messed-up family lives like mine.

But Erik, the way that he was looking at me, struck me as a totally different kind of criminal. He struck me as a psychopath. I had known my share of those guys as well and they were the scariest criminals of them all. The psychopath had no conscience, no remorse, and no true feelings. At his core is nothing but blackness. They were always the ones I knew I had to give a wide berth to and not get sucked in, because it was easy to get sucked in by them. That was what made them so scary – they had a casual kind of charm that made you think they were good dudes. They knew how to play a good dude quite well. But, underneath it all, underneath their casual glibness, their obvious intelligence and their charm, lay a monster. A monster who would get you into his good graces, and, before you knew it, you were caught up in his web. He would be the one who would not only kill a man in prison just because he looked at him wrong, but would then turn around and convincingly blame it on somebody else.

I straightened my shoulders, trying to get back on track, but the way Erik was studying me still rankled. "Who do you want me to give you?" Erik finally asked. "Who do you want to focus on for this murder? I know you have to come up with some kind of plausible alternative and I can give you some names. Mainly they're people I want out of the way, and this would be a good way to kill two birds with one stone, as they say."

This was always where my own conscience got to me. I always wanted to give my clients the best representation, but I always had a difficult time trying to throw somebody under the bus if they had nothing to do with the murder. When I had an alternative suspect in mind, I tried to make sure it was a *plausible* alternative. That he or she could very well have done it. I didn't like it when my clients offered somebody else up on a silver platter because, more often than not, the person offered up was somebody my client didn't like. Maybe it was a guy who slept with my client's wife, or perhaps a guy who stole money from my client. I didn't feel comfortable pointing a finger at just anybody, let alone somebody who my client indicated was his enemy.

"That's okay," I said. "I don't want you giving me names unless they're names of people who might have actually had a hand in this. If you know somebody like that, then, by all means, give me that name. I'll check it out. But don't name names just to name them. That's another one of my rules."

Erik shook his head. "You have an awful lot of rules. Listen, I know your job, and you have only one job. You work for me and your only job is to make sure I walk these charges down. So if I tell you I have the name of somebody I want you to use for this case, then you use it."

I stood up. I would have to take control of this interview and make sure this Erik kid knew who was running the show. Yes, he was technically my boss. That was always the case. But he wouldn't dictate trial strategy to me. I would make damn sure about that.

"Now, you listen to me. I'm the one trying this case, which means I'm the one who will dictate strategy. I'm the expert here. If I tell you we're going a certain way, then that's the way we're going. And I'm telling you I don't want you to throw out random names to me. If you give me a name, you better be goddamned sure that person might be good for this crime. You got that?"

Erik's face was expressionless as I yelled at him, which unnerved me all the more. "You're the boss," he said. "You do your investigation and try to figure it out. I got nothing for you."

I wondered if I overplayed my hand. I looked over at Harper to see if she disapproved of the way I was treating Erik, but it didn't seem she did. I couldn't necessarily discern if she approved, either. Her face was that of a poker player.

"Okay, then," I said. "I think I have the information I need. I have an investigator who will be turning over every stone and I hope to have some kind of firm grip on the direction I need to go for this trial. Assuming there is a trial." I looked over at Harper. "Ms. Ross, do you have any questions for Erik?"

Erik cocked his head and looked at Harper. "Yeah. You've been sitting there, as mute as a mime. My father said you're going to be my attorney, yet you haven't said word one. What do you have to contribute?"

Harper bit her lower lip and I wondered what was on her mind. "Mr. Gregorian," she said. "I have complete confidence in my associate, Mr. Harrington. He's highly skilled and experienced. He's thoughtful and sure of himself. I'll defer all strategic decisions to him."

Erik didn't seem happy with that announcement. "You mean he's going to be my lawyer here, not you. Is that what you're telling me?"

I looked at Harper, wondering if that *was* what she was thinking. If so, she and I would have words, because I did not think I would be first-chairing this thing. I didn't anticipate that and I didn't want that. I had my own cases to work up and the understanding that Harper and I had was that I would assist her in her cases. Conduct interviews, lay the groundwork, brainstorm with her, help her out in a pinch. I didn't imagine she would just dump a case on me without warning.

She sighed and put her hands to her temples. "No, Erik, Mr. Gregorian, that's not what I'm saying. I'll be trying your case. What I'm trying to tell you is that Mr. Harrington and I are on the same page as far as trial strategy goes. I agree with him 100% - we won't finger just anybody for this crime. We have to find somebody who might really have done it. Otherwise, we just go into the trial and try for reasonable doubt and let the jury come to their own conclusions. In other words, we don't necessarily have to show the jury proof that somebody else might have done it. We just have to put doubt in their minds that you did it."

"But it helps a helluva lot if you can show that somebody else did it, and name that person. I know that."

"That's true," Harper said. "The jury does abhor a vacuum. It's always helpful to actually present an alternative suspect to the jury, but that's not always easy to do. That said, we will do a thorough investigation on this case and, hopefully, we'll pinpoint somebody else for this crime. But we won't throw just anybody under the bus. I hope I have made that point perfectly clear."

Erik glared at both of us but finally shrugged and stood up. "Well, okay," he said. "You guys do your investigation and come up with a plausible alternative theory. But I hope you know I won't be a fly on the wall and not put my two cents into the discussion. I'll give you my opinion on every move you make, so you have to keep me informed every step of the way."

"We will," Harper said. "We promise."

He grimaced. His face told me he didn't really trust either one of us. I trusted both of us, especially Harper. She had a lot on the line on this trial.

"And one other thing," Erik said, pointing right at me. "You said something earlier about the possibility there won't be a trial. I can tell you there will be a trial. Unless those prosecutors choose to drop all charges against me, there will be a trial. Because I won't spend a single day in prison for this. That means that any and all plea deals will be null and void. I won't take one of them. I hope I make myself perfectly clear about that point."

It was my turn to bite my lower lip. I knew what he was saying. It didn't mean I had to agree with it. He was the boss, though. If he didn't want to take any plea agreements, we couldn't force him.

"Crystal clear," I said, looking at Harper. She nodded in agreement.

"Okay, then," he said. "This is where I leave you. You get that investigator on the case. Hopefully he can figure out who did it and what happened."

At that, he left.

FIVE

Harper and I continued to sit in the conference room. She had her notebook out, but she was doodling in it, not writing out a word.

"Harper," I said. "What's going on?"

She tried to plaster on a smile but I saw right through that. I had seen that look before, on Sarah's face, 1000 times. Tight lips, stone face, eyes that didn't light up. Her smile was fake, as fake as Sarah's breasts. "I don't want this case," she said. "I don't want it and I resent having it. I've never been forced to represent somebody before. Except for when I was a baby lawyer with the Public Defender's Office."

I somehow didn't know that she, too, came from the Public Defender's Office. She obviously was there long before I got my attorney to defend me after the Innocence Project attorney, Chuck Riegel, got me a new trial and Colleen took my case. I wondered if she knew Colleen and I asked her.

"Colleen Sutton, of course, of course," she said. "She was one of my closest friends at the PD's Office." She looked out the window. "I remember going out with her and some of the others on New Year's Eve one year. It turned out that many of us were not only single but also dateless for the evening, so we went out as a group that night. I think Colleen and I ended up dancing on the tables. That was obviously during my drinking days."

"During your drinking days. Meaning?"

"I'm in AA. I'm recovering from yet another setback, two, actually, I experienced in Los Angeles. So, I don't drink anymore."

There goes my idea about tossing back shots in a bar and telling war stories.

"I'm sorry to hear that," I said. "My mother had a drinking problem." I threw that last part in there to let Harper know I wasn't necessarily a kindred soul but I understood. I didn't want to tell her that my mother's drinking problem was really the least of her problems, though. Prescription drugs – OxyContin, the "Hillbilly Heroin," was her main issue, and then, when her doctors refused to give her any more prescriptions, actual street heroin. That was the main reason why she prostituted herself - she needed those drugs like she needed oxygen. She still prostituted herself, even after I came along, and I used to hear her with her johns while I played with my toys in my bedroom. I never quite knew what those sounds were until I got a little older and suddenly understood everything. And it made me literally vomit.

"So," Harper said, obviously wanting to change the subject. "Now that you know your boss is an incorrigible drunk, it's your turn to tell me something I don't know. I mean, I know you went to a top-rated law school, much better than the one I went to, and you were a late bloomer. You didn't start college until you were 23. What did you do before you were 23? You left that part of your resume blank."

I ran my hand through my hair, suddenly shy about telling her the truth. I never knew what to say to people who asked me this question. It always seemed so convoluted to tell them I was wrongfully imprisoned when I was 18 and the Innocence Project saved my bacon. Harper would understand, of course. If anybody would understand something like that, it would be Harper. Yet, I couldn't quite bring myself to tell her. "I went to Europe," I said. "To find myself. Did the whole hostel thing. Rode bikes through the Alps. It was a freeing experience, one I'm really glad to have had."

She nodded. "I've always wanted to do something like that myself. Just get a bike in Europe, go all around, look at castles, eat pastries and talk to all the locals. Learn a different language along the way. I've never done it, though. You're very lucky to have had a chance for an experience like that. From what I understand, it's a once in a lifetime thing, something you never forget."

I nodded. I had actually been through Luxembourg and France, not on a bicycle, but as part of a tour. If Harper asked me about my experiences, I could relay them. But she didn't ask me. She seemed preoccupied.

"Well, okay, then," Harper said. "I resent Erik being my client, but he is my client. In fact, he's not only my client, but I must represent him and must get an acquittal for him. If I don't, suffice to say I won't be long for this world. So, we have to put our brains together on this thing and look at every angle. Where would you like to begin?"

"Well, I want to begin with his dad and this Vardan Dorian guy. They're the most likely place to start because they essentially brought Shelly into the organization. Vardan literally found her and brought her in and Sargis gave his blessing. Something is rotten in the State of Denmark right there if you ask me."

"I was thinking the same thing, but I can't figure that one out. Why would Sargis want to throw his son under the bus, and why would he be so adamant to see Erik is set free for this? Unless he's playing some kind of elaborate game with me. I don't discount that, but I don't want to chance it, either. I mean, if he's playing a game, then I need to call his bluff and see what Sargis does. Right? But if I'm wrong...." She sliced her hand across her neck. "There goes me and there go my girls. Me, I don't really care all that much. I live, I die, what do I care? I mean, I like life, don't get me wrong, but if I die, it's not like I'm really going to know. But my girls, that's a different story. I would go to the ends of the earth to protect them, which means there's no way in hell I'll test this theory."

I wrote that down. "Okay, we begin with the dad and Vardan Dorian. We find out more about Vardan Dorian especially. But I have to admit, I'm intrigued about Shelly's background as a hacker. That seems like that could also bear some fruit. Find out who she knew as a part of that world. Maybe there was somebody from her hacker days who wanted her dead. Somebody who knew that, because Shelly was embedded with the Gregorian clan, she would be a target to be killed by somebody in the clan. Maybe somebody saw her work with the Gregorian clan as a convenient cover. That's what I'm thinking. That's where I'd like to direct Garrett to begin his investigation. Do you have the same ideas about it?"

"Yes," she said. "I was actually thinking the same things. Of course, we also need to find out if she had any kind of romantic entanglements, somebody who might have wanted her dead for other reasons. And, of course, we always have to look at other angles, such as whether or not she had a life insurance policy, and who was the beneficiary for it. I still think Erik did this. I think he's good for it. All day long. But, if we can find at least a few plausible alternatives, we can start working up a good strategy."

I nodded as I studied my notes. "Who's on the other side of this?"

"Nick Wright," she said. "I know, I know. He's a grandstander and a blowhard. I can't stand him. But it's the luck of the draw, I guess. And the judge is Judge Clarion. Division 40."

I smiled as I realized that Judge Clarion was the judge we drew for this case. I always got along well with him, although I was one of the only ones. He reminded me of an old-time justice like you might see in the movies. White-haired, cantankerous, not one to take shit from anybody. I guessed the reason why I liked Judge Clarion so much was because he reminded me of some of the guards I befriended in prison. They were gruff and menacing but if you knew just how to talk to them, they became like pussycats, for the most part. They never gave me shit, namely because I knew how to handle them. I was the same way with Judge Clarion. He and I got along because we understood one another. I understood he had a job to do, and he did the same with me. He let me do my job and I let him do his.

"Well, okay, then. We know how to strategize around Judge Clarion and Nick Wright. It's always helpful to know just what you're up against and how much you can get away with. Which isn't much with Judge Clarion, I have to say. But that's okay. If you know it going in, it's not so bad."

Harper smiled. "I think I made the right choice in hiring you," she said. "You really seem to know your stuff."

"I do. Not just because I worked at the Public Defender's Office for the past five years. But also because I'm a student of human nature. I've known and seen every kind of person in my life, and I've got a handbook on how to handle all of them."

Harper narrowed her eyes at me when I said that and nodded. "Yeah, I've known all types of people myself. My father always said there's only 7 different types of people in the world. Everyone fits into one type of archetype or another. Do you believe that?"

I shrugged. "I guess. I've heard the theory that there are seven types of personalities. The King, the Warrior, the Wise Man, the Priest, the Scholar, the Artist, the Server. But you read about the personalities and none of them talk about the criminal type. About the type of person who is pathological in some way. The pathological personality is what we're dealing with most of the time. And there's very little we can do to help them."

Harper seemed to be in a reflective mood. She seemed to absorb my words as she looked down at the conference room table. "I think you're right. I think most of our clients have a pathology of some sort. Either a personality disorder or a true mental illness. Mostly I see people with personality disorders, though. But what does that say about us? If our clients have a pathology, and they're out there committing crimes, aren't we enabling them just to keep on committing more crimes? Take this Erik kid, for instance. Let's just say we're successful. We manage to convince the jury that Erik didn't kill Shelly. The jury acquits. What are we doing except putting a known criminal back on the streets? Because you know Erik is good for all kinds of other crimes. Maybe not murder. But he's the leader of a clan that controls a good part of the city and that clan is up to no good. They're kidnapping innocent girls and selling them to the highest bidder. They're stealing. They're hacking into computer systems. They're selling street drugs. They're making a lot of money off the backs of hard-working people." She shook her head. "The only thing that Erik is doing I don't have a problem with is the prostitution angle. The girls get compensated richly and going into it with open eyes. But with everything else Erik is doing..."

I knew what she was talking about. It was something that all defense attorneys felt in their core. We all like to think we're doing God's work, representing the down-trodden and the defenseless. It's an ethos drilled into every person working in the Public Defender's Office. Every person deserves a good defense. It's in the Constitution. The Sixth Amendment right to counsel. And it's true. Every person deserves a good defense. But, in reality, our roles weren't all that lofty. In reality, we were trying to get acquittals for people who really don't deserve them because they're bad for society.

Harper bit the bottom part of her mouth. "I was responsible one time for a murder," she said quietly. "I had a client a few years back. He killed a man. Told me it was self-defense, and I never really believed him. I wanted to, though. I got him off on a technicality. He gave a polygraph that he flunked. Of course, the polygraph wasn't admissible in court. But the prosecutor accidentally introduced it. Quite unexpectedly. I jumped on that, asked for a mistrial, and got it. Then I badgered the prosecutor to drop the charges against my client. They finally relented." She shook her head. "I felt I was giving him my best defense. And I was. Then he murdered his girlfriend in cold blood. Left two girls orphaned, the girls I have in my care right now."

I nodded. I didn't quite know how Harper felt, because I hadn't experienced that. Yet. It was only a matter of time, however, before the same thing happened to me. It was only a matter of time before a person I get acquitted goes on and murders somebody else. That type of thing just came with this job. I knew that. But I truly believed in the maxim that it's better for 10 guilty men to go free than to see one innocent person get convicted. That one innocent person was the person I worked for. He or she was the person that made this whole job worthwhile.

Because that one innocent person was me.

SIX

I went to the hospital that night. The same thing I did every night. Go to the hospital, take off my coat, wash my hands, put on rubber gloves and a mask, and go in and see my daughter. She was awaiting a bone marrow transplant and had been given powerful chemotherapy and radiation, so her immunity system was very low.

Amelia was lying in the bed, looking pale – paler than I had ever seen her. She was pale, anyhow, because she took after her mother. Her brother Nate took after me – he had the olive skin, the green eyes, the wild curly hair. But Amelia was pale, thin and blonde, just like her mother. Anybody who saw Nate and Amelia together would never guess they were siblings. People who saw me with Amelia probably thought she was adopted. Likewise people who saw Sarah with Nate.

Funny how genetics worked.

She saw me come in and smiled. "Daddy," she said, reaching out her arms. I sat down next to the bed and didn't touch her. I was afraid to. I was always paranoid I still had germs she might catch and those germs would kill her. I wanted to touch her, though. I wanted to smooth the blonde hair covering her forehead and kiss her cheek. I wanted to hold her in my arms and tell her that everything would be okay.

I wished I knew that everything would be okay. At the moment, however, things didn't look so good. Amelia had been battling her non-Hodgkin's Lymphoma for the last two years, since she was only four years old. We tried immunotherapy, chemotherapy, radiation and blood transfusions. I had witnessed her suffering for the past two years, and it was wearing on me, but I was determined to stay strong for her. Now she was in the hospital because she was going to undergo a bone marrow transplant.

I sometimes wondered if I was doing all this for her or for myself. Was I being selfish, wanting to keep her, even though everything in the universe was trying to take her from me? If I was spiritual, which I really wasn't, but if I were, I would just let her go. Let her suffering end. But I just couldn't. I had to go through every experimental treatment, every conventional treatment, everything the doctors said might help her. I had to because I needed her in my life.

This caused a rift between Sarah and me, one of many. At first, Sarah was on board with all the treatments we were trying with Amelia. But, eventually, Sarah had decided we had put Amelia through too much. She had watched her brother die in much the same way – for two years, Sarah's brother was put through the chemotherapy, radiation and surgery ringer. He died at the age of 14. Sarah felt it was unfair that he had to go through so much suffering only to die anyhow. She feared the same thing was happening with Amelia and that we were playing God. She was Catholic. She prayed on it and came to the conclusion that it was God's will that Amelia should be taken and we were only prolonging the inevitable.

"Hey, kitten," I said, sitting down next to Amelia. "How's it shaking in here?"

She shrugged, her blue eyes dimming. "It sucks," she said. "When can I get out of here? And where's Sarah?"

We went through this every time. Sarah had long since decided she wouldn't participate in Amelia's treatment because she was

against it on principle. That meant that, for this current hospitaliza-
tion, she hadn't yet seen Amelia. Amelia had been in the hospital for
two weeks at this point and Sarah hadn't darkened the doorstep of the
hospital yet.

"She's battling a cold," I told Amelia. "She's a kindergarten
teacher and she's exposed to germs all the time. I know I told you
nobody can visit you if they've been exposed to a virus."

Amelia nodded but looked skeptical. "She doesn't want me to be
treated, does she?"

I had to admit that children knew more than what we gave them
credit for. "It's not that," I lied. "Mom can't be around you because
she might infect you with a bug and that could kill you. We need to
make sure we get this bone marrow transplant without a hitch."

"Okay," Amelia said. "It's really boring in here. They won't let
me play with my iPad because they can't assure me the iPad doesn't
have germs. They won't let me have books. I can only watch TV.
Apparently the TV doesn't have germs. I'm going crazy in here,
Dad."

"I know, kitten, I know. But it's only for a few more days. You'll
get your transplant on Saturday, and then, hopefully, you can come
home."

Amelia looked skeptical. "What if it doesn't work? The transplant. What if it doesn't work?" Her eyes got big. "What happens,
Dad, if it doesn't work?"

I sighed. I didn't want to tell her the bone marrow transplant was
the last resort. We had gone through all the clinical trials and all the
conventional treatments. I didn't want to tell her this was the end of
the road.

"Let's not talk about that," I said. "Let's just be positive. Think
positive." I tried to ignore the lump in my throat, tried to keep my
tears from flowing. I wished, more than anything, that Sarah was here
next to me, holding my hand. But she wasn't. It was true she wasn't
feeling well, but she was apparently feeling well enough to get a
massage and get her nails done. She made excuses for not coming and

felt her excuses were good. After all, the doctors did tell us we couldn't be in Amelia's room if we were suffering from any kind of a virus or infection. Sarah, as a kindergarten teacher, was always exposed to just about everything.

She probably couldn't visit Amelia directly but she certainly could come to the hospital and stand outside the room. That might not do Amelia any good, but it would certainly do me some good. She could stand shoulder to shoulder with me and fight the good fight. She could bring Nate here, which would certainly do Amelia some good. Nate usually came with me when I visited, but lately I've been coming straight from the office, as Children's Mercy was in mid-town Kansas City and my office was on The Plaza, which meant it was only about a ten minute drive in traffic from my office to Amelia's hospital. My home was in Leawood, Kansas, in the opposite direction, so I didn't go home and get Nate before I visited Amelia in the evenings.

Sarah got off work at 4 so she certainly could bring Nate to the hospital. He would have to wait for the weekend to see his sister, and that wasn't fair.

I stayed in Amelia's room for about an hour. By then, it was 8 o'clock and she was getting tired. The time had just changed, which meant the sky was pitch black outside by the time I left her in the hospital room.

I went home and found Sarah was still somewhere. The babysitter, Heather, a sixteen year old who lived next door to us, was sitting in the living room, surfing the net on her phone. "Nate's in his room," she said. "Sarah heated up a frozen pizza for dinner. There's some in the oven if you want it."

"Have you heard from Sarah?" I asked Heather.

"Yeah," she said. "She called to say she was getting a drink with an old friend tonight at this place called the Brick House. She said not to expect her in until at least midnight."

The Brick House was currently in the same space as my old haunt, The Velvet Dog. It was in midtown Kansas City, right by the large radio tower that used to be called the KCMO Tower but was currently called KCTV Tower – this was a tower I used to imagine was The Eiffel Tower, because it was shaped like the famous Paris tower. It always lit up the night like a beacon and I was fascinated by it. I was likewise fascinated by The Velvet Dog – it was once the hippest martini bar in town. Retro vibe, dark red walls, two levels and a patio, and the best selections of martinis in the city. I never quite understood why it went out of business. Something about problems between the owners of that bar and another bar called The Empire Room. Both of those bars had the same kind of retro hipster vibe and gave Martini Corner its name.

Now there was the Brick House, just another neighborhood bar and didn't have the distinctive vibe The Velvet Dog had. And my wife was apparently drinking there while our daughter lays in a hospital bed, scared to death. And, even worse than that, I suspected Sarah was drinking there with somebody who wasn't a female. I suspected that Sarah was drinking with John Gibson, who was, ironically enough, one of my former co-workers at the Public Defender's Office and was currently making the big bucks in a large personal injury firm.

I knew Sarah was having an affair but I was all out of fucks to give at that point. My only focus was on Amelia getting well. Everything else in my life was secondary.

Of course I was also worried about my different cases I was working on. That was always a point of stress. I wanted to make sure that Betsy Ward, Austin's mom, got some modicum of justice for losing her son in such a way. As much as I secretly thought the whole thing was a blessing because Austin was really, really sick, I also thought it was a travesty. He shouldn't have died like that.

Or should he have? His death was literally painless. He went to sleep for his surgery and never woke up. That doctor possibly saved him many years of pain and relapses. That doctor possibly saved his mother years of stress – getting her hopes up, having them crash down, again and again. The endless cycle of thinking this was it, my child is cured, only to get the bad news, once again, in the doctor's office. The tears begin anew, the panicking re-starts, everything re-sets to the moment when you first found out how sick your child is. You have to have hope but that hope dims with every passing day. Cancer is impossible for families and impossible for the children suffering from it. Watching your child's light slowly dim was inde-scribably heart-breaking.

Was Betsy merely spared years of that kind of agony? She had no choice, at the moment, but to make her peace with what had happened. She could get some closure on Austin's life and his illness. For many families, the ones who went through years of hopes that bloomed, then were cruelly dashed, their closure never would come until their child either got permanently well or passed away. Betsy's healing could begin.

Yet there had been hope for Austin. Hope that another experi-mental treatment might have been his ticket. That he might yet fulfill his dream of working for NASA. It was that kernel of hope that was taken by the careless doctors in his case. It was that kernel of hope I needed to sell to the jury if I was to get any kind of settlement for Betsy.

I checked on Nate who was sitting in his room playing a video game. I spent about an hour with him, making sure his homework was done and just chatting about life, before I went to my home office and examined my cases. I had a full roster of things on my plate, from robbery and burglary cases that were sure to plead out – most cases pled out – to these two large cases that probably would result in a trial. Betsy Ward and Erik Gregorian. Two people who couldn't be more different, yet both of them needed me all the same.

Erik was technically Harper's case but I had the feeling she would lean on me to get the acquittal she desperately needed. Both of these cases were in their nascent stage, which meant they both could take a turn at any moment. Something would pop up during investi-gation that would either be the saving grace or the death knell. That was usually how it worked. It was my job to either run with the saving grace or find every way possible to ensure the death knell wasn't actually fatal.

I checked the clock. It was only 10. Garrett was no doubt still awake. That man hardly slept. Maybe he and I could grab a drink together and I could pick his brain on what he was finding out on the Austin Ward case. Give him the facts on Erik's case and see what he could find out there. I was restless that evening, and, deep down, spoiling for a fight.

I called my overnight baby-sitter, whose name was Emily. I couldn't get Heather to work late on school nights, but Emily was a bit older and in college. She also lived in the neighborhood and was always happy to make some extra money sitting for Nate when I had to work really late and Sarah was out doing God-knew-what. I knew she just came over and worked on her schoolwork, cramming for a pop quiz in one of her humanities classes while Nate slept, but that was okay. I obviously needed somebody to stay with Nate, so I was happy to get Emily to do it.

She agreed to come over and, when she got there, I put on my leather jacket and left.

I arranged to meet Garrett at the Brick House.

Yeah, it was spying, but so what? Sarah deserved it.

SEVEN

I met Garrett at the bar. He was already there, sitting at a table, a vodka and water in his glass. He smiled and waved his glass in the air as I walked in.

"Hey, buddy," he said as I sat down. "I know why you chose this place." He gestured to the loft area upstairs. "Your wife is here with some guy."

Some guy. I think I knew who that some guy was, but I would wait until one of them came down the stairs to find out. There was a bar upstairs, however, so it might be awhile before one or both of them made their appearance. In the meantime, I would pick Garrett's brain.

Tom Garrett was a guy I came to know in prison. He was a street guy, just like myself, who joined a gang when he was only 10 years old. He had the same kind of home life I did – an alcoholic mother, an absent father, men in the house who would come and go. Many of those men were violent and abusive. Of all the prison types, Garrett and his ilk were the ones I got along with the best. We bonded over our shared stories.

Garrett was serving a five-year stint for armed robbery when I met him. He was good for the robbery so he wasn't too upset to be serving time. In fact, he was happy his Public Defender got him such a light sentence in the first place. He had to roll on the instigator of the robbery in order to get that sentence, so he was always looking over his shoulder, but that was a small price to pay. Once he was out, he vowed to go straight, so he hung out a shingle as a private detective. He was good at what he did, mainly because he still knew the players on the street. He could get information from snitches and rats much easier than any cop could, because he was friends with just about everybody in the underground world.

Besides, Garrett was a big guy – 6'5" of solid muscle. He was one of those guys always pumping iron in the prison gym so he ended up packing on as much muscle as an NFL linebacker. Nobody would mess with Garrett. He was always afraid that somebody would pump him full of lead as revenge for him rolling on his robbery partner, Freddy Lithgow, but he never lived in fear that somebody would get the best of him in hand-to-hand combat.

What was funny to me was that Garrett had a dog, but it wasn't the kind of dog you would associate with a huge guy with a body covered with tattoos. It wasn't a Pit Bull or a Rottweiler or a Doberman or any of those "manly" dogs. It was a little Shih Tzu who Garrett named Trudy. And since Garrett wasn't married or had any kids that he knew about, Trudy was the current love of his life. He bought little dresses for Trudy and took her to the grocery store and to any restaurant that had a dog-friendly patio. To me, there was nothing funnier than seeing Garrett walking that dog with her silly little dress and little bows in her hair.

"What does this 'some guy' look like?" I asked Garrett as the waitress came around and took my drink order.

Garrett shrugged. "He looks like an asshole, if you ask me. Slicked-back hair, a golf shirt, khaki pants. You know the type. I'm sorry, but that slicked-back hair always says 'prick' to me."

I laughed, because I usually thought the same damn thing. And, I had to admit, the description matched John Gibson. He looked like an asshole and really was one. That was why he ended up working at the Public Defender's Office for the trial experience, not because he was actually interested in defending the indigent. He high-tailed it out of there for the big bucks as fast as he could.

The waitress came back with my scotch and water and I took the drink and tipped her five bucks.

"Keep 'em coming," I said, and she nodded.

"That kind of night, huh?" Garrett said. "I wondered why you called me to come out tonight."

I shrugged. "Yeah. I didn't think I could sleep. Anyhow, I need to pick your brain about a case I'll give you. Erik Gregorian. You know anything about him?"

Garrett snorted. "What, do you think I wouldn't know about that psycho? The Gregorian branch of the Armenian Power are a bad bunch of dudes even by my standards. I mean, I'm no angel, as you well know, but even I find kidnapping innocent girls and selling them into slavery to be disgusting. But, yes, I know Erik and I know his whole filthy clan. Why?"

"He's my client. Actually, he's Harper's client, but I have a feeling I'll be taking the lead on this one. Harper doesn't seem to have the stomach for it."

Garrett shook his head. "To each his own, buddy, but why did she take his case if she doesn't have the stomach for it? Seriously, isn't there a serial killer she could represent? I have much more respect for those dudes than I do for somebody like Erik Gregorian. At least they have an excuse – they're pretty much insane. But Gregorian just does that shit for money."

An interesting distinction, I thought, but didn't say as much. "She was forced into taking it by Erik's father, Sargis Gregorian. He's one of the largest bosses in the Southern California area and he apparently has Harper's number. He's threatened her – he told her she has to take Erik's case or else he'll kill her and have her daughters kidnapped and sold. So she's terrified. She also has to somehow get an acquittal for Erik. She obviously doesn't want anything to do with this case, so I think I'll take the lead on it. Anything you can tell me about Erik would be helpful and then I'll have you do the investigation on the murder of Shelly McMason. I'm sure you've heard of that case. Everybody has."

When I mentioned Shelly's case, Garrett shook his head. "That poor girl," he said. "She had everything going for her and then she got mixed up with that clan, and that was that."

"What do you know about her case? Have you heard anything?"

He shrugged. "No, but I'll surely ask around and see if anybody bites. I do know she was infiltrated in Gregorian's group as a computer hacker. I know some of the guys who worked with her when she was doing that shit underground. That was how she earned her money for school from what I understand. Her parents are richer than Croesus, but I've heard they cut her off because she was engaged to a Muslim man. It's ridiculous how prejudice works."

I cocked my head. Shelly McMason was becoming more interesting to me by the second. I didn't even know her parents had cut her off. I found the reason for them cutting her off to be ridiculous, but, then again, maybe there was something more to the story. Maybe her parents cut her off for some other reason.

"Her parents cut her off," I said. "Just because she was engaged to a Muslim man? Are you sure that's the only reason why they cut her off?"

"That's what I heard. Her parents are old money. They live in Mission Hills. I'm pretty sure they're the type who are horrified by people who aren't like them. Listen, with people like that, there are any number of reasons why they cut their kids off. Maybe the kid likes somebody poor, or maybe they want to pursue some kind of profession that doesn't make them wealthy. Maybe they refuse to go into the family business. Who knows? What I do know is that Shelly's parents obviously used their money to manipulate her to do what they wanted her to do. That's pretty safe to say."

"So," I said. "What you know is she made money to pay for her schooling by doing underground hacking and her parents cut her off financially. Do you know anything else about her? Anything else about her murder?"

Garrett steepled his hands and took a drink of his vodka. "I did hear a few other things about her, all unconfirmed. When her murder started making the news, I started asking around. I figured I could maybe drum up some business with the person representing Erik Gregorian. I never dreamed that person would be you, but that's pretty lucky that it is. But, yeah, I found out a few other things about her."

"What are these other things?"

"I've heard the Muslim man wasn't the only guy she was banging. She was also apparently involved with Wells Armstrong."

"Wells Armstrong? Where have I heard name before?"

"He's been in the news lately. He was the CEO of Armstrong Pharmaceuticals but was forced to resign when it was discovered his company was involved in tainted chemotherapy drugs. You might have remembered that happening about six months back. When that scandal hit the news, Armstrong's stock dropped like a stone and Wells was forced out. He landed on his feet, though – his company gave him a golden parachute worth $50 million." Garrett shook his head. "Nice work if you can get it. Your company gives people tainted drugs, your stock drops through the floor, you get forced out but get millions on your way out the door. Where can I sign up for such a gig?"

"Where can any of us sign up for such a gig? So, Shelly was involved with this Wells guy. So what? I mean, is that important?"

"Well, yeah, it is. Wells is married. No biggy, of course. Lots of married guys banging around with young girls. But you have to understand that Armstrong Pharmaceuticals was the big rival for Andrew McMason's company. You have to remember Andrew's grandfather founded Argyros Pharmaceuticals. That's the largest company founded in Kansas City and also one of the oldest. Who do you think benefited the most when Armstrong's stock took a dive?"

"Argyros, obviously, since those two companies were the biggest players in the area." I nodded. "Sounds like we have some pretty decent leads on other people who might have killed Shelly. See what you can do to follow up on those leads. See what you can find out."

"I will." Garrett shook his head. "But Erik Gregorian is still looking good to me for her murder. At least, somebody in the Gregorian clan is looking good to me. Since he's the head of the Kansas City clan, if anybody in the clan killed her, it was approved by Erik. There's no getting around that, and there's no getting around the fact that Shelly was about to expose the Gregorian's foul deeds to the world."

"Be that as it may, we have to find alternative suspects, and that's where you come in. See what you can find out." I paused. "And what did you find out about Vardan Dorian?"

"Vardan Dorian," he said. "He was Erik's friend and he referred Shelly to Erik." He looked at his notes. "There wasn't much I could find about him, except he knew some of the hackers Shelly worked with and those hackers told Vardan that Shelly was on the up and up. That was all I found out about him. I found no indication he was trying to sabotage Erik or knew what Shelly was up to. You have to understand that there wasn't any tracing Shelly to the newspaper. Because she was an investigative journalist infiltrating a dangerous mob, the newspaper was extremely secretive about her employment. I had difficulties trying to find out she worked for the newspaper. I had to really know who to ask about her. So, there really isn't any reason to suspect Vardan knew what Shelly was doing. As far as he knew, Shelly was a hacker, and that was that."

Garrett saluted me and returned to his drink. "Anything else on your mind?"

"Yeah. Have you found out anything else about my other case? The med mal case? I know I just gave it to you a week ago, so I don't expect anything just yet. I just thought I would ask."

Garrett shrugged. "Nothing yet. I'm doing some digging on that anesthesiologist who gave that poor kid the drug and I don't see anything dirty with Dr. Kim just yet. That doesn't mean there's not something there, though."

"I know. I'm just going to have to figure that case out myself. I have some depositions scheduled with some of the key players next week. I'll see if I can do some digging of my own and find out what I can about what happened. I know there was a mistake made, but I'm really trying to see if there's an angle where we can get punitive damages. If we can't, I think this case will literally be nothing but a money sink."

That was always the problem with something like a medical malpractice case. When you tried one, and you sunk $100,000 into the investigative process before everything is said and done, you had to try for a jury verdict in the millions to make it worth your while. There was just no way the actual damages in Austin's case would warrant that. If I couldn't prove there was some kind of willfulness or intent, then Harper was probably right. I would have to abandon that case as painful as it was to do so.

Just then, I looked up and saw my wife coming down the stairs. She met my eyes and looked away. The man behind her, John Gibson, looked at me quizzically and then looked at her.

There would be a confrontation at last. And I didn't think it would be pretty.

EIGHT

HARPER

I stayed late in the office after Damien left. Sophia was watching the girls, and I just needed some time to myself. Time to decompress. Time to reflect on what was going on. My headspace was always threatening me and I always had a tough time turning off the negative voice.

The lights were off in the suite so my office was the only light on. I turned to the window, looked at the people below, and, as always, I wondered about them. They were down there on The Plaza, shopping and going to restaurants and bars and maybe to the movies. I wondered if they were as free as I thought they were, or maybe, like me, they just had on a really good façade.

I swiveled around to my desk and looked over the prosecutor's file for Erik Gregorian. The Statement of Information, the pictures of Shelly, pictures of the car, the police report, and the transcript of Erik's statement to the police. Erik's rap sheet was also included in this initial discovery, and, of course, it was a long one. Mainly petty theft, a few burglary charges here and there, but nothing major. That was because Erik, after he became the leader of his clan, was protected by the soldiers beneath him. They did the dirty work.

When he was coming up, he was a soldier, even though Sargis was his father, so he was convicted for minor things. I knew he was good for much more than what his rap sheet indicated, but he was just never caught for those things.

Until now.

I read Erik's statement to the police, found no confession, and moved on. He professed his innocence to the cops, even though the cops were hammering away at him, apparently, for hours. The transcript was that long.

There were also some witness statements in the file and I read them too. They were mainly people at the scene of the accident. They all said Shelly was going at a high rate of speed on I-70, and then she crossed the median and hit a semi head-on. The highway patrolmen cut her out of the car, but there was very little of her to cut out. Her body, like the car she drove, was completely mangled. It looked like a tragic accident until the car was examined and it was found her brakes had been tampered with. That, of course, was why she was driving at such a high rate of speed.

Or was it? That actually made little sense to me. Yes, she had no brakes, but didn't anybody ever teach her about what to do in that case? Take your foot off the gas and pull up on the emergency brake. You don't hit the gas harder. That made little sense that she would have been driving so erratically, tampered brakes or no.

Maybe she just panicked when she figured out she didn't have brakes. That was the most likely scenario. She panicked and hit the gas when she should have been doing just the opposite.

Just then, I looked up and saw a familiar figure coming through the door. Sargis Gregorian. My nemesis. He was the one who threatened me into taking this case. He was the one who made me afraid for my life. Yet he had an odd charisma. When I was in his presence, I somehow forgot just what he was – a thug, a kidnapper, a killer and an overall bad guy.

He came into my office and sat down across from me, his pale green eyes – the same color as Erik's – framed by long, dark eyelashes.

His dark hair was still cut very short and he was dressed the same as he ever was. A perfectly tailored suit in charcoal, a silk lavender shirt underneath, a tie and perfectly buffed leather shoes. Because it was starting to get cold outside, he was also dressed in an overcoat and fedora.

He took off his hat and coat and smiled. "I have to say, I always forget how cold it can get in this part of the country. I've been spoiled living in Southern California all these years." He shook his head. "But even this weather is nothing compared to Armenia in the mountains." He visibly shuddered. "That's why our people settled in Los Angeles. We were tired of the freezing weather."

In spite of myself, I smiled. It was the middle of October, for the love of God! It was probably 40 degrees outside, maybe a bit less, as it was unseasonably cold. But it was hardly a reason for complaining. Just wait until December, I couldn't help but think. *Then you'll know what cold is.*

"Sargis Gregorian," I said. "You're actually just the man I wanted to see."

He shrugged. "I wanted to drop in and see how things were going with my son's case. See if you're earning your keep here."

I bit my lower lip. "What keep? I'm not getting paid on this case, remember? I'm doing it as a favor to you, so you don't kill me and kidnap my girls. Or is that fact lost on you?"

He smiled and laughed lightly. "Oh, don't worry about that. Check your bank balance. Your trust account balance. You'll see you've been handsomely rewarded for this case after all."

I was skeptical, but I booted up my laptop and checked my bank account. I gasped as I saw my trust account was flush with cash – somebody had made a $100,000 deposit in there, dated today. I cocked my head.

"Okay, now we're talking. I'm glad you've made this more of a real attorney-client thing, and not some kind of blackmail thing." I got out my standard contracts, which explained I billed $700 per hour for my time, $150 per hour for paralegal time and $450 per hour for associate time. "Since we're making this more of a business arrangement, I'd like for you to review this contract. It will explain my billable hours."

I felt a sense of relief that Sargis actually would pay me. I was fretting, just a little, about how I would keep the lights on. Running a law practice wasn't cheap – there was always money going out the door for experts, personnel, rent and utilities. Now I had an associate and a full-time investigator working for me as well. And I still had two girls at home, both of whom were in private schools, both of whom had ambitions of going to an Ivy League college. Money was a bit of a worry for me. The last thing I wanted was to take a full-blown murder case *pro bono*.

Sargis looked at the contract and nodded. "This looks pretty standard," he said, and then he signed it. I took the contract, made a copy of it and handed it to him.

"What made you change your mind about paying me?" I asked him.

"I always intended to pay you. I just wanted to see if you would actually accept my terms. And you did." He nodded approvingly and I suddenly understood. He was testing me, just like Damien thought. I wondered if the other parts of this deal – that if I lost this case, I would lose my life and my girls would be kidnapped – was also a part of the test.

Then again, after what Erik told me, it was entirely possible this entire case was nothing but an elaborate mind-game for Sargis. If Erik was telling the truth, and Sargis did actually clear Shelly to work for the Gregorian clan, then that raised some huge red flags for me. It did for Damien, too.

I leaned back in my chair. Sargis had already found out he had the upper hand. I went along with the case, thinking I wouldn't be paid, because I was frightened. There had to be some way I could regain control. Some way I could ensure my safety if things went south with this case, as it looked like it would.

"So," I said. "You were testing me and I guess I flunked. Is that it?"

"Something like that." He smiled. "I'm a great student of human nature. I can pinpoint just how much I can get away with. I do that with everyone I meet. And I see fear in you, Harper. I see a woman who is unsure of herself, which makes you assume the worst about everybody you meet. I don't pretend to know where your deep well of insecurity comes from. I only know it's there. You're easily exploited."

"That's not a very good trait for a defense attorney – easily exploited."

He shook his head. "On the contrary, it's an excellent trait for somebody in the business of defending criminals. Your clients can manipulate you into thinking they're innocent when they really are not. That helps you defend them and it gives you an air of believ-ability to the jury. I can tell you believe it when a man tells you he didn't kill somebody or he didn't break into somebody's house." He nodded his head. "In your case, I would have to say your certain naïveté is a great asset. Now, if you were a prosecutor..." He shook his head.

For some reason, Sargis' words were cutting me to the core. I couldn't believe I was so transparent to this man. It was like I was made of glass and this man could see straight through me. "What about your son? Is he manipulating me? Does he also think I'm weak and easily exploitable?"

Sargis laughed. "You'll have to ask him that question."

"What about you? You've already targeted my weaknesses. You already seemed to have figured me out. At least you believe you do."

"I do." He smiled. "Rest assured."

"The reason why I ask you that question," I said to him, "is I have some real questions about your son's case."

"What are they? I will answer any question you have."

"Why would you have cleared Shelly to work with Erik? Erik told me he asked you directly about her, and you assured him she was clean. She wasn't clean, of course. She was trying to infiltrate Erik's organization. I'm quite sure you would have known about that before telling him she was clean. Or, at the very least, you should have known about that."

Sargis smiled and shook his head. "I do not want to impugn my son's integrity," he said. "But I am afraid I will have to on this point. I can assure you that Erik never asked me about Shelly. That is not something that happens between my son and me. I gave him his territory to run and that means I am hands-off. I am not a micromanager. I have my own territory to run, Ms. Ross, and how am I supposed to advise my son about personnel decisions from 1,500 miles away?" He stared at me, his smile having disappeared. "Ms. Ross, your common sense should have told you Erik was lying when he told you I approved of Ms. McMason's hiring."

I bit my lower lip, now trying to figure out who was lying – Sargis or Erik? What Sargis was saying made sense – how would he necessarily know if Shelly was on the level or not? Sargis was in Los Angeles. Erik was here in Kansas City, as was Shelly. The only way Sargis would know about Shelly's background would be if Sargis himself sent Shelly in to infiltrate Erik's clan. And why would he do that? That didn't make a lick of sense to me.

I wouldn't let that point go, however. Somebody was lying. I just didn't know who.

"So, you're telling me you didn't know Shelly. Is that right?" I leaned back in my chair and tried to read Sargis. It was impossible to do, but I would try.

"Yes, that is correct. I had never heard of Ms. McMason before my son was accused of murdering her."

"Okay, then," I said. "If you say you didn't know her, and you didn't approve of her working for Erik, then I guess that's the only real question I have for you."

Sargis cocked his head. He apparently was surprised I didn't want to press the issue. Then he appeared to shrug. "Very well. How is this case coming along? What have you done for the case?"

"Nothing yet. I just spoke with your son today to get his story. I will tell you that the case will go through the Grand Jury process, because that's how it's done in the 16th Circuit. Murders are one of many cases that go through the Grand Jury process, as opposed to going through the Preliminary Hearing process. Erik most likely will be formally arraigned for Shelly's murder."

"And you're not going to fight that?"

"No. There's no reason to. I'm sorry to say, Preliminary Hearings just aren't available for murders in this circuit. And I'm sure you know about Grand Juries – they indict, 99 times out of 100. I don't have any say on whether or not they indict, either. They're conducted in secret so I don't even know when your son's case will be presented to them."

Sargis looked as if he disapproved. His lips were pursed, and his pale green eyes were trained on my face. "What kind of motions will you be presenting to the judge? What kind of pre-trial motions do you foresee?"

"Well, I'll obviously present a pre-trial motion to examine the car Shelly was driving. There's some questions I have about that car – apparently the witnesses who saw her driving said she was driving at a high rate of speed. I'll have an expert evaluate that car. Other than that, I'll have to delve more into the case to see if there is anything else that should be addressed pre-trial. There's the possibility that I'll be filing a motion to dismiss if I get the report back from my investigator and I don't see any evidence Erik was involved in Shelly's murder. At the moment, though, I don't anticipate filing a Motion to Dismiss. Even if Erik didn't kill Shelly, there's reason to believe he might have ordered it. He had motive to kill her. He had opportunity to kill her. He had the means."

"And you are so sure he had the motive, means and opportunity to murder Ms. McMason?" Sargis asked me.

"Yes. I do. He has an entire network of soldiers assigned to kill. That takes care of both means and opportunity. And he certainly had the motive – Shelly was going to expose his network to the entire world. From where I sit, Erik looks like he certainly committed this murder. I won't lie."

Sargis just nodded his head. "That is what it looks like right now, perhaps. But I believe that, once you get more into the facts of the case, you will find there is a different story. I have confidence you will work your magic on the jury just like you always do. Just like you always have."

"How do you know so much about me and the cases I've tried?"

"Ms. Ross, do you believe I would entrust my son's case to just anyone? Of course not. I've done my research. I have found you have had an extraordinarily high percentage of wins in court. You seem to have the magic touch with juries. Again, I believe your success comes, at least in part, because of your naïveté. You are a true believer. Now, I do not believe your associate, Mr. Harrington, is the same. But perhaps that's a good thing – the Yin and the Yang, as one might say. His cynicism might balance out your naïveté. The two of you might make a good team."

"How do you know about Damien?" I asked Sargis.

"I've done my research on him. I know more about him than you do, I'm quite sure."

"What kind of background research have you done on him?"

"I've spoken with his colleagues at the Public Defender's Office. And it turns out I know some of his personal friends. They all, to a man, tell me Mr. Harrington is a ethical and moral man. They all tell me he's also a skeptical man. I believe he has had a rougher background than you know about."

I wondered about exactly what Sargis was talking about, and I wondered how he knew.

"What does that mean? I admit, I don't know much about him aside from his professional life. I know what cases he has won and I know what cases he has lost. I know what clients he has had. But I don't know much more about him. Perhaps you can fill me in?"

Sargis shook his head. "You can't get every answer you seek from me." He stood up. "Now, I must leave you. I came into town mainly to see how Erik's organization is functioning without him. I will have to appoint a new boss, at least temporarily, while Erik is absent. I understand, of course, he is out on bail, but I also understand a condition of his bail is that he cannot work with his organization. Believe it or not, Ms. Ross, I try to stay within the bounds of the law as much as I can."

I tried to suppress a smile when he said that. Sargis might be many things, but a law-abider wasn't one of them.

"Please shut the door behind you," I said.

"I will. I will just show myself out, if you do not mind."

At that, he turned and walked out of the suite, shutting the door behind him.

NINE

DAMIEN

"Hello, Sarah," I said, looking her right in the eye. I looked at John, who looked embarrassed. I raised my right eyebrow and crossed my arms in front of me. My insides were completely coiled, like a snake ready to strike.

Sarah looked me in the eye as well. "You're here," she said, her words slurred. "And where is Nate?"

"Nate is at home. Emily is watching him."

"Why would you just leave our son at home like that?" Sarah seemed indignant, which I felt was rich, considering the fact that she, too, was in a bar while our son was at home. And, unlike me, she apparently was up to no good. "Nate needs you to be with him at home."

I looked over at John who looked like the weasel he was. "Sarah, we'll talk later," he hastily said, and then walked rapidly towards the door. In a second, he disappeared into the night.

I was happy he left, but, at the same time, I really wanted to punch his teeth in. I used to work with John at the Public Defender's Office, and I was never that friendly with him. But I had never found him to be a rat or a weasel. Those were two animals he resembled to me at the moment.

Now, it was just Sarah and me, face to face. Garrett was still sitting down at the table.

"That's really rich," I said to Sarah. "That's really rich of you to be accusing me of being neglectful to our children. Considering the fact it's been me who has been at the hospital every single evening with our daughter, and it has been me who has come home to an empty house, night after night. I mean, it's not empty – Nate is there. But you haven't been there. I've been helping Nate with his home-work. I've been picking him up from basketball practice." Our son was playing in a Junior League and his coach was telling me how much potential Nate had. "I've been the one who has been constantly trying to quell his fears about the possibility that he will lose his sister. And where have you been this whole time? Apparently at a bar, or maybe you've just been with John Gibson in some hotel room somewhere. You don't get home until after I've gone to bed. It's been going on for weeks, Sarah, and it ends tonight."

Sarah's blue eyes burned with fury as I berated her. "I just haven't had anything to say to you lately," she said. "And I don't want to pretend anymore I do. I haven't wanted to come home. I'm sorry you can't understand that. But there's nothing at home I'm interested in anymore."

I knew this was coming. Obviously. It was a hard thing to avoid. I knew she wanted out of the marriage – that much was obvious. I even knew why she wanted out of the marriage. She resented me for continuing Amelia's treatment. She hated me for that. She constantly accused me of torturing Amelia when I should be making peace with Amelia's impending death. That was a huge barrier between us. Apparently Sarah couldn't take it anymore and she had already checked out. Already checked out and John Gibson was there to pick up the pieces.

"Fine," I said. "Fine. If you want to divorce me, that's just fine. But know this – I'll fight for sole custody of our children. And if the judge awards joint custody, I'll fight to be the primary caretaker. I'll get the kids full-time and you'll just be relegated to part-time parent status. And any judge will award me the primary custodian status over you, because you've been an absent parent."

"That's okay with me," she said. "We both know Amelia won't be around much longer, so it'll just be you and Nate together. And that's fine. He needs his father more than he needs his mother."

Her words struck me like daggers. She was so cold about losing Amelia. So matter of fact. Amelia was fighting for her life in a hospital room and Sarah apparently couldn't care less. I had never struck a woman in my life. Had never hit a woman. I had hit plenty of men, but never a woman. But, right at that moment, I had never wanted to punch anyone's face so much as I wanted to punch my wife's face. If it weren't for the fact that we were out in public and people were watching us, I probably would have hauled off and hit her.

I realized my fist was clenched at my side and I loosened my fingers so they hung down at my waist. I turned my face, not wanting to see Sarah's eyes. I once thought she was so beautiful. And she was. Objectively, she was. Perfect features, creamy skin, gorgeous blonde hair, a fit and curvy body. She really kept up her beauty routine with regular facials, manicures and pedicures, waxing, and massages. She worked out all the time, going to the gym and lifting weights and riding her bike around town. She spent so much time on her outward appearance but so little time on her soul. She was ugly inside, and, because she was so ugly inside, she no longer appeared beautiful to me.

"Sarah," I said, trying to be as even as possible. "Please move out as soon as possible. I'll help you find an apartment. But I don't want you in the house anymore. I can handle the children on my own. You can go to your boyfriend, I would imagine your boyfriend is John, and you and he can be very happy together. I'll be at Amelia's side while she battles for her life. I'll be there for Nate as he has to live through Amelia's illness as well. I can be mother and father to both of our kids. I don't want you around either of them and I don't want you around me."

Sarah opened her mouth and then shut it again. "Okay," she said. "I'll move out. I've already consulted a divorce attorney. I know what property I'll be entitled to. He's already drawn up a settlement decree. All you have to do is have your lawyer look at this document and you can sign it and I guess we can be done. I won't fight you on custody issues. Nate needs his father. I won't take that away from him."

I once again wanted to hit her. She didn't even mention Amelia. She apparently just assumed Amelia wouldn't be around. "What about Amelia? She's a girl. She needs her mother. What about her? She needs her mother. She needs her mother. She needs her mother." I couldn't stop repeating that last line. It just came out, again and again, and every time I said it, I saw Sarah flinch. That was why I kept saying it. I wanted to see the pain on Sarah's face. I needed to see she wasn't the cold bitch she was coming off as right at that moment. "What about Amelia? Are you really just going to abandon her right when she needs you the most?"

"She'll get over it," she said crisply. "Are we done here?"

"Yes. We're done."

She nodded and then disappeared into the crowd. I saw her go through the front door and I felt hollow. I just couldn't believe I had ever loved her. She was such a weak person. Such a shallow person. I didn't know what happened to the Sarah who was such a happy person. The Sarah who would explode into peals of laughter at my stupid jokes. Amelia getting sick exposed the fissures. Now those fissures just exploded into a chasm. Right there at the bar.

I went back to my table where Garrett was still sitting. I sat down and he patted me on the back. "It's tough," he said. "You'll get through this, buddy. God knows you've gone through much worse than this. Any dude who can spend five years in prison for something he didn't do, and live to tell the tale without so much as a scratch, isn't a dude I would ever count out."

I smiled, not feeling the smile at all. "I need to finish my drink and go home," I said. "I have a long drive ahead of me."

"Sarah doesn't. That guy, that prick with the slick hair, he lives around here. In Hyde Park. In one of those remodeled mansions."

"Oh?" I chuckled. "And how do you know this?"

He shrugged as he took a sip of his drink. "It's my business to know stuff like that." Then he grinned as he lifted up John's wallet. "And I got his wallet."

At that, I laughed out loud and patted him on the back. "You do know you're going to have to turn that into the bar, don't you?"

"I know. I just lifted it from him because I wanted to see where he lives. At any rate, he lives around here if you want me to do some stake-outs for you."

"No." I shook my head. "At this point, I don't really care if they're together. I just need to move on with my life." I finished my drink. "Find out what you can about Austin Ward's case. And follow up on all the leads you have on Shelly McMason. Those are the two people I care about right now. Them and my two children. Other than that..." I shook my head. "I'm all out of fucks to give."

Garrett finished his drink and we stood up and hugged. "I'll see you later, buddy," he said.

"Later."

And we left.

But not before Garrett went to the bar and turned in John's wallet.

TEN

I needed to pay Betsy Ward a visit, so I did. I wanted to see how she was doing, and I also wanted to reassure her I was on Austin's case. I didn't yet know how things would go on Austin's case, but I wanted her to know I would work on it.

Truth be told, however, I was somewhat reluctant to commit to Austin's case. While I knew there was medical malpractice involved in Austin's death, I just didn't think actual damages would ever cover the cost of trying the case. If I couldn't come up with some way to stick punitives on the case, I didn't know if I could go forward. So part of the reason why I would speak with Betsy was to see if she could tell me anything I could hang my hat on. Anything that would perk up my ears, make me think the case wasn't a lost cause. Make me think there was a chance our recovery on this case would be large enough to make it worth everybody's while. The last thing I wanted was for the jury to come back with $50,000 damages, which wouldn't touch our cost of bringing the case to trial. Our firm would only recover about $20,000 if the award was $50,000, because the contractual obligation was our contingency fee was 40% of the total award. We would end up way in the hole on any award less than a half million.

I went to Betsy's house, a Tudor home in the Armour Hills area, not too far from where I lived. I knew Betsy now lived alone. Her husband, Austin's father, had passed away from the same type of cancer that struck down Austin – leukemia. From what I understood, Betsy and her husband Robert were newlyweds when Robert was diagnosed. She was already pregnant by that time even though she didn't know it yet. Robert lived another five years after his diagnosis, going through chemotherapy, blood transfusions and finally a bone marrow transplant. Betsy told me that losing Robert that way was the toughest thing she had ever done. Seeing him waste away before her eyes was something she couldn't forget.

"He was 225 pounds when we met," she said. "A big, strong guy. All muscle, really. By the time he passed, he was only 120 pounds and too weak to even get out of bed. Nobody should have to go through that. Nobody."

Her words struck me like daggers as I thought about Amelia in her own hospital bed, awaiting her own bone marrow transplant. She had a different kind of cancer than did Robert and Austin, but her treatment had much in common with their treatments. Chemotherapy, blood transfusions and bone marrow transplants. It was crazy that Austin got his leukemia 16 years after Robert was stricken and the treatment protocol hadn't really changed all that much in all those years. Yes, there were clinical trials where they tried different things. But the overall protocol hadn't changed significantly in all those years. Where was scientific research? What was the government doing with all those scientific grants? All those brilliant scientific minds – why hadn't they come up with a less barbaric way of dealing with the dread disease of cancer?

I knocked on Betsy's door and she answered it. I was astounded when I looked at her. She looked like she hadn't showered in days – her hair was greasy and matted. She had enormous bags under her blue eyes and had lost a considerable amount of weight just since the last time I saw her. She had a blank look on her face, almost as if she didn't quite recognize me as I stood in front of her.

A cat came up and wrapped itself around her leg and two dogs bounded to the door to bark at me. Yet she made no move to let me in the door.

I had called her to arrange this appointment. I wondered if she remembered that. The way she was acting right at that moment told me she didn't remember I was coming over. She probably didn't remember things from minute to minute.

I wondered if this was my fate, too. If I lose Amelia, would I be a depressed mess with no will to live? I had to think that wouldn't happen to me. I had Nate to consider and a hectic and stressful job. Lots of clients who needed me. I didn't know about Betsy's job – all I knew was she was on FMLA leave of absence from her place of employment, and, from the looks of things, she hadn't yet gone back to work.

She finally opened the screen door without a word and I stepped into the home. One of the little dogs scampered onto the porch and ran out onto the lawn, and I finally heard Betsy speak.

"Sparky, come back. Come here," she yelled as the dog ran safely back into the house. "You know better than that."

Somehow, the dog running onto the lawn brought Betsy back to life. "Excuse my mess," she said, her hand waving around her living room. I saw empty pizza boxes on the coffee table – three of them, all from Dominoes – and untold boxes of Kleenexes strewn along the floor. On the fireplace mantel were three Chinese takeout boxes stacked up, the top one half-full with shrimp and vegetables in a light sauce. There were magazines and newspapers strewn all around the floor. On the big-screen TV there was a Netflix series playing – I recognized it as *Orange is the New Black*. It was paused on the scene where the lead character gets served a bloody tampon in her English Muffin and my stomach turned. I couldn't stand that scene the first time around, and having it paused there made me want to get sick, so I turned away.

She shook her head. "I've been doing nothing but binge-watching shows for the past week," she said. "This is my second time on this show. I just got finished with binge-watching *Game of Thrones*," she said, "and before that, it was *Lost*. Which pretty much sums up my state of mind these days – I'm lost."

"I hated that show," I said. "Because of the way it ended. So many questions left unanswered."

"I know, right?" she said with a smile. "The ending made about as much sense as the series did, but that's okay. It was a good series anyhow. Anyhow, those aren't the only series I've watched this past week. I haven't been sleeping. All I've been doing is watching shows and ordering delivery Chinese and pizza. As you can probably tell."

She cleared off a spot on the couch by throwing some magazines on the floor and I sat down.

"I would offer you something to drink," she said. "Which is another thing I've been doing, pretty much non-stop. I have to go back to work on Monday and I don't know how I'll ever manage it. But maybe it will be good for me. Give me something to do other than drink, eat shitty food and watch shitty television. Shitty streaming, that is."

I put my hand up. I tried not to drink alcohol during the day. I was a social drinker, anyhow, not one to drink until I got drunk.

"Thank you for the thought," I said. "But I don't drink during the day. I will take some water, though."

She went into the kitchen and brought back a bottled water. "Here," she said, handing it to me. "I actually have plenty of bottled water. That's the only thing in my fridge. I haven't gone to the store in God-knows-how-long, but I always buy my bottled water at Costco, which means I always have a shit-ton of it in my fridge."

"Thanks," I said, taking a sip. "How are you?"

"How do you think?" she asked. "Seriously. Austin was the only thing I had. At one time, I had a family – a husband and son. And a dog. Not these current dogs, but another dog. His name was Toby. He was a beautiful German Shepherd, very protective and very loving. Now I don't have Robert, I don't have Austin, and I don't even have Toby." She hung her head and put her thumb and forefinger on the bridge of her nose. "And I'm pissed. So pissed."

She got up off the couch and then got a piece of paper she handed to me. "Here," she said. "I got results back from my son's genetic test. It turns out he had a certain gene that caused leukemia. I would imagine Robert had the exact same gene. It's called the BCR and I've been looking it up on the internet. I'm really angry because my doctor didn't even think to have Austin genetically tested. I just had this done because a friend of mine told me I should try to figure out if Austin's leukemia was genetic because he had the same type of leukemia his father had. Why didn't my doctor advise me to get Austin genetically tested? He could have been treated with gene therapy. That probably would've helped him much more than what they were doing to him."

I looked at the paper detailing Austin's genetic profile. It did seem he had that gene. I would have to do my research on it and find out more about it. If what Betsy was saying was correct – Austin might have responded to genetic therapy – then that might be significant in terms of our case. I was searching for some way to show Austin might have lived a long and prosperous life if he wasn't killed by a drug he was clearly allergic to. That was my main sticking point – the fact that Austin's life expectancy was a matter of months, not years, and certainly not decades. The bone marrow transplant he received was a last resort and certainly wasn't a sure thing. We would have dueling doctors on this case as it was – my doctor would have to testify that Austin could have lived many years if he wasn't given Propofol, and their doctor would testify that Austin was on death's door, and nothing would change that.

But could this genetic testing have changed things? Could Austin have been saved by genetic therapy? That might make a difference in the jury's eyes. Austin might have had a chance for a complete cure, but for him dying on the operating table. It was certainly an argument worth a shot.

I sighed as I thought about the fact that this genetic test was a shot, but just barely. This case was still risky. It was a risky strategy to try to hang my hat on the possibility that Austin could've been cured with gene therapy. Plus, it meant I would have to hire one more expert – I would have to hire a geneticist to explain to the jury about gene therapy and why Austin could've been helped by it. That just made my case even more expensive to try.

"Does this help?" Betsy asked me. "That Austin had that genetic marker, does it help? Can you sue his oncologist for not recommending the test?"

"I'll have to inquire with my expert about that one," I said. "I'm not sure if not recommending a genetic test would be a breach of the doctor's duty to his patient."

"If it's not a breach of his duty, then what happens?"

"There's not a negligence suit against your oncologist," I said, "Dr. West. For a negligence case, you have to show duty, breach, causation, damages. So, you have to show a duty and a breach of that duty. The standard for a breach is reasonable standard of care. If a doctor's actions were somehow outside the reasonable standard of care, we possibly have a negligence action. If they aren't outside the reasonable standard of care, then we don't. That part is pretty simple. So, my expert will have to tell you whether or not Dr. West breached his duty to Austin by operating outside the reasonable standard of care. I'm not quite sure if he did or not. I'll have to ask Dr. Kaur about that."

"And that means..."

"That means we can't bring a suit against Dr. West. The state of Missouri is pretty strict about that. If my expert witness doesn't sign off then I can't bring a suit. Dr. Kaur has to find a breach of the standard of care."

Betsy nodded. "Well, it's worth a shot."

"Yes. At any rate, this genetic test thing might bolster my case against the anesthesiologist. There's the possibility Austin might have been cured by gene therapy. If that's the case, we might be able to sell the jury that Austin had a chance to go on to realize his NASA dreams. That would make the award much greater but it's still an uphill climb."

"Does that mean you won't take the case?"

I shifted uncomfortably in my seat. "No. I'll go ahead and file the case. I just don't know if I'm the man to try this case. Maybe you would be better off with one of the big guns in town. There are firms that try these medical malpractice cases by the hundreds. They're familiar with the defense attorneys on the other side. They can probably get you a settlement where I probably couldn't. That might be what you need."

Betsy stared at the TV, which still had the still image of the bloody tampon wedged in the English Muffin. "No," she said softly. "I don't want to become a number to somebody. I want somebody who gives a crap about me. Somebody who knew Austin and gives a crap about him. I want you to have this case not some asshole in a thousand-dollar suit. If you don't want the case, I understand. You've explained it all to me and I know the case might not be worth much money because Austin's life expectancy was so short. But if you don't want the case then I guess there won't be a case. I don't want to deal with those other assholes like you see on TV all the time." She shook her head. "It's you or nobody."

I smiled and put my arm around her as she hung her head and grabbed a Kleenex and sobbed into it. "I appreciate your faith in me," I said. "I just don't know if it's warranted."

"If it's not warranted, it's not. I think it is, though. You're my friend. You and I bonded. I pray for your daughter every night at the same time I'm praying for Austin's soul. You know what I'm going through. You understand. That means a lot to me. It has to be you taking Austin's case."

"No pressure," I said lightly, hoping she would laugh at my little joke.

To my relief, she smiled when I said that. "No pressure." Then she glanced at the TV. "Oh, God," she said. "I just realized I paused that show at just the wrong scene. Gross." She clicked play on her remote and the scene came to life. Piper, the lead character on the show, looked at the English Muffin in horror and then ran out of the room to get sick. I smiled as I realized I knew how Piper was feeling.

I felt a little sick myself.

No pressure.

ELEVEN

The next day, I met Garrett. He told me he had a preliminary report on our vic, Shelly McMason, and told me I would be interested in what he found out about her.

I brought Harper along with me to the restaurant where Garrett wanted us to meet. It was called the Grand Street Café, a restaurant right off the Plaza. It was tucked away off the street, so it was difficult to even know it was there, but it was, right behind Winstead's. Winstead's was a hamburger joint on the corner, and, I had to admit, it had the best damned hamburgers I had ever eaten. Grand Street was right behind Winstead's and I hadn't actually been there before. Harper assured me the food was excellent.

"Garrett has good taste," she said. "If he picked this place out."

We went in and saw Garrett waiting for us at the front of the restaurant. We followed him and our hostess to a back table right next to a window. This place didn't have much of a view but that was fine. We weren't there for the scenery.

"So," I said to Garrett. "What did you find out about Shelly?"

"Well," he said. "I found out something very interesting about her. Very interesting indeed. Now I told you about Wells Armstrong, the CEO of Armstrong Pharmaceuticals, and how Shelly was his mistress. At the time when I found out that piece of information, I wasn't aware of how Shelly met him in the first place."

The waitress came around and took our orders. I got the filet mignon, Harper got the cornbread encrusted trout, while Garrett ordered the pork chop.

"Everything is fantastic here, I can assure you," Garrett said. "Anyhow, where was I?"

"You were about to tell me about what you found out about how Shelly met Wells Armstrong."

"Yes. Shelly met Wells Armstrong in Los Angeles about a year ago. I talked to Wells' wife. She told me Wells is one of those businessmen who gets call girls when he's away on business trips. She knows all about it and apparently doesn't care. Personally, I get the feeling Mrs. Armstrong is a lesbian, but I can't be sure. At any rate, I have the feeling the marriage between the Armstrongs is strictly one of convenience."

Harper nodded her head. "Sounds about right. Go on."

"I asked Mrs. Armstrong about Wells and about his call girls. Mrs. Armstrong, her name is Naomi, she tells me she thinks Shelly was one of Wells' call girls out in LA. Like she was a regular girl for Wells when he went on business trips one summer."

Harper's eyes started to get wide as she started to understand what Garrett was telling us. "She worked there for a summer?" Harper asked. "Last summer, I would imagine?"

"Yeah. I mean, she was obviously living in Columbia, Missouri, for the school year. I checked out her school records and there wasn't any indication she ever took a leave of absence from school or anything like that. She was very active in her sorority as well. I interviewed some of her sorority sisters and none of them seemed to have any clue Shelly had any kind of a double life. They all described Shelly as being a prankster, fun-loving, and was always on different committees to make floats and house decs and was active in putting together their winter and spring parties. Attended all the football games, dated fraternity dudes, you know the drill. She was apparently the quintessential sorority girl. Her little sister in the sorority apparently idolized her."

I nodded my head. "So, in other words, there wasn't anything about her university or sorority life that gave anybody pause."

"Right. Shelly apparently kept her moonlighting activities very secret. I know why she did it. I managed to get my hands on her bank account and also managed to get a printout of her expenses. She was paying for her college completely out of her own pocket. Her parents really didn't contribute anything to her tuition or room and board or her sorority expenses or any of that." Garrett shook his head. "All over her dating a Muslim man. I guess it didn't help she was also dating Wells Armstrong, but still. Some people."

I had to smile. Garrett did have a sense of outrage for injustice and he obviously thought it was an injustice for Shelly's parents to cut her off financially.

"So, Shelly was a call girl in Los Angeles one summer," Harper said. "Are we sure she met Wells that way?"

"Yes," Garrett said. "I'm sure about that. I actually found her Madame, if you will. Her name is Irina Kovokosky, and, as you can tell from her name, she is a Russian national."

"And you spoke with Irina?" Harper asked, stirring her drink with her straw.

"I did. I spoke with her and she told me Wells was one of Shelly's regular clients. Wells apparently traveled to Los Angeles on a regular basis, and, that summer, Shelly and Wells were together quite often. Irina went through her books and told me Shelly and Wells met in Wells' hotel room 12 times that summer. I guess Shelly must have been pretty good at what she did. Either that or the two actually started to like each other. Considering the fact Shelly and Wells started an actual relationship after that summer tells me the two of them hit it off on different levels, not just sexually."

Harper rolled her eyes. "It's a regular *Pretty Woman* story. Successful businessman, prostitute, the two fall in love. Guess fairy tales really do come true." Her tone was sarcastic and she rolled her eyes and shook her head to emphasize the point.

I smiled, thinking Harper was sounding like me about love at that point. She seemed just as cynical about it. I wondered if all was okay between her and Axel.

"I wonder if any of this is significant," I said. "Irina is a Russian national. Does she have any mob ties? To the Russian mob or maybe the Armenian mob?" I knew the Armenian mob sometimes worked with the Russian mob. Irina might have some connection to Erik or even to Sargis. Most likely she would have a connection to Sargis if she was out in Los Angeles.

"I'm working on that angle," Garrett said. "She told me she didn't have any organized crime connections but she's going to say that to cover her ass. I'll have to uncover whether or not she is actually involved in organized crime. That will be my next step."

"Figure that out," Harper said. "And get back to us about what you have found. In the meantime, find out more about her relationship with Wells. Go through her financials, find out if he was paying her here in Kansas City. I somehow get the feeling we're really onto something." Harper was looking intense at the moment. Her green eyes were focused on Garrett's face and her fingers were stirring her drink faster and faster. "And see what you can find out about any other clients she might have had out in LA. This is a good lead but we need something more concrete. Not to mention the fact that her hacker background might have put her in contact with some people who literally want to kill her. She was a criminal hacker, underground, which meant she was involved in stealing people's identities and was also probably involved in other activities that would piss somebody off. Maybe she stole from the wrong person. Find out about her activities in that regard."

"What are you thinking about?" I asked Harper. "What kind of theory are you working on in your head right now?"

"I don't really know," Harper said. "Sargis paid me a visit yesterday. And he insists he didn't know Shelly was a journalist trying to get a story. Obviously, either he is lying or his son is. I don't know which one at the moment. I'm just trying to figure out if this Irina person might have been involved with Sargis. She's Russian, she's shady, but does she have mob ties? And just because she might have mob ties to the Russian mob, does that mean she also knows Sargis? It's kind of a six degrees of separation type thing at the moment but I need to get the thread to connect somehow."

I nodded my head. "At any rate, it's interesting information. It's information we didn't know before. I don't even think the media knows this story. They're obviously running the hacker background but they didn't know about the call girl thing."

That was an odd thing, I was thinking. Shelly was a call girl and a hacker. Yet, somehow, the media hadn't yet figured out she was a call girl. I wondered about this Irina Kovokosky person – I wondered how many girls she was managing and why none of the girls had come forward about Shelly's activities. That was usually what happened in situations like this – the media would figure out the popular blonde sorority girl was screwing men for money in her spare time and would be all over that like flies on shit. They would be talking to everybody Shelly knew in Los Angeles. Yet, the media never found out about it, and neither did the prosecutors or the cops here, apparently. Why would that be?

"Find out more about Irina," I said to Garrett. "Find out what kind of girls she manages and whether or not these girls were tight with Shelly. There's something about this whole situation that's not sitting right with me."

"I'll find out," Garrett said. "I'm working on that, anyhow. Irina is supposed to give me a list of Shelly's clients but she hasn't yet. I suppose that will happen any time now."

"Well," Harper said. "If Irina doesn't want to give you the list of clients we can issue a subpoena for them. And if that doesn't work, I have my own hacker who can find this out for us. Her name is Anna and she's amazing. There's nothing she can't find. She doesn't do it criminally, though. I mean, she does, in that she finds out information she's clearly not supposed to. But she doesn't steal and doesn't plant viruses and nonsense like that. I like to think of Anna as being more of a white hat hacker as opposed to a black hat hacker like Shelly was."

Our food came around and I realized I was starving. "And what about the other case I have you working on? The med mal case? You find out anything more?"

"Yeah," Garrett said. "I found out some more information about the anesthesiologist. Dr. Kim has apparently been involved in multiple cases over the years. I suppose that's probably not a huge surprise to you."

I shook my head. "No, not a surprise at all, unfortunately. It's usually my experience that doctors who screw up once like this, and I mean really screw up, tend to have left a trail of settled malpractice claims in their midst. I was pretty sure Dr. Kim would be much the same."

"Yeah," Garrett said. "He's been sued more than once, that's for sure. He's settled a lot of cases, though. That might be a good thing for you. It means he's willing to settle as opposed to dragging this case to trial."

"At this point," I said, "I hate to say it, but I'm probably going to bite at any kind of settlement offer they float to me. As I've been telling Betsy, it costs much more to try these cases than the money we'll make off this. Keep digging, maybe we can find that perfect angle that will give us the right leverage to make Dr. Kim and the Menorah Hospital to settle the case. In the meantime, I have a mandatory mediation meeting with Angela Hughes in two months. That will be after the discovery period has ended. The judge in this case has ordered this mediation so I have to go."

I felt good to have a fruitful path on the Dr. Kim case. I had the feeling he had been involved with other cases over the years, so I would have to hammer him about these cases when I finally got to depose him. I had sent out discovery requests to the other side – request for production of documents and interrogatories – but I hadn't yet gotten them back. I had the feeling that when I got them back, I would have even more areas to cover with Dr. Kim.

The waitress came around and served our food and the three of us just chatted throughout the rest of the evening. By the end of the evening, however, Harper asked if I would like to come for dinner and meet her two girls and boyfriend, Axel. As I understood it, Axel and Harper had been dating for a number of years. I didn't know much about him, except he was a police detective for the Kansas City Police Department and had been for a number of years. And Harper also said Axel was from Australia. Other than that, I was flying blind.

Yet, I was looking forward to meeting her family. I was starting to feel Harper was warming up to me just a bit. At first, when I came to work for her, she was just a little bit stand-offish. She had explained to me that she had been going through a battle for her sobriety in the past few months and was having issues with coming to terms with some dark parts of her past.

Her past couldn't possibly be darker than mine, however. I wondered when I would get the gumption to tell her about my stint in prison and all I had to go through to get to the other side. I wondered if she would judge me when I told her my three best friends growing up were all serving prison sentences. Connor's life sentence was without the possibility of parole. The others were up for parole next year. They had served 17 years of their sentence and I knew all three hadn't caught any other cases while on the inside. I knew all three of them had been model citizens on the inside. I thought the three men would have a decent chance of making their parole but I had mixed emotions about that. Connor would be devastated to lose them. I felt the most sorry for him because he was literally a kid when that all went down. A kid. It didn't seem fair that he would spend the rest of his life behind bars for something he did when he was only 16.

I wondered if there was a story there. If the other guys managed to get their parole, I wondered if I could get my Innocence Project attorneys on the case to try to free Connor. Not that Connor was innocent. He wasn't. But he was a completely different man. He was no longer the wild kid who idolized his older brother Jack. That was part of the reason why he brought the gun into the robbery – he wanted to impress Jack. Jack was always telling Connor he wasn't allowed to do much whenever the four of them would rob people. Connor always insisted on coming along but Jack would always tell him he had to stay in the car. Connor was assigned the permanent position of lookout guy and he didn't like that. That was why he ended up in that liquor store with a gun. He wanted to show Jack he could be useful.

That was the irony. He wanted to please Jack and show Jack he was adult enough to be in on the jobs. That was the reason why the four of them went down so hard for that robbery. If only nobody was killed, the guys probably would be gotten a sentence of 10 years, out in 8. The prisons were overcrowded so guys were getting out after serving 20% of their time. But for a Rob One, there's a mandatory minimum of 85% of the prison time served. The guys had a clean adult record, though, and their Juvenile Records were sealed and couldn't be used against them.

Connor only wanted to help. Instead, he signed their death warrants. Not literally, thank God. I think the jury took pity on the guys because they really never meant to hurt anyone. That was why the jury chose to sentence the guys to life in prison with the chance of parole.

I would have dinner with Harper the following evening. But first, I would have to visit Amelia and tell her the bad news about her mother. That was something I wasn't at all looking forward to.

TWELVE

I went to see Amelia that night. She was sitting up in bed, looking healthier than I had ever seen her. When she saw me, she smiled and I went over to the bed. I still had to wear a mask and gloves because I still had to be sterile. But the way Amelia was looking, I thought there was a glimmer of hope. No matter how slight.

"Dad," she said with obvious delight. "I'm so happy to see you tonight. I mean, I'm always happy to see you, but especially tonight."

"Especially tonight, huh?" I asked teasingly. "Why especially tonight?"

She shrugged. "I feel pretty decent tonight," she said. "For the first time in a long time, I actually feel like getting out of bed. I need to do something other than watch those stupid television shows all the time. I wish I could have a sterilized iPad or something like that but my nurses tell me I can't. I just can't wait until I get my surgery, though."

"I can't wait for you to get your surgery, either," I said. And then I paused. I would have to tell her about her mother. Not she would be surprised in the least. I knew she wouldn't be. She had to know her mother and I were having problems. It was obvious Sarah had checked out on Amelia long ago. Really, Amelia didn't have a mother, and hadn't had one for quite some time.

"But Kitten, I have to tell you something."

"You and Sarah are getting a divorce," she said in a matter-of-fact tone. "I know. Sarah was by earlier today to tell me all about it." She rolled her eyes. She had recently started referring to her mother as "Sarah." I knew why – Amelia apparently wasn't feeling Sarah was her mother anymore. Sarah was really a stranger to her. "It's no big deal, of course. Sarah hasn't been my mom pretty much since I got sick. It's not like I'll be missing out on some kind of undying devotion or anything like that. She wasn't like Austin's mom. That woman was dedicated."

I blinked. It never occurred to me that Amelia might know Austin. "You know Austin Ward?" I asked her. "I mean, you knew him?"

"Yeah," she said. "When I first got here, before I started all that chemotherapy and stuff that lowered my immunity system so much, I could go around and see other kids in the cancer ward. Austin was one of the kids I saw. He taught me how to play chess. That was before he was isolated, too, for his surgery. Turns out I'm a natural, or at least that's what Austin tells me. I'm gonna take lessons when I get out of this place."

"You know what happened to him, right?" I asked her.

"Yeah. That's pretty sad. He was a good guy." She looked down at her hands and then looked up at me. "I met his mom, too. She really loved Austin. Austin thought it was kinda weird, though, because his mom was dating one of his doctors. Nobody really knew about it but Austin did. He didn't like that his mom was dating his doctor, though."

My ears perked up when Amelia said that. "Dating one of Austin's doctors? Do you know which one? Did Austin tell you which doctor his mom was dating?"

"Yeah, he did. He told me his mom was dating a doctor in the hospital. He wasn't really Austin's doctor, but he does lots of surgeries. He's one of those guys who puts people to sleep before they get operated on."

I closed my eyes. "Was his name Dr. Kim, by any chance?"

"Yeah," Amelia said, pointing at me. "Dr. Kim. How did you know that?"

"A hunch," I said. I wondered what was going on. That was the strangest thing. Betsy never told me she and Dr. Kim once dated. I would have thought that was really odd, to say the very least. She dated him and now she's suing him?

I didn't really think much of that fact, other than I knew I would have to have words with Betsy about what Amelia just told me. I couldn't have my clients hiding such huge facts from me. It was bound to affect her case against Dr. Kim and against the hospital. I was happy that Amelia outed the two of them, however. If she didn't I might not have figured out what was going on until it was too late. Garrett was bound to find out but hadn't so far.

I wanted to change the subject. I would get to the bottom of the Dr. Kim thing with Betsy in due time. For now, though, I needed to really see how my daughter was doing emotionally. Now that she knew her mom and I were splitting up, it had to affect her.

"How do you really feel about your mother and I splitting up?" I asked her.

She shrugged. "It's fine. Most of the kids around here have parents splitting up. We had this group therapy when I first got here and most of the kids talked about that. The therapist told us all that splitting up is what sometimes happens to parents when their kids get sick. I guess people can't really handle their kids being sick and maybe gonna die and they end up breaking up. It happens." She shrugged again. "But are you going to start dating again?" She scrunched up her nose and shook her head. "Tell me you're not going to bring a lot of women to the house."

That was something I wouldn't do. I didn't tell her why I wouldn't do it but I knew the truth. After the way my mother brought guy after guy to our trailer home, I promised myself I would never do that to a kid of mine. That pretty much meant I wouldn't bring a woman home to meet Amelia and Nate until I was sure I would marry the woman. And that wouldn't be for a long, long time. Maybe never. After the way Sarah burned me, I didn't think I could trust anybody for awhile.

"I won't be bringing women to the house," I said. "I promise."

"Pinky swear?" she asked me, holding out her pinky.

"Pinky swear," I said, holding out my pinky. We both wiggled our pinkies at each other since we couldn't actually touch.

"That's good," she said. "I mean, Sarah already has a dude. His name is John and he looks sleazy. Hair all greased back like a douche. He brought me a gift, it's over there," she said, pointing to a stuffed animal on a little table next to her bed. "Guess he thinks I'm some kind of baby or something."

I closed my eyes, feeling the rage bubbling to the surface. "Your mother brought her new boyfriend here? To your hospital room?"

"Yeah," Amelia said. "You're much cuter than he is, though," she said. "And much cooler, too. He's so weird. He just tells stupid jokes. Knock knock jokes." She rolled her eyes. "Again, he must think I'm a baby. Or in kindergarten. I told him I'm in the second grade and he's all 'knock, knock.'" She rapped the air. "Lame."

Amelia was in the second grade even though she was only six. That was because she skipped a grade. My daughter was brilliant and I still couldn't believe Sarah had given up on her so quickly. She would be sorry one day when Amelia wins the Nobel Prize for finding a cure for cancer. If anybody would go on to cure cancer, it would be Amelia.

I straightened up in my chair. "Tell your mom not to bring him around anymore," I said. "That's not right she would do that."

"I don't care. Sarah is dating a douche. I guess that's news to the world, but it is what it is. I just don't want you to bring women around because I'll apparently be living with you. Sarah told me that too."

I smiled. "Is there anything that escapes you?"

"No." She laughed. "Nothing."

I wanted so badly to smooth back her hair. Tell her a story like when she was three years old and wanted to hear *Half Magic* for the eightieth time. That was a book I loved when I was a kid, and I wanted to share it with her. She understood it, even at a young age. I told Amelia that story and so many others. But there wouldn't be any of those stories anymore. She had already outgrown them. That made me sad, in a way, but I was also looking forward to the day when she really outgrew them. I was looking forward to the day when we could put cancer behind us and her doctor actually tells me Amelia can expect to live a long and fruitful life.

The nurse came around. "Visiting hours are over," she said. "I know you're her parent so technically you can visit her anytime, but she needs her rest. Her big day happens next week."

She was referring to the date of Amelia's surgery. I looked forward to that day yet also dreaded it. After all, Betsy was looking forward to her son's surgery, too. She obviously had high hopes. Her son never came out of surgery.

Would that happen to Amelia?

THIRTEEN

The next day, I decided to do some digging of my own. Garrett's report about Wells Armstrong got me curious. I decided to call Irina myself and ask her some questions over the phone. Hopefully she would answer them truthfully.

Harper and I met in the conference room to get a status update on the Erik Gregorian case. We often did this to brainstorm and I would tell her what was on my mind. I needed to clear with her what I would do.

She brought in some Krispy Kreme donuts. "I know, I know," she said. "Donuts are crap. They're terrible for your health, clog your arteries and there's way too much sugar in them." She looked at me apologetically. "But they sure taste amazing."

I picked up a jelly-filled one, finding it was warm. "Are these right off the line?" I asked her.

"I wish," she said. "No, I just come in here and put them into the microwave for about twenty seconds." She went over to the Keurig machine and made me a cup of a coffee and sat down with her bottled water. I was starting to learn that Harper wasn't fond of caffeine. I never saw her drink coffee or even tea. The only thing I saw her drink was bottled water. I wondered if she ever got bored.

"Now," she said, "we found some pretty good information from Garrett. That might be why Nick Wright just called to see if I was interested in a plea deal. We have our first pre-trial conference next week with the trial judge, Judge Clarion, so I want to get a lay of the land before I go before him. He'll want to see if we can plea this case out but I want a better idea of how strong the DA's case is before I commit to anything."

"What are you thinking about?" I asked.

"Well, obviously, we have to find some major holes. I got a court order allowing us to inspect the car and I'm sending an expert down there to do just that. I thought it was pretty odd that witnesses told the police that Shelly was driving at a high rate of speed. If it was simply that her brakes weren't working, why was she slamming her foot on the gas? Most people would try to slow down by taking their foot off the gas and hope to coast to a stop that way. Or they might be even smarter than that and would pull up on the emergency brake or turn the car off. Shelly didn't strike me as being a stupid woman. Surely she was smart enough to figure out how to maneuver a car that didn't have brakes."

"She might have panicked," I said. "That's what I think happened. She was driving on the highway during a busy part of the day. She was probably going 70 or 80 before she realized she didn't have brakes. So, she's driving at a good clip, she puts her foot on the brake, and nothing happens. At that point, she panicked and puts her foot on the gas. That happens when people panic – their brain confuses the pedals. When I was in law school, I interned for an insurance defense firm. They had a case where somebody got behind the wheel, got confused and hit the gas instead of the brake. He ended up pinning a woman's legs against the wall. She lost both of her legs from the knee down. I'm telling you, it happens more often than you might think."

"I know," Harper said, nodding . "And I totally get what you're saying. I'm saying that it needs to be looked into a bit more. So I found an expert to examine that car. His name is Joseph Savolo and he's been a car mechanic for twenty years. He'll testify in court if we ask him and he finds anything out about the car that is suspicious."

"I guess I don't really know what that will prove," I said. "So, he finds out that there was something else wrong with the car. How does that exonerate Erik?"

"It's a causation thing," she said. "Yes, her brake lines were completely cut but that didn't actually cause her death. Maybe there was some other kind of defect that caused the car to careen out of control. If we can present to the jury that Shelly wouldn't have died but for the other defect, then..."

I shook my head. "I know what you're saying, but it sounds like a losing strategy to me. You can't show Shelly wouldn't have died if the car wasn't defective in some other way. Assuming you find some other kind of defect. The truth of that matter is, she was driving on the highway when her car went out of control and she was killed. Just having her brake lines cut would possibly be enough to kill her even absent some other defect. Go ahead and have your expert, Joseph Savante, take a look at the car, but I don't think this is something to hang our hat on."

"Savolo," Harper said. "Joseph's last name is Savolo, not Savante."

"Oh," I said, shaking my head. Truth be told, Nick Savante was on my mind and had been every day for the past 17 years. Him and Tommy and Jack and Connor. All the guys were on my mind constantly. "Savolo."

Harper cocked her head and stared at me. She seemed to know that something was bothering me.

"Anything you want to tell me?" she asked.

"No," I said. "Why?"

"I don't know. You just got this funny look on your face. Not funny ha ha, but funny strange."

I shook my head. "Nothing, nothing. I was just thinking about a buddy of mine I used to know. Wondering how he's doing. What he's up to."

"You should visit him," Harper said. "If you're thinking about him I'm sure he probably thinks about you, too. Trust me, it's always a good thing to reconnect. I had a girlfriend I haven't seen in about 10 years. Then I looked her up on Facebook, we had dinner and it was just like we never stopped talking to one another. I always used to think about her and now she and I are friends again. I wondered why we ever lost touch in the first place."

I swallowed hard. I wanted to tell her it wasn't exactly like that. If I wanted to see Nick I would have to go to Cameron prison to see him.

"Yeah," I said. "Maybe I'll just do that. What you say – look him up on Facebook and see if I can catch up with him." I cleared my throat. "Anyhow, I'm going to call Irina Kovokosky today. I'll see if she can tell me anything more about Shelly and the work she was doing for her. I hope she talks to me. I'll get a feel for her and see if she might make a good witness for Erik's trial."

Harper nodded. "That's a good idea. I'm going to put in a phone call to Wells Armstrong myself today. I'm hoping he'll meet with me. Maybe you work the Irina angle and I'll work the Wells angle, and we can meet here after both of us talk to our respective witnesses. I have a feeling we'll be going down a fruitful path if we work it this way. At any rate, it will give us some indication on where this case will be heading and what our strategy will be."

Harper gathered together the documents she had spread out on the table and looked at her watch. "Well, I have to get going. I have a pre-trial conference on a different case. It's also a murder case but I think that this one will plead out. It's death penalty eligible but I have an offer on the table for 30 years. I'll tell my client to jump all over that one."

I nodded my head. "Careful, though, Harper. You know what they say when you sell your house and somebody takes your offer within a day. That means you priced your house too low. If the prosecutor is offering you 30 years on a death penalty case, that might mean there's something you're overlooking about the case. Something the prosecutor knows that you don't. All I'm saying is this — if it sounds too good to be true, it probably is. Look closer."

Harper nodded. "I know what you're saying, and you're probably right. I'll have to figure that out, though. In the meantime, get on the horn with Irina and see what you can find out. I'll set up an appointment with Wells in the next few days. I'll see you later."

At that, she walked rapidly out the door of the conference room and disappeared down the hall.

FOURTEEN

I called Irina after Harper left the conference room. I fully expected to get her voice mail, so I was surprised when she answered the phone.

"Irina Kovokosky," she said. "How can I help you?"

I cleared my throat. "Ms. Kovokosky," I said. "My name is Damien Harrington, and I would like to speak with you about one of your girls. Shelly McMason."

"Yes," she said. Her voice was dripping and strong, like honey. She had a definite accent, although I could distinctly understand every word she said. "Mr. Harrington. I was expecting your call. That is why I picked up the phone. I usually let it go to voice mail, because nobody calls me on my cell phone except those sleazy telemarketers trying to sell me everything under the sun. But I recognize your phone number – 816 area code. I thought it might be you calling me."

This was encouraging. I thought she might be reluctant to speak with me. After all, her business was technically illegal – she was sending out call girls. Garrett told me Irina billed her company as an escort service but it apparently was no more an escort service than all those Las Vegas "escort services" were. I always had to laugh when the street vendors handed out those little flyers with the naked women on them on the streets of Las Vegas. They were advertising for escorts but the girls in the pictures were naked, so you had to know they were offering something other than just a date for lonely men.

I could hear her puffing away on a cigarette. "What would you like to ask me about Shelly?" she asked. "I'll tell you anything you need to know but won't testify in court. Not unless you subpoena me and pay for my travel. I have no desire to go to Kansas City in the dead of winter and your investigator, Tom Garrett, told me the trial is scheduled for December. My tits are freezing just thinking about going there at that time. I left Russia to get away from the cold."

I had to stifle a smile as Irina told me about her frozen tits. "Don't worry," I said. "I don't anticipate you'll have to testify but I reserve the right to change my mind. If I issue a subpoena, you'll be required to attend trial, of course. But I will pay your traveling expenses."

She snorted. "Big whoop. You couldn't pay me enough to go there in December. So I hope I can tell you what I know and that will be that."

"Okay," I said. "What can you tell me about Shelly? How did she come to work for you?"

"Well, I can tell you one thing about Shelly. She's a live one. But she never did strike me as a working girl. Her heart wasn't in it. She specifically wanted to meet wealthy men in the Los Angeles area and specifically was interested in men high up in the pharmaceutical business. I don't judge. I have plenty of wealthy men like that, including CEOs and other kinds of officers working in the pharmaceutical business. I liked Shelly. She was a beautiful girl, great tits and tight little ass, but that wasn't why I liked her. I liked her because she was whip smart. I knew I could send her out on dates with wealthy men and they wouldn't be offended. She came from that world, too, so that helped. She spoke the language and she had impeccable table manners. That's what I look for in my girls when they want to date wealthy men. They must have excellent manners, they must look the part – I don't like my girls to be trashy – they must be extremely intelligent and it helps if they come from wealth. Shelly fit all the bills so she was very much in demand in that world."

"So you send your girls out to wealthy men. And do they end up taking the girls out, or-"

"Yes," Irina said. "I'm not operating a sex ring here. If the man wants to have sex with the girl, she has to, of course. But many of my men don't even want my girls for sex. They might actually need a date for some kind of high society function, or a wedding or something like that. Sometimes they want a girl they can travel with because their wives don't want to travel with them. My girls are not just there for the sex but also for companionship. They're also there because these men need some kind of stress relief and they're not demanding like other girls are. These men like my girls because they aren't trying to trap them into a relationship – they're only around for these men's enjoyment. Nothing more and nothing less."

I nodded, making notes as she spoke. "So, Shelly was interested in meeting players in the pharmaceutical industry. Is that right?"

"Yes, that's right. She explained her father was a big-wheel in the pharmaceutical industry in Kansas City. Apparently her father never allowed Shelly to go to industry functions so she didn't actually know people in that industry. I thought it was a bit odd she was so specific but then I figured she was looking for somebody like her father. I get that a lot. Lots of girls with daddy issues."

"Did she mention that she had a boyfriend? His name is Yasin Ahmadi and he's apparently a native of Iraq. He came over here when he was a small child and his parents obtained refugee status. From what I understand, Shelly and Yasin were very much in love for several years. Did she talk about him at all?"

"No," Irina said. "She never mentioned a Muslim man. That doesn't mean this Yasin wasn't in the picture. Do you know when she broke up with him?"

I thought about what Garrett had scribbled in his report to Harper and me. That stood out to me – Garrett had spoken with a number of Shelly's friends who all told him that Shelly and Yasin were still together at the time of Shelly's death. At first, the friends thought Shelly was only dating Yasin because she wanted to piss off her father. Which she did, of course. She pissed him off but good. Obviously - her father cut her off financially when she started to date Yasin. But her friends soon came to the conclusion that Shelly and Yasin were made for each other. Yasin was Muslim and his parents were from the old country but he was completely American and liberal. He was observant of the Muslim faith but didn't have the antiquated ideas about women that many traditional Muslim men have.

That said, Yasin's father and mother were apparently much more old-school than was Yasin. Abdullah Ahmadi and his wife, Rimsha, had very orthodox views about life. Culturally, according to Garrett, Yasin and his parents couldn't be more different. Yasin was Westernized – he wore blue-jeans and button-downs, he played video games with his friends and met with his co-workers for beers after work. He listened to rap music as much as he listened to classical music and he never listened to Traditional Arabic music like his parents did. He and his parents apparently clashed about this, but Yasin didn't seem to care. He was too busy having fun with his friends.

That said, according to the report, Garrett indicated that Yasin was observant in the Muslim religion. He had a prayer rug and said his Islamic prayers several times a day. He observed Ramadan and all the Muslim holy days. He even kept the dietary restrictions of the religion. He understood his religion to be one of peace even though he knew that many Muslims, like his father, had a more radical view of the Quran.

I wondered how Abdullah and Rimsha felt about Yasin seeing Shelly. And what if they found out about Shelly's extracurricular activities with the wealthy men in Los Angeles? For that matter, what if Yasin found out about it? Could he have been angry enough to kill Shelly?

"I don't think they broke up," I said. "As far as I know, Shelly and Yasin were still seeing each other when she died."

"Oh, well, there you go," Irina said. "Shelly was seeing these wealthy men behind Yasin's back and he killed her. Happens all the time, especially with those Muslims. There, I solved the case for you."

"Thank you," I said. "But I'm Erik Gregorian's lawyer. He's been charged with Shelly's murder. I owe it to him to do more than a cursory examination of the likely candidates for her murder. That means I need to know more from you about Shelly and her relationships with her clients. I understand she was seeing Wells Armstrong on a regular basis and they came back to Kansas City and resumed their relationship. Is that right?"

"Yes. That is right. Wells Armstrong became one of Shelly's regular clients, and, by the end of that summer, Wells was her only client. I didn't mind because Wells had her more or less full-time so she was getting paid a lot of money to be his escort. That kept the money flowing to me, too, so I let her keep seeing Wells and excluding her other men."

"Did she explain why she was seeing Wells full time?"

"No. She didn't. But I assumed the two of them hit it off. That happens sometimes, you know. A client becomes infatuated with a girl, the girl becomes infatuated with the client, and the two of them start an actual relationship. It doesn't happen often, but it does happen. I assumed that was what happened here. I didn't know Shelly also had another man in Kansas City. She never spoke of that."

I made notes, but that seemed odd to me. From Garrett's report, Shelly and Yasin really seemed to be in love. Those friends never even knew this Wells fellow existed in Shelly's life. She never spoke of him to her friends. They never met him. She went out with her friends but always with Yasin in tow, not Wells. Yet supposedly Shelly was also in a relationship with Wells. I wondered if he kept paying her when they got back to Kansas City and Shelly resumed her "normal" life, whatever that meant for her.

"Okay," I said. "I think I have the picture of what was going on with Wells and Shelly. Can I ask you just a few more questions?"

"Certainly," she said. "As I said, I'm eager to help you over the phone because I don't want you to call me as a witness in trial. I hope we can avoid that at all costs."

"I won't make any promises," I said. "But I'll certainly try to avoid calling you at trial. Now I need to know if you have any connections to the Russian mob." I certainly didn't think she would tell me the truth if she did, but I still wanted to get her reaction. "And if you are familiar with a man named Sargis Gregorian."

"Sure, sure," she said, to my surprise. "Not to the question about my having connections to the Russian mob, but to the question about Sargis Gregorian. I know him. Just about everybody knows him here in Los Angeles. He runs a large part of LA and many of us have to pay him in order for us to work in his territories."

My ears perked up. "Do you have to pay him? Are you in his territory?"

"I'm not at liberty to say," she said. "You can take what you will from that answer."

"I'll take that to mean you have to pay him," I said.

"Listen, that is how it works here in Los Angeles. Sargis makes everybody pay him. Everybody from the lowly guy running a convenience store to people like me who run less-than-legal businesses. And I don't mind paying him, either. He has most of the LAPD in his pocket. I pay him and he keeps the cops off my doorstep. I consider that to be getting quite a lot for my money."

I cleared my throat. "Would it surprise you to know that Erik is implying his father might have been behind Shelly's hiring? That Sargis Gregorian told my client, Erik, that Shelly was above-board when she really wasn't?"

"So? What are you trying to say here?"

I wasn't quite sure what I was getting at. Something was nagging me about Irina especially since I figured out that Irina and Sargis not only knew one another but were financially connected to each other.

"I'm not sure," I said truthfully. "I don't really know what I'm getting at. I'm trying to put the puzzle pieces together."

"Well, if you ask me, I would look at that Yasin fellow. I know those Muslims and how they treat women. They would consider it a real dishonor to find out their woman was an escort for wealthy men. It's always the boyfriend, anyhow, but in this case, I would seriously consider it's the boyfriend this time, too."

"I'll do that."

I would keep both Yasin and his father in mind. Either one of them might have been angered into killing Shelly. But, at the same time, maybe not. It seemed sabotaging Shelly's car would be too subtle. I knew about honor killings, which was what this might fall under, and they usually killed the girl outright with a knife. They didn't go to elaborate means. They just came right out and did it.

Besides, this wouldn't be an honor killing, *per se*. A true honor killing involved a member of the person's family. Usually the girl would be killed because she had sex with a boy or even if she was raped. The girls might also be murdered because they renounced the faith, they refused an arranged marriage or they had feminist ideas. I didn't think it was customary to kill somebody who was only dating a guy from a Muslim family. I really didn't think Shelly's case fell under the auspices of a traditional honor killing.

I hung up the phone and stared at my notes. I was eager to get with Harper and see what she could tell me after she spoke with Wells. I wondered if the stories would match up. Would Wells admit to that he met Shelly through an "escort service?" Did Wells know about Yasin? If he did know about Yasin, what did he know about him and how much did he know? Did Shelly and Wells have an understanding? Did Shelly and Yasin have an understanding? And what about Irina? She had a monetary relationship with Sargis. Was that significant?

So many questions, so few answers. My trial strategy was starting to take shape, however. There were enough candidates who might have reason to want Shelly dead that it would be fairly easy to steer the jury away from Erik. While I was with Harper – we both thought Erik was good for the crime – I was encouraged there appeared to be enough alternate suspects that we could build a decent case.

I called Harper and she answered from her car. "Yeah, Damien," she said. "What did you find out?" Then she groaned. "When are they ever going to coordinate these goddamned traffic lights a little better? I swear to God, I'm sitting here at a red light and the light ahead of me is green as a Christmas tree. So, when I get up to that light, it's going to be just turning red. This kind of shit drives me crazy even after all these years."

I heard her humming along to the radio. "I just spoke with Irina," I said. "I found out some interesting tidbits."

"She knows Sargis, doesn't she?" Harper asked.

"Well, yeah, and that's interesting, too. But Shelly went to Los Angeles to sign up with this service specifically because she wanted to meet wealthy men highly placed in the pharmaceutical industry."

"Hmmmm," Harper said, drawing out that word. "She specifically wanted to meet wealthy men highly placed in the pharmaceutical industry. Out in Los Angeles, specifically. I wonder what's up with that? Hopefully I'll find that out when I speak with Wells himself. I hope he'll give me something to go on with this."

"I have a feeling he's going to. Provide some kind of clarity, that is. In the meantime, I-"

I looked up and saw Pearl was peeking her head through the door. "This came for you," she mouthed, seeing I was on the phone. "I mean, it came for Harper. But it looks pretty important so I need you to review it."

It was a FedEx package. I examined it while I spoke with Harper, wondering what it was. It was a box that wasn't very large at all – it was the size of a ring box, maybe just a bit larger.

"You what?" Harper asked. "I'm sorry, you cut off in mid-sentence just now."

I had lost my train of thought. "I forgot what I wanted to say." Usually, when I forget what I was about to say, I try to fill the conversation with small talk. That usually got me back on track. "In the meantime, I'll be seeing you tonight for dinner. I'll bring the dessert." For me, bringing dessert usually meant I would go to the Hen House, a grocery store near where I lived in Leawood, and pick up a Tiramisu. But, for tonight, I actually special ordered a Tiramisu from a gourmet grocer across the street from the Hen House. I didn't want to go too cheap for Harper.

"Yes. Bring the dessert. I'll see you at 7."

We hung up.

I never did remember what I was going to tell Harper.

FIFTEEN

I tore open the FedEx package and saw a small portable drive inside.
I immediately put the drive into the USB port on my computer and
booted it up.

There, on the screen, was Shelly. Her blonde hair was pulled up
in a ponytail and she was fresh-faced. This was the first time I had
actually seen the girl, except for in pictures in the newspaper after
she died. Other than, of course, her gruesome death photo.

I was struck by her beauty. She had creamy skin, big blue eyes
and a tiny frame. She was dressed in a t-shirt that said *I'm not always
rude and sarcastic. Sometimes I'm asleep.* I had to smile just a little at
that. Even though she looked the part of the sorority girl, she seemed
to have the fuck-you attitude I always found appealing.

She was staring at the screen and shook her head from side to side
for a few seconds. Then she bit her lower lip.

I soon realized this was a video diary. She stated the date as
August 9 of the previous year, so this video diary was presumably
filmed over a year ago. "There's not much to tell," she said. "My dad
is a fuck-head, as usual, but I don't give a shit about that anymore. He
seems to have a problem with Yasin. I mean, of course he has a

problem with Yasin. That's why he won't pay for the rest of my schooling. I'm in my last year and want to go to NYU and get my master's, but it looks like I'll have to be paying for that on my own. Thank God I got that job last summer. That was a pretty lucrative job, too, paid very well. I can pay my tuition, books, apartment and everything else I need this year, and be paying it all out of pocket. I don't need him or his money." Then she raised her eyebrow. "And it looks like I'll have to keep on working that job if I'll make a go of Yasin and me. He just found out he's been accepted into medical school at UMKC. He wants to get married but his parents don't exactly approve of the two of us, either. I'll have to be the bread-winner for a little while because I don't want Yasin to go into too much debt."

I made notes as she spoke. So far, she was confirming a few theo-ries I had about her. Specifically, I now knew exactly why she was working as a call girl. She wanted to marry Yasin and support him while he went through medical school. Since her parents cut her off and his parents apparently did the same, she would have to make money. Lots of money. Yet, she was a journalist, working for the *Kansas City Star*. That surely didn't pay much money. I had to wonder why she chose that field if she had to make enough money to support both herself and Yasin while Yasin attended medical school.

I then wondered if she kept doing her call-girl routine in Kansas City. Was she working as a call-girl at night? Yasin was presumably very busy as a first-year medical student. It was likely he wouldn't even notice if she went out at night to meet men. Maybe she was working as a call girl while working for *The Star*. All while infiltrating Erik's clan as a computer hacker. If that was the case, she was a busy girl indeed.

That video diary soon ended and a new one began. She began this diary entry like she began the last one, stating the date, October 18 of last year. This time, she was wearing some makeup and was dressed in a button-down and a jacket. Her lips were bright red and she was clearly wearing eye-shadow and mascara. "I'm sorry I didn't make more entries," she said. "I've been busy. Because, you know, life. But I'm on my way to a job and I wanted to check in. I'm graduating this December, so yay." She pumped both of her fists into the air. "And I got a job lined up with *The Kansas City Star*. I would like to think I got that job because of my grades at MU but I suspect I got that job because Andrew is a huge benefactor." She rolled her eyes. I recognized the name "Andrew" was her father's name, so she must have been referring to him. "Yeah, I'm not going to refer to him as 'Dad' anymore, because he's not. He hasn't returned my phone calls in three month so I've officially wiped him clean from my memory banks. Or something."

She ran her pinky along her lower lip as if she was putting on lip gloss, and then appeared to adjust the camera a bit. "Anyhow, I have this job I have to do." She rolled her eyes. "I don't want to do it but I have to. I wish I could just work my job at *The Star* and do my hacking, but it kinda looks like I'll have to make more money so Yasin and I can get married. Being poor sucks. I've never been poor, but I'm starting to experience what's it's like and I think I hate it. So I'll do something to make sure I'm not poor anymore." Then there was a knock at her door. "Okay," she said, taking a big breath. "Looks like it's showtime. I'll do another entry when I have something new to talk about. Bye."

I wondered why I was in possession of this video diary. I looked at the package and it was anonymous. I didn't know who sent it. I therefore didn't know the motivation of the person who would have sent it. That bothered me. Somebody obviously wanted us to have it but who? And why?

I watched several more episodes of the video diary. It was much the same. She lamented about her life, talked about what she was doing for the newspaper, talked about working with the Gregorian clan and talked about marrying Yasin. She was animated when she spoke about working with the Gregorians. That seemed to make her come alive.

"This is such a cool assignment they've given me," she said in one of her video diaries she made in February of this year. "They found out about my hacking skills, so they've arranged for me to work for the Gregorians. They're an Armenian mob clan that's operating on the East Side." She rubbed her hands together with glee. "I need some excitement in my life. Yasin just started his medical school classes and he's never around. I knew that would happen, of course. He's always in class or in the library studying. Either that or he's in labs." She rolled her eyes. "And he'll be doing rotations in his third and fourth years. And then he'll be a resident working 100 hours a week. I'm obviously going to have to fill my time in some way. I'll have to satisfy my adrenaline-junkie side some way and working for the Armenian mob is the perfect way to do it."

Her eyes got wide and she grinned. "I love to live with danger. Life is so boring without it. I love knowing I might be killed at any moment for doing what I'm doing. I mean, I don't want to die, but I love the possibility of it."

I took a deep breath, wondering what these video diaries meant. I was getting a good picture of Shelly the girl by these diaries. But it was weird she never spoke directly about Wells. She talked about doing jobs in the evenings but never said what those jobs were. It was almost as if she was thinking ahead – she was thinking these video diaries might one day be viewed by somebody other than herself and didn't want to put it out there what she was doing.

Then, in the last video diary, I suddenly understood why I was in possession of this thumb drive in the first place. For the last video entry told me everything I needed to know.

As I watched it, I suddenly understood. The person who sent this thumb drive to Harper wanted her to see this last video entry specifically.

It was a video entry that sounded like a woman on the verge of suicide.

SIXTEEN

HARPER

I answered my phone, seeing it was Damien calling and I picked up. I was in the lobby of our building, waiting for the elevator. My pre-trial conference for my other murder case didn't exactly go as planned. My client, David Wilson, was there and he informed me that he wouldn't take the prosecutor's 30-year plea deal. I wanted to brain him when he said that, and I reminded him that he was facing the death penalty if we took the case to trial.

No matter. He wanted his day in court.

I had stewed about this case all the way to my office building, but, at the same time, Damien's words rang in my ears. *Be careful about taking an easy plea deal. The prosecutor probably knows something you don't.* Or something like that. And that made sense. It *did* seem the prosecutor was trying to get rid of this case. I hadn't yet gotten her discovery on the case, either. I calmed down as I wondered exactly what Montel Jefferson, the prosecutor on this case, might be hiding.

So, it looked like I had another murder trial on my hands and I felt like I would go bonkers.

"Yeah, Damien," I said, picking up the phone.

"Harper, are you close to the office?" he asked.

"I'm in the lobby, actually, waiting for the elevator. Why? What's up?"

"There's something you need to see."

I was immediately curious. "What?"

"You're in the lobby? You'll be here soon enough. I'll show it to you when you get here."

Now I was good and curious. I hoped it was good news. After the day I had, I needed a pick-me-up.

I got into the office suite and went to Damien's office. He wasn't there so I went down to the conference room. He was in there, staring at his computer and shaking his head.

"Hey," I said. "What's up?"

Damien looked up at me. "What is the possibility Shelly was suicidal?" he asked without preamble.

"I don't know, why?"

"Somebody sent us this in the mail," he said, taking a thumb drive out of his computer and holding it up. "It's a video diary. I've been watching it for the past several hours. It's a fascinating look at Shelly's life. She documented her frustrations, her fears and her dreams. She was really quite funny in a sarcastic type of way. But it's her final video diary entry I really want you to see."

I cocked my head and laid my bag on the conference room table. I went over to Damien's computer and paused. Shelly's pretty face was frozen on the screen. She had bags under her eyes and it appeared she had been crying.

"Now," Damien said. "I'll give you a brief synopsis of what she was saying in her earlier entries. She talked about how she hates her father and how she was excited to marry Yasin. She also seemed amped about her job with Erik's clan. She said she loved danger and loved the feeling she was endangering her life by working for the Gregorians. She was that type of girl, apparently, the thrill-seeker. The kind of person for whom boredom is the deadliest feeling of all. Bear in mind, in every single one of her entries, her demeanor was the same. She didn't seem depressed in any of her entries. She seemed annoyed in a lot of them, happy in others, but not depressed. But look at this one."

He backed up the video several minutes and then Shelly came to life. Her shoulders were slumped and she had been crying. Most worrying of all, there was a large bruise covering her left eye. "He hit me," she said, her voice cracking. She shook her head. "I don't know what to do. I think he's dangerous. I never thought he was dangerous. And I'm scared. I'm so scared because I've been feeling this isn't worth it anymore. None of this is worth it anymore. And I've been having nightmares lately about the baby. I don't think I want to be here anymore. I don't want to give him the satisfaction of my death, but I feel there's nothing to live for here. There's nothing here for me. Tell my mother I'm sorry. Tell-"

And it cut off.

Damien looked up at me. I just shook my head. "Well, that muddies the waters. Couldn't the girl be more clear about what she was thinking? And what was up with that video just cutting off like that in the middle of her speaking? Seriously."

Damien stood up. "It sounds like she wanted to commit suicide to me."

"Yeah, maybe. It also sounds like she was afraid of somebody. And what's up with that talk about 'the baby?' She wasn't pregnant when she was killed. If she were, I would have seen something about it. And who was being violent to her? She was going to say goodbye to different people, it sounded like, or she was sorry. She was trying to apologize to her mother and it sounded like she would go down the list. Then she cut off."

That video should have been my saving grace. If Shelly were suicidal, and she actually did commit suicide, then that would explain why she was traveling at a high rate of speed and crossed the median. That was one way to kill yourself. I always hated people who did that, though, because they often took out others. It was like an airline pilot who deliberately crashes a plane because he's suicidal. Yes, kill yourself, but don't bring others into it. If Shelly killed herself by crashing her car, that's what she was doing – she was endangering other people because she wanted to die. That wasn't right.

"Let me get the report back from my car expert," I said. "Savolo is supposed to look at the car in a couple of days. He can tell me if there was some kind of a defect. If there wasn't, then maybe you're right. Maybe Shelly committed suicide. But there's not enough here on the video to establish that. And we're still faced with the fact that somebody had the intent to kill her. We don't yet know who it is but if there's one thing I know, it's this – it makes zero sense for a suicidal person to tamper with her own brakes. If she was suicidal and wanted to die in a car accident, she would have just driven recklessly and crashed her car. Right?"

Damien shook his head. "No. Maybe she wanted to frame somebody for murdering her."

"If that were the case, then wouldn't she have made that last video diary entry a little bit differently? For instance, if she was trying to frame, let's say, Yasin, for killing her, then she would have said Yasin's name. She would have said 'Yasin is violent and I'm afraid of him. He hit me, causing this bruise on my eye. And then, just so there wasn't any question, she would have probably said something like 'If something happens to me, Yasin did it.' At least, that's how I would have done it if I was trying to frame somebody for my murder."

For some reason, that video diary entry irritated me. I wished the girl had stated who she was afraid of. Who hit her. Explained more about the baby. And I wished she would have figured out when her recorder had quit recording.

"I'm sorry, Damien, but it's not a smoking gun. I'll have a look at the rest of the video entries and see what I can glean from them. It sounded like she was suicidal but it also sounded like she was afraid of somebody. We don't know who she was afraid of just yet, but she was obviously afraid of somebody. I do wonder why she didn't name that person, though. At this point, it could be she was afraid of Yasin, Wells, Erik or even her father. I just don't think she would have cut her own brakes, though, so I think we'll have to come up with a better defense than suicide."

I had to admit, Damien looked pretty crushed when I said those things. He seemed to really believe Shelly committed suicide and that it was a matter of convincing the prosecutor of that fact. If he thought Nick Wright would go for that and just dismiss the case, though, Damien had another thing coming. Nick wasn't the type who would back down from a fight. A fight was exactly what he had on his hands. He really had a hard-on for Erik, too. He wanted to put Erik away, mainly because he knew Erik was good for so many crimes he couldn't touch him on.

Crimes he couldn't touch him on. Nobody had been able to touch Erik yet on anything he did. Yet the DA's office could get to Erik on this one. Why was that? Once again, the name "Sargis" popped into my head. Why wasn't Sargis protecting Erik on this murder? Sargis apparently could protect Erik against every other charge that might have been brought against him. Why was that protection taken off for this case?

There was still a thread there. There was a confusing web of people surrounding this murder and none of them exactly seemed to be related to one another. Some of the people I suspected were related – Yasin and Andrew McMason, Shelly's father, had a thread tying them together. They hated one another and Shelly seemed to hate her father, too. Erik stood alone in this web, unless you considered that Sargis might have also been involved. And then there was Wells. He had a connection to Irina, who also had a connection to Sargis. But that might be playing six degrees of separation there. Just because Wells had a connection with Irina and Irina had a connection with Sargis did not mean Sargis and Wells were connected.

I got out a piece of paper and drew a diagram of all the key players in this drama, and also wrote the word "baby?" in the middle of it. For now, I would not consider the issue of suicide. Considering that just confused me and took the whole thing off-kilter. And then I handed the paper to Damien.

"Here," I said. "Here are all the people who might have had a reason to off Shelly. We need to not eliminate any one of them until we can get more evidence in this case. We might never eliminate any of them. But I think we have enough here to confuse the jury. We have enough culprits that we can put reasonable doubt in their minds. That's all we're going for, remember - reasonable doubt.

"Tell me what you're thinking," Damien said. "Tell me each of your theories for each of these people."

"Yasin, that's obvious. He was the boyfriend and Shelly was having sex with Wells, possibly still for money. There's no indication that the people in her normal life, the life that included Yasin, knew about Wells. There's also no indication that the people in her alter life, the life that included Wells, knew about Yasin. She was good about keeping the two worlds separate. But if Yasin found out about what she was doing..." I sliced my hand across my neck. "So, that's a possible motive I'll tease out."

Damien nodded his head. "Go on..."

"Wells, same thing. Let's say he fell in love with Shelly but didn't know she had a fiancé. That would give him reason to kill her if he found out the truth."

Damien made some notes. "And..."

"Erik, our client, had motive because she would expose his organization. So, there's that. There's always that."

"And Sargis..."

"Maybe he wanted his son out of the way. So he kills Shelly and lets Erik take the fall. Again, I don't quite know how that theory holds up. We'll get Garrett do some investigating to find if there was a rift between father and son, but that seems like a possibility."

"Don't forget Abdullah Ahmadi, Yasin's father," Damien said. "He might have killed her when he found out about Shelly's extracurricular activities. Protecting Yasin's honor and all that."

"Right." I wrote that down. "And then there's Andrew McMason."

"And why would he have wanted her killed?"

"Because he's a bastard. And she mentioned a baby. What if Andrew was raping her and he impregnated her? He's not just a bastard but a wealthy bastard. That would give him reason."

"But Shelly wasn't pregnant when she was killed."

"I know. But maybe it happened in the past. Maybe something came up and she was threatening to expose him. You never know."

I was just throwing theories out there, saying them out loud to see if any of them sounded just right. So far, none of them did, but at least I was throwing them out there. It was all a part of the creative process for me. I had to bounce theories off people. Throw the ball to them and see if they ran with any of them. In this case, Damien wasn't jumping on any of the theories. He seemed skeptical about all of them.

"What are your theories? Besides suicide, I mean?" I asked.

He shrugged. "I think you've come up with good ones. Preliminarily, at least. None of them sound quite right yet all of them sound right. None stands out above the rest. I still think we're missing something."

"Maybe so. We have time, though, to develop our theories more. With some more intense investigation and maybe some pre-trial discovery, we can find something that might stick. That's the hope, anyhow."

Damien nodded, not seeming convinced. "That's always the hope."

SEVENTEEN
DAMIEN

I think I found my smoking gun on my medical malpractice case. In fact, I was certain of it. I picked up my newspaper in the morning, intending to read it with my morning coffee and a bagel, same as every other day. Then I saw it.

Angel of Mercy, Angel of Death. First page of the paper. I read past the headlines and saw what the article was about: Dr. Kim. He had just been arrested and had confessed to what he said were "Mercy Killings." According to his confession, he had deliberately killed 35 patients by giving them either overdoses or giving them medicine he knew the patient was allergic to. He stated in his confession that he had done this with terminal patients because he wanted to end their suffering. He had apparently seen both of his parents die a slow death from cancer and didn't want any other family to experience that kind of agony. He stated that he knew that what he had done was legally wrong but felt in his heart that he was doing a just and moral action.

In spite of myself, I smiled after reading the article. Not because I was so happy that 35 people were dead at Dr. Kim's hand. Rather, I was happy because I knew I would get the punitive damages I was seeking. It would be so easy to prove causation in this case and it would also be incredibly easy to prove Dr. Kim's actions were intentional. He intentionally killed Austin Ward. I felt as if this investigation into Dr. Kim's background was the smoking gun I needed to continue with the case. It was the smoking gun I needed to force a settlement.

Sure enough, when I got into the office, Pearl gave me a message to call back April Kennedy. April was the defense attorney representing Dr. Kim. She was working for a large firm downtown, a firm that specialized in defending medical malpractice cases. I was quite sure she was getting paid the big bucks and would have had every weapon in her arsenal trained on me and my case. That was what these firms did – intimidate everyone into either dropping their case or settling for less than what the case was worth. Or not filing a case at all. That was obviously the most preferable scenario for April's firm.

Well, guess what? It would be none of the above for me. I was not only going to pursue this case, but I wouldn't let up. Not for a second.

I called her back, and her secretary put her right on the line. "Hello," she said. "April Kennedy."

"Hi, April," I said, "This is Damien Harrington. I was returning your call."

"Yes, Damien," she said. "I'm sure you read about Dr. Kim in the newspaper today. It was surprising to our firm that this happened. We would like to schedule a settlement conference in our office today at 3 PM. Are you free at that time?"

"Sure," I said, nodding. "I'll be free at that time. I'll check with my client and see if she's free, though. I'm not sure. She might be working."

"Well, if there's a scheduling conflict, let me know. For now, though, I would like to invite you to this settlement conference. We're lining up plaintiff's attorneys to come in for these conferences. We'll have more openings next week if you would like to check with your client and call me back."

"I will."

I hung up the phone and immediately called Betsy on her cell. She picked up. "Damien," she said, almost breathlessly. "I was hoping you would call me. I saw the newspaper. I was going to call you. It's great, isn't it? Austin will finally get some kind of justice."

"Are you at work?"

"No. I haven't gone back to work yet. I haven't had the energy to go back to work. I'm still on FMLA and have another two weeks left. For now, I'll take every day of FMLA I can."

"Good. We can go to this settlement conference today We'll see what they offer us, and then you and I can discuss it. I'm thinking that the offer on the table for us will include at least a million in puni- tive damages. They won't call it punitive damages, but they have to take into consideration that any case they try that has Dr. Kim as one of the defendants will result in a pretty substantial punitive damage claim. I'm thinking in my head that actual damages might be in the range of around $50,000 or less. Actual damages take into account pain and suffering – that doesn't apply here, because Austin suffered no additional pain and suffering due to Dr. Kim's actions. These damages also take into account lost earnings, and that includes future earnings – that's dicey because Austin wasn't expected to live very long, even if this didn't happen to him. The actual damages also take into account medical bills that might have accumulated from the time of the negligence until the time of the death. Unfortunately, in our case, that would be zero. We could have possibly also gone for loss of consortium, but even that was shaky, because that usually goes to the surviving spouse or the children of the deceased. But loss of consor- tium literally tries to put a dollar value on companionship, and we certainly could have tried for that, since Austin was your only child and your only family."

I was speaking rapidly. I was so excited for this turn of events that I was practically bouncing off the walls. I felt badly I was that happy about Dr. Kim's actions. After all, Austin was dead. There was no changing that. No getting around that. No amount of an award would be enough, in the end, to make Betsy Ward whole. But I would try for as much of an award as I could. Maybe I could get enough of an award that she could quit her job and find something that made her truly happy. Maybe she could take a mental health break to Europe and find some kind of joy in that. Or whatever. Money couldn't buy happiness, but it never actually hurt matters, either.

"And what about the punitive damages, then? What are you going to ask for?"

I took a deep breath, trying to figure out what a jury would award in a case like this. The doctor deliberately killed Austin Ward. He admitted to it. He confessed. I would have to do some research on other jury awards with similar fact patterns before I went to the settlement conference.

"I don't know yet. I'll have to do some research. Juries are a strange phenomenon. I know that and so do defense attorneys. Everyone in the legal profession knows that. One jury will hear a case and award millions in punitives. Another jury will hear a substantially similar case and award no punitives at all. It's a roll of the dice but not really. A scientific formula should be able to guide how much I'll ask for in this case. I'm not really sure exactly what that formula is just yet."

"Well, figure it out. When is our settlement conference?"

"Today at 3 if you can make it."

"I'll be there."

I SPENT the rest of the day looking at jury verdicts. I had to be careful about this case, though, because it was different. It was no longer just a negligence case. It was an intentional tort. Chances were that Dr. Kim's malpractice insurance carrier wouldn't pay. I would have to figure out if Dr. Kim had the assets to cover my claim and all the others that would be coming down the pike.

That was why I wanted that settlement conference to happen soon. I wanted to be at the front of the line in collecting. He couldn't declare bankruptcy on my claim, but, then again, there might be only so many funds available.

That was another thing I would have to look into. I hadn't asked Garrett to find out about Dr. Kim's wealth, because, up until this morning, his personal wealth wasn't relevant. I would try to collect against the malpractice insurance. Now, all of a sudden, whether or not Dr. Kim was wealthy became of paramount importance to me.

"Garrett," I said, calling him. "I need to find something out. I need to find it out in the next few hours."

"Sure, Damien, what do you need?"

"I need to know how much Dr. Kim is worth. Personally. I need to know all of his assets and how much they're worth. Can you do that for me in the next few hours?" I didn't want to postpone the settlement conference, but I also didn't want to fly blind on this.

"Sure," he said. "Let me do some asset checking and I'll get back with you in about a half hour."

A half hour later, Garrett called. "Yeah, Garrett," I said. "What did you find out?"

"You're in luck. Dr. Kim is a very wealthy man. He has several homes around the world and is also in possession of precious art work. He apparently bought several paintings over the years from auction houses, and these paintings alone probably are worth in the neighborhood of $250 million. We're talking Francis Bacon, Kandinsky and Pollock. He came from inherited wealth, but he's also made a pretty penny at his job for the past 20 years. He's making about a million a year right now just from his anesthesiologist job. If you're afraid he can't pay a judgment, relax. He'll be good for any judgment you want to ask for. Ask away."

I let out a sigh of relief when I got off the phone with Garrett. *So, Kim is a wealthy man.* I no longer felt I had to be first in line for the settlement conference, but, in this case, I thought I better keep my appointment. Betsy Ward was expecting to get this case settled and, by God, I would make her happy.

In the end, I decided to shoot the moon. Ask for $10 million and negotiate down from there. It certainly didn't hurt to ask.

It never hurt to ask.

RIGHT AT 3, I went to the building that housed Edelman, Lathrop and Thomas, the largest law firm in the Kansas City area. The firm was situated on the 41st and 42nd floor of One Kansas City Place, the tallest building in the area. Since this glass and steel structure only had 42 floors, this meant the law firm occupied the top two floors of the building, a sign of the firm's prestige. I got downtown and walked into the building and was impressed and slightly intimidated at the same time.

I walked to the elevator and pushed it. There were actually two sets of elevators – one set of elevators took you to the 20th floor. The other set of elevators bypassed the bottom 20 floors and went from floor 20 up to the top. Once I got into the elevator, it whooshed so quickly up to the top of the building I almost had a sense of vertigo.

The settlement conference I was supposed to attend was on the top floor. The glass doors to the suite were etched with the law firm's name, and, when I opened the door, there was an enormous circular structure that was manned by a petite blonde girl with bobbed hair and an obvious fake rack. She smiled at me.

"Can I help you?"

"Yes. Damien Harrington here to see April Kennedy. I'm scheduled in for a settlement conference for one of Dr. Kim's cases."

"Is your client here?"

"No, not yet," I said.

"I'll call Ms. Kennedy and let her know you are here but that your client is not at the moment. Do you expect your client by the appointed time?"

"Yes." I nodded. "I called her to let her know."

She smiled again and got on her phone and dialed. "Ms. Kennedy, there is a Mr. Damien Harrington here to see you." She looked up at me while she spoke. "I'll let him know." Then she hung up the phone. "Ms. Kennedy told me to escort you back to her conference room whenever you're ready."

I took a deep breath and got my briefcase out. "Thank you," I said. I opened up the briefcase so I could be ready for the conference. The file was in there in a brown accordion folder that opened up. Inside the folder was individual manila folders with tabs.

One manila folder was for medical records for Austin, another was the information about Dr. Kim, another was information about Betsy, still another housed relevant information about Austin. Included in this file was Austin's grade reports from his private school, his SAT scores – a 1575 out of a possible 1600 – and his ACT scores. He scored an average ACT of 34 out of a possible 36. His math score was a perfect 36. He had already been accepted at MIT at the time of his death. I found this out when Betsy received the MIT acceptance letter in the mail two weeks after Austin passed. Also included in this file was the acceptance letter to Harvard. All this showed Austin's potential. I also decided to include the results of the genetic test that demonstrated that Austin had the BCR genetic marker and that he could have fully benefited from gene therapy. Included were some scholarly articles I found that showed that gene therapy had been successful in treating other hard-to-treat leukemia cases and that it was successful in actually curing many different people around the world.

In other words, if Austin didn't die by being given the wrong drug during his surgery, he might have been saved by gene therapy. That might have been the most important piece of information I had. Austin had the possibility of living a long life, and had the possibility of becoming a NASA engineer. The current NASA aerospace engineers were being paid around $100,000. By the time Austin graduated with his bachelor'a degree, he probably could have started making $125,000 or more. Lifetime earnings for Austin therefore could have been well in the millions.

Granted, this was not an easy argument to make, considering

Austin's prognosis, but these people were not in the position to bargain. It was in their interest to quietly settle as many cases as they could, because they also had Menorah Hospital as a client, and Menorah Hospital was where Dr. Kim primarily worked. Dr. Kim was finished as an anesthesiologist, of course, and his reputation was being dragged through the mud. But Menorah Hospital wanted this story off the front pages as soon as possible and the only way to do that was to make sure there weren't any loud victims' families going to the paper every day of the week.

This case would blow up huge. It already was on the front page of the paper and had the potential to be on the front page for weeks. I remembered one case where there was a doctor diluting chemotherapy drugs. The doctor was not only on the front page of the paper for weeks, he was on the evening news every single night. He eventually became a national scandal. Dr. Kim had the same potential – to become a national scandal. He could become the subject of documentaries and could easily have his story featured on the national 24-hour news channels such as MSNBC, CNN and Fox. That would be Menorah Hospital's biggest nightmare.

Yes, I had April Kennedy over a barrel. I had the feeling that, since I was no doubt one of the earliest settlement cases for them, I could ask for much more than I would even be entitled to in a trial and get it. All I had to do was tell them that if they didn't meet my demands I would send Betsy to the nearest reporter to sob and cry and give her story. Betsy made a very sympathetic character, considering Austin was her only child and only family.

I looked at the clock and saw that it read 3 PM. I glanced into the hallway, hoping to see Betsy, but I didn't. I decided to call her.

"I'm almost there," she said when I called. I could tell she had been crying – her voice was cracking as she spoke. "I'm sorry I'm running late. I'll be there as soon as I can."

I hung up. I hated that she was running late. I liked to be prompt to my meetings, especially something as important as this one. Especially since I knew that April had probably scheduled several of these settlement conferences back to back. I was slotted for an hour, and I knew that at 4 PM there was probably somebody coming in, and another at 5, and probably late into the night. There were 35 victims in this case, and I knew this firm would want to settle with all of them in a matter of days.

At 3:15, I was becoming more concerned. I kept seeing the blonde receptionist glance at me, and, from time to time, she received a call from April inquiring about where I was. "His client isn't here yet," she would say. "I'll let you know when she shows."

Finally, at 3:20, she showed. "I'm so sorry," she said. She sounded out of breath. "I need to tell you something before we go in there. I'm late because I was at home, debating on what to do."

I rolled my eyes. "We need to get in there. She's waiting on us. We only had an hour to negotiate as it is. Now we only have 40 minutes. I'm quite sure that April is tightly scheduled on this."

"This will only take a minute," she said. "I need to speak with you out in the hall. I don't want any of those lawyers to hear me."

I opened the door to the suite. "I'll be right back," I said to the blonde receptionist.

Betsy and I got into the hallway. "Okay, we're here. Now what? What were you going to tell me?"

She glanced down at the floor. "There are a few things you need to know. The only reason why I'm telling you this is because it might come up. I don't know if those lawyers know about this."

I rolled my eyes. "Know about what? And why are you waiting until now to tell me something that is apparently important?"

She ran her foot along the glossy marble floor. "I didn't know how to tell you about this. But I need to. I need to, because I think that Min-jun might have said something to them."

"Who is Min-jun?" I shook my head. Min-jun was the first name of Dr. Kim. He was from Korea, and that was a common boy's name. I just didn't know why Betsy would be calling Dr. Kim by his first name, so I was confused.

Then it dawned on me. Amelia, my daughter, told me that Betsy and Dr. Kim were having an affair. That would be why Betsy would be calling Dr. Kim by his first name.

"Min-jun Kim," she said. "Dr. Kim." She continued to look down at the floor. "I started having an affair with him because I knew what he was doing. I knew what he was up to. And I wanted him to do the same thing to Austin."

I was comprehending what she was saying. It didn't make a lick of sense to me. Betsy *knew* that Dr. Kim was deliberately killing people and she didn't tell me about it? And what did she mean, she wanted Dr. Kim to do the same to Austin?

"I'm sorry?" I asked her. "I don't understand?"

She looked furtively around. "I wanted Austin to die peacefully," she said. "And I wanted Dr. Kim to do it."

EIGHTEEN

I bit my lower lip, feeling the rage coming in from my chest area and spread. I took a deep breath.

"You knew what Dr. Kim was doing," I said slowly. "And you wanted him to kill Austin." I looked up at the ceiling. I actually understood. Betsy wanted Austin to die peacefully because she had seen her husband linger with the same disease and it was the most painful experience of her life. I got that. I didn't condone it. To me, she was no different than my feckless and unfaithful wife, Sarah, who, no doubt, would love to arrange the same thing for Amelia. She probably would do that if she could. So, yeah, I understood why Betsy would do what she did.

But why wouldn't she tell me she knew that Dr. Kim was deliberately killing people? And why would she turn around and want to sue Dr. Kim after she, herself, arranged for this to happen? And how was I going to, in good conscience, go into that settlement conference and demand millions of dollars for the life of her son, knowing what I knew? No matter, I would go in there and still demand millions of dollars for Austin's life. I would do that and pretend I never heard the vile things Betsy was telling me.

"Yes," she said. "I'm only telling you now because I think it might come up in that conference."

"You think?" My voice was loud, too loud. I didn't want anybody to be suspicious, so I had to work on modulating my tone of voice. "Now, we have to get in there in that settlement conference. We've already eaten up half of our allotted time. But before we do, I need to know the answer to my question. You knew what Dr. Kim was doing, yet you didn't say a word about that to me. Why?"

Her voice was a loud whisper. "I didn't tell you about that because you would ask me how I knew and I didn't know what to say. Plus, I promised Min-jun I wouldn't tell anybody about what he was doing. I promised him that. He told me that if I told you what he was doing that he would go to prison for the rest of his life. I didn't want that. I'm actually very fond of him. He helped me when I needed it. He helped Austin die a peaceful death in his sleep. That was all I wanted. Min-jun gave that to me, so I wouldn't tell you something that would send him to prison."

"And how did you find out what he was doing? How did you know you could single him out as somebody who would do something like that for you? And why would you turn around and sue him, when you were the one that arranged for it to happen?"

She made a motion for me to lower my voice. "One question at a time."

"We don't have time for one question at a time. Answer all those questions I just posed. Answer them all or, I swear to God, I'll walk out of here with no settlement at all."

She took a deep breath. "I knew what he was doing because I overheard some people talking about it. They suspected he was doing that. I don't know who I overheard speaking about it, but it was just a rumor going around the oncology floor. You know, it was idle talk. People talking about how so many patients had died while Min-jun was administering the anesthesia. People thought he might have been deliberately killing them. They were talking about how many lawsuits he had against him and were whispering about how many times the hospital had quietly settled with people without them even filing a lawsuit. There's a lot of talk around the oncology ward between parents."

I shook my head. The hospital was settling with the next of kin for anesthesiology overdoses and other deaths resulting from the improper use of anesthesia, before these people had even filed a lawsuit? Why would the hospital be protecting Dr. Kim like that?

I suddenly realized there was the distinct possibility that there wouldn't be 35 clients that April Kennedy would try to settle with. Most of those 35 people had already gotten their millions without even filing a lawsuit. They were no-doubt given confidential settlements that would have never shown up in my research on this doctor. They were quietly paid to go away, yet Dr. Kim continued with his hospital privileges. That was disgusting to me.

It was disgusting to me, yet I would use it as leverage. If April didn't meet my demand, which I had decided would be $15 million, I would threaten to expose the hospital for what it was doing. I knew I could get Tom Garrett to do some deep investigation into Dr. Kim and the hush-hush settlements and I could show that the hospital could be on the hook for hundreds of millions of dollars in punitive damages if I really wanted to go down that route. I could literally bankrupt that hospital.

I had all the leverage to ask for the moon. I didn't want to sue the hospital, mainly because I wanted this case to be over. Betsy had just confessed to me that she arranged for her kid to be killed, so I wouldn't risk going to trial and having that fact uncovered for the jury. No, somebody else would have to sue Menorah for what it did. That wouldn't be my hill to die on. I would just use that fact as a bargaining chip.

"Okay," I said. "So, the damage is done. You're going to walk out of this building a very wealthy woman. A very wealthy woman, even though you asked for it in the first place. I don't know how I feel about that. What I know is I'll have to take a shower when I get out of here."

At that, we walked back into the suite of the law firm. "We're ready," I said.

Blondie nodded her head. "This way, sir," she said, and I followed her through the maze of offices to an enormous conference room. It had floor-to-ceiling windows that looked out over the expanse of the city. Plush white carpet, a long cherry wood table in the middle, leather seats, high ceilings and a modern chandelier that hung from the ceiling.

At the table were six lawyers – three men and three women. Also seated at the table was Dr. Kim. I recognized April, the lead attorney. I had worked with her before.

She saw me come in and stood up, and so did the others. April Kennedy was small – only about 5'2" and probably weighed about a buck nine. She had dark hair cut in a shaggy bob and was wearing a dark blue suit with black piping and heels. She was an attractive woman, with her dark brown eyes, olive skin and perfectly straight teeth. She walked over to me and shook my hand, gripping it as hard as any man.

"Mr. Harrington," she said. "Thank you for coming in."

"Thank you for seeing me."

"Please have a seat." She gestured to one of the black leather chairs. She got a water for Betsy and me and the two of us sat down.

I looked over at Betsy, hating her. I couldn't believe what she had just confessed to me. How could she snow me like that? Seriously. How could she have knowledge about the crimes that Dr. Kim was doing, and not tell me? And how could she be suing Dr. Kim after she arranged for him to kill her son? It wasn't like his malpractice insurance would cover his deed. It was an intentional act, and his malpractice insurance didn't cover-

His malpractice insurance didn't cover intentional acts. That was it! That was why Betsy didn't tell me the truth about what Dr. Kim was doing. That made sense. She didn't want me to know. She probably didn't expect this would come out in quite this way. Betsy was no fool. She had to have known what the implications would be if it came out that Dr. Kim had intentionally killed her son. That would negate the malpractice insurance and would mean the money would have to come out of Dr. Kim's own pocket. She clearly didn't want that to happen.

I fiddled with my file, wondering how to approach this. I had to wonder if they would ask me in this conference about Betsy's relationship with their client. They had to know that Betsy and Dr. Kim were having an affair. They had to suspect what was going on.

I cleared my throat. I looked April right in the eye and decided to shoot the moon and ask for a crazy amount of money and see what she did.

"In light of what was revealed in the newspaper just this morning, I would like to make a demand of $20 million." I nodded my head. "I have some documentation here about Austin's grades and his SAT and ACT scores, and I have two letters of acceptance. One is from Harvard and one from MIT. I also have my client here, who can testify that her son had the ambition to be a NASA aerospace engineer, and the average salary for that kind of engineer for NASA is currently $105,000. I have an actuarial table that has been prepared by an actuary that shows that, over Austin's lifetime, he could have earned $8 million from the time he got out of school until the time he retired at age 65. I am not demanding damages for pain and suffering, obviously, but I have also calculated damages for loss of consortium. I figured those damages would be $2 million. That is because Austin was my client's only family, and, while you cannot put a value on companionship, the law requires I do just that."

"Loss of consortium does not figure into this case," April said. "That is only for surviving spouses and for surviving children. It does not go to parents."

"Nothing in the law says that parents cannot get loss of consortium," I said, knowing I was standing on shaky legal ground. "But I understand that a jury probably wouldn't award this type of damage, so I am willing to strike that out of my demand."

April nodded. "So noted. Please proceed."

"So, I've calculated $8 million for lifetime earnings, and $12 million for punitive damages."

April shook her head. "$12 million for punitive damages is excessive. We do not believe that a jury would award that large of amount. Plus, I think you know as well as I do that your client's son, Austin Ward, was terminally ill. Therefore, you cannot extrapolate lifetime earnings to age 65."

"I also have the results of a genetic test that showed Austin had a genetic marker for leukemia. I have studies in my file that show that, with Austin's kind of genetic marker, gene therapy could have been effective enough for a cure. If Austin would have lived, he could have pursued genetic therapy and he might have been cured."

I closed my eyes as I remembered how I found out about Austin's genetic marker. Betsy told me that day in her house. She had just gotten the results back from the genetic test and was very upset.

I now knew why she was so upset. She probably realized, too late, that Austin had a chance to live. He had a chance and she took that away from him. She did. Dr. Kim probably wouldn't have killed her son if she didn't ask him to do so. And Betsy knew what Dr. Kim was doing. Or she suspected it, at any rate. She could have requested that Dr. Kim not be the anesthesiologist for her son's case.

That had to kill her. She took away Austin's only chance to live. And he had a chance to live a long life. With the right gene therapy, he could have beaten his leukemia. That had to devastate her.

"Mr. Harrington," April said. "We understand your argument, but it's weak. Your client was terminal. Yes, he had a genetic marker and yes he could have been cured by gene therapy. Those are contingencies we are prepared to take into account. According to the research we have done independently, Austin had a 70% chance of surviving if he was properly given gene therapy. Therefore, we calculate that Austin's lifetime earnings would be 70% of what your actuary estimates. That would be $5.5 million over his lifetime. However, Austin had not yet pursued a career in aerospace. There was no guarantee that he would have actually become an aerospace engineer. We'll take into account that his chosen profession was likely to happen, but there was a chance it wouldn't. We understand that he had acceptance letters from Harvard and MIT, and we further note that Austin had perfect mathematical scores on both his ACT and SAT. We calculated there was an 80% chance that Austin could have achieved his ambitions of being a NASA engineer had he lived. Therefore, we are prepared to offer your client $4.5 million in actual damages."

That sounded good to me. April was correct. There was no guarantee that Austin would have lived if he would have gotten gene therapy. There was no guarantee that Austin would have pursued a career in aerospace engineering with NASA. There was always the chance that Austin would have just decided to become a guitar player on the street. Plenty of super intelligent people dropped out of society to do menial work and Austin was a decent guitar player. He was driven, however.

"$6 million," I said. "In actual damages. "I believe that Austin had at least a 90% chance of fulfilling his dream if he would have lived. And I also believe that Austin had more like an 80% chance of living if he would have gotten gene therapy. My research on the issue shows that gene therapy is very promising for Austin's type of genetic marker. $6 million is a fair amount."

April stared at me, as did the other five people on the other side of the table. She was in no position to bargain. Not when the hospital would be on the hook for untold millions if I really wanted to play hardball. The hospital wasn't her client, because that would be a conflict of interest to represent both Dr. Kim and the hospital, but, at the same time, I was pretty sure the hospital and its culpability would weigh heavily in these negotiations.

She turned to Dr. Kim, who silently nodded his head.

"$6 million is a fair amount," she said. "For actual damages."

I nodded. I was entitled to 40% of the award, and I was calculating that in my head. $2.4 million would be my cut. I would share at least part of it with Harper, even though she hadn't really participated in this case. Not a bad chunk of change. It was, by far, more money than I had ever had in my life. That number was staggering to me, and I hadn't even gotten in-depth to the topic of punitive damages.

"Now, for punitive damages," I said. "I had asked for an award of $12 million. I think this is a fair request, considering Dr. Kim's culpability. Plus, I have it on good authority that the hospital has been quietly settling cases with many of the people Dr. Kim has deliberately killed. My research shows that Menorah Hospital has been quietly settling with these individuals before a lawsuit was even filed. They've kept a killer anesthesiologist on their staff for years, knowing what he was doing. If that gets out to the public, the hospital will be on the hook for hundreds of millions of dollars in punitive damages. I believe, in light of that fact, that $12 million in punitive damages in this case is a steal."

"So you're saying that if we do not settle for your amount you will file a new lawsuit against the hospital?"

"Well, no. The hospital is already one of the defendants in this case, of course. What I am saying is I will drop my lawsuit against the hospital in exchange for your agreeing to $12 million in punitive damages in this conference. I can make the award of punitives contingent upon my dropping the hospital as a defendant. If you don't give me what I'm asking for, I will pursue the hospital with vigor and it could end up costing that hospital hundreds of millions of dollars. As I see it, $12 million is a bargain."

April turned to Dr. Kim, who silently nodded. He clasped his hands together tightly, his face a mask of shame.

April turned back to me. "Okay. $12 million in punitive damages is reasonable, in light of the extensive amount of culpability that could result if this case came to trial. As you said, in order for you to receive these funds, you must dismiss your entire lawsuit with prejudice. Once you do that, we will make an ACH deposit into your account and into your client's account for the funds due. It's my understanding you are entitled to 40% of the award and your client is entitled to 60%. Is that correct?"

"Yes, that is correct. Now, I need to see some settlement documents before I agree to anything. As I understand, we have agreed in this conference on a total award of $18 million - $6 million for actual damages and $12 million for punitive damages. Please draw that up and we can sign it."

April nodded and one of the lawyers at the end of the table got up and left the room.

"Henry Jackson will prepare the document for you to sign," she said.

Fifteen minutes later, Henry came back, a document in his hand. I read it over carefully. It had boilerplate settlement language, and I read over that rapidly before getting to the good part. I nodded and signed it. I passed it to Betsy, and she signed it as well. Then Dr. Kim signed it, as did April.

When all of us signed it, Henry left the room again and quickly came back with four copies of the document we all signed. He handed me my copy and I tucked it into the file. Betsy looked at her copy with wonder. Her face showed she couldn't quite believe she was, suddenly, a millionaire. Especially since she arranged for all this to happen.

April stood up and offered me her hand. "Thank you for coming in," she said, as I shook it. "Cecilia will show you out."

I looked at the clock and saw that it was 4 PM. No doubt there was another lawyer with another client waiting in the wings. These settlement conferences would be rapid-fire. Quietly settle each one, hope there were at least a few parties who didn't know that Menorah Hospital had kept a murderer on the staff and hope for minimal damages and fallout. If every victim settled rapidly, that would obviously be the best thing, PR-wise. The quicker the victims were subjected to gag orders due to having settled their cases, the quicker this whole story would die.

"Thank you," I said. And then Betsy and I got up and left the conference room. On the way out, I saw the B-Shift waiting in the lobby of the suite. A lawyer dressed in a three-piece suit and an African-American couple sat on the leather seats, flipping through magazines and looking nervous.

They were about to become millionaires. All of them.

I hoped they could handle it.

I hoped *I* could handle it.

NINETEEN

As I drove to Harper's house, I had to process what had just happened. I had just settled a case for $18 million. I was entitled to 40% of that. I would have to discuss with Harper what cut I would give her. She had expressed interest in working on the case, although she didn't do anything yet. She hadn't had the chance to really get into it. Still, I was a generous guy and decided to contribute 10% to the law firm. That would certainly give Harper's firm a nice boost, because 10% of $18 million was $1.8 million.

And my cut would still be $5.5 million. I had to let that sink in. I was a multi-millionaire. It was time to get a new roof, which my older home needed, and a new car. I was still driving a 2005 Explorer. Working at the Public Defender's Office wasn't exactly lucrative. It was invigorating work, but you don't get rich there. I hadn't yet worked for Harper for long enough to really make better money, so that meant I was driving a beater car and my roof leaked.

Now, I was officially wealthy. That was the oddest thing in the world.

Harper would be astounded when I told her. Or, maybe she

wouldn't. After all, she probably read the paper as well. She had to have known this was coming.

I just couldn't get over how quickly it all went, however. As of this morning, I had no clue this was coming. Now, not even 12 hours later, I was a millionaire. It was as if I had won the lottery.

I had a crisis of conscience, however, at the way it all went down. Betsy had arranged for this to happen. She got Dr. Kim to do it for her. And yet, she would be even wealthier from this whole arrangement than I was. After I took my cut, her award would be over $10 million. And she was the one who made sure that it happened! She was Austin's killer as much as Dr. Kim, yet she would profit over it. That didn't seem right. If I had any ethics at all, I would have admitted the truth to April and be done with it.

Yet I knew I couldn't. Betsy had told me in confidence about what she had done. Attorney-client privilege dictated I couldn't say one word. What I could have done, however, if I had a decent bone in my body, would have been to withdraw from the case. Let Betsy find somebody else to settle for the blood money. That's what this was. Blood money. It was tainted, so I couldn't feel entirely good about it. I hated that, too. I hated that I had to always look at this money as tainted. I had to know I got this money because a kid was dead. A kid who had a decent chance of living if only his mother hadn't arranged for his death.

Still, she was the one who had to live with what she had done. I was sure she believed, at the time, she was doing the right thing. She had seen her husband slowly pass away in agony from the same dread disease Austin had. That had to weigh into her thinking. But still, she should have waited until she got the results from the genetic test before she did anything. She should have tried that one last thing — the gene therapy. Austin could have lived a long, happy and productive life. He could have contributed much to society and to the field of aerospace engineering. Betsy took that chance away from him. She had to live with that. Perhaps that was punishment enough.

I arrived at Harper's beautiful home in the heart of Brookside. I had secretly wanted to move to this neighborhood myself one day. I had a home in Leawood, also a desirable neighborhood, even though my home was tiny compared to Harper's. Maybe that was what I would do with this windfall – I could buy a historic home in this district. I loved the way these homes looked. The architecture of the 1920s, when these homes were built, fascinated me. Homes just seemed so much more solidly built in the 1920s, compared to more modern homes. My own home was mid-century and was typical for that era – it was built ranch-style and was rather small. Only 1500 square feet. But these Brookside homes were two and three story. Many were Tudor-style, others were Colonial and still others were Cape Cods. Many featured large porches and many were built in stone.

Harper's own house was a shirt-waist and was three stories with a large porch and sun room. I had my Tiramisu in my hand as I knocked on the door. A large, friendly Golden Retriever and a friendlier Rottweiler came bounding to the door when as I stood there, and Harper opened the door and greeted me with a smile. "Welcome," she said. "Come on in. I'm so excited you're here to see my home and my family."

I walked in the door and immediately saw two identical girls. They both had black hair and green eyes, and both looked to be around 13. I also saw a tall man with salt and pepper hair and large muscles. I figured that was Axel and the two girls had to be Rina and Abby. Harper talked about them all the time.

"I have a potato casserole in the oven," she said. "And a baked chicken, plus salad. I hope all that is good for you."

"Sounds amazing," I said. "Here's my dessert. I hope it's good."

Harper smiled, took the Tiramisu and put it on the island in her kitchen. "It looks amazing."

· · ·

DINNER WAS excellent and her girls were hilarious. Rina talked a lot, and Abby sat quietly, not wanting to interject. She let her sister have the floor, who took it with gusto. I heard everything about Rina's life, including all the school gossip and all about the streaming shows she loved to watch.

Abby, for her part, just quietly sat there, occasionally talking about some of the books she was reading. She also came alive when Harper told me that Abby was an excellent flute player and had just made first chair in the Middle School band. She beamed about that and told me all about some of the pieces she was practicing for sectionals and how she had a solo.

Harper seemed to have an amazing life and I yearned for that myself. I envied that both of her daughters were healthy and that neither girl was facing an uncertain future. *Maybe Amelia will come home and she'll be just as vibrant and alive as these two girls. Maybe they can all be friends.* I took a deep breath as I listened to the girls talk, thinking about Amelia and silently praying I could have this kind of life one day.

One thing was for sure. If God came down and told me I could either have the $5.5 million coming to me from this medical malpractice award, or I could have Amelia healthy – I couldn't have both – I wouldn't hesitate. I would give up that money so fast...

After dinner, the girls went up to do their homework, and Axel and I enjoyed some wine while Harper drank water.

"So," Harper said. "What did you think about Rina and Abby?"

I nodded my head. "Amazing girls. You're doing a great job with them."

"You have two kids, right?" Harper asked. "You should bring them next time. They're a lot younger than my girls, of course, but I still would love to meet them."

I took a deep breath. I still had a hard time talking about Amelia. I never liked to tell people how sick she was. I sometimes felt that if I didn't talk about Amelia's illness out loud that it somehow didn't exist. That was silly, of course. It *did* exist. She *was* sick. She was possibly going to die. I had to face that. Still, I wasn't ready for the questions.

"I'll bring them next time," I said. "But I would love to have you over for dinner, too. I don't cook a whole lot, but I make a mean pot roast."

As Harper cleared the dishes, Axel and I bantered. I liked him. He was a man's man. Plus, he really seemed to love Harper. He looked at her the way I used to look at Sarah. That seemed like so long ago. Sitting at that table, seeing Axel get up and help Harper in the kitchen and watching them tease each other, I somehow had problems picturing my doing the same with Sarah. It was as if I had never loved her. I intellectually knew I did at one time, but I just couldn't conjure up the emotions I felt when Sarah and I were in love. Those emotions seemed foreign to me.

After Harper cleared the table, she came back in about ten minutes and I knew it was the right time to tell her the news.

"Betsy Ward," I said. "You probably read in the paper about what happened."

"Yes," she said. "I wanted to ask you about that. I would imagine they're willing to settle."

"They actually did settle. Today. I think that when the news broke, they knew they would have to settle everyone's cases as rapidly as possible. The quicker the victims get confidential settlements the quicker this story will die. That's PR 101, really."

"Right." Harper nodded. "Still, wow. They already got you in to settle the case. How much?"

"$18 million," I said, and Harper gasped.

"Oh my God," she said. "I wish I would have gotten on this case with you sooner. Congratulations." She raised her glass and I clinked my glass with hers. Axel did the same.

"Don't worry," I said. "I've already decided to give you 10%. That means your firm will soon be $1.8 million richer."

Harper rapidly shook her head. "No. That's not right. I didn't do anything on this case. Thank you, that's very generous of you, but I can't accept that."

"Of course you can. Listen, you gave me a chance. You hired me and gave me a chance. And I figured my cut will be $5.5 million even assuming I give you 10%. Trust me, that's more money than I ever thought I would see at one time. It's more than enough for me. I'm a simple guy with simple tastes. I'll have both of my kids' colleges completely funded, and can get a new car, a new roof and maybe a house around here. If I can do all that, I'm good. I want you to have 10%. This was a windfall I never expected, considering the circumstances, and I want to share it."

Harper continued to shake her head, but Axel put his hand on her forearm.

"Mate," he said. "Your new associate wants to do something nice for you. Accept his generosity with a smile."

Her face flushed red. "I didn't do a damn thing. You did all of it. You did the discovery, you hired the actuary, you did all the research. You went to the settlement conference. You met with the client. You did it all. I didn't do a thing. I can't-"

I cleared my throat. "You won't have a choice. I'll make a direct deposit into your bank. I'll do that whether you like it or not, so please accept that."

She finally nodded. "Thank you," she said in a small voice. "I think that's the nicest thing anyone's ever done for me. I don't know how I'll ever repay you."

I smiled. "You've already repaid me by taking me into your firm. Now there's one major case off my plate, and we can focus on Erik Gregorian's case. I'm glad I can really focus on that one, because it'll be a doozy."

"Yes," she said. "It is. Going to be a doozy. But I think we can win it. I think we have enough other suspects that might have done it. We can just throw spaghetti against the wall and hope something sticks."

The three of us talked long into the night. By the time I finally stumbled home at midnight, I was exhausted and happy. I was a wealthy man and Harper and I had a solid game plan for Erik's case.

It had been a good day.

It would have been an even better day if I didn't know that Betsy Ward made the choice to have her son deliberately killed. She had blood on her hands and had tainted everything about this settlement.

But I would have to try to forget about that.

TWENTY

"Okay," Harper said. "Trial is next week. It's time for us to really prepare for it."

We were in the conference room, with everything we had prepared for trial spread out in front of us. We had the strategy to go for and were fairly confident our strategy was sound. Still, one never could tell exactly what would happen. Juries were fickle to say the very least.

"I'll be taking the lead on this one," I said. "And you'll be second chair. I know how much Erik turns your stomach. I can feel the contempt you have for him. I don't want the jury to also feel that contempt, so it's probably best I try the case."

"Go for it," Harper said. "You're right. Erik is scum, and I think he's a sociopath. It makes me want to vomit to know that, if we get an acquittal, we'll be letting that vile snake back on the streets. But it is what it is."

"Yeah," I said. "That's true. It is what it is. It's what we do, of course. Erik won't be the first violent sociopath we let loose on the street and he certainly won't be the last. We just have to let that go and forge ahead with the best plan we can come up with for his acquittal."

Harper shook her head. "I know. So, let's see. I got the witness list from the prosecutor's office so let's go over it. It looks like they'll be calling their automotive expert first to the stand. He's going to testify about the brake lines being cut. There's not really a whole lot we can do to counter his testimony. I say we don't even try."

I nodded. "Do we have the report back from your expert – the one you hired to find out if there was some other defect we didn't know about? The person who might be able to testify about why Shelly was going at such a high rate of speed when she died?"

"Yeah." Harper nodded her head. "He did a thorough examination of the car and found nothing wrong with it. Aside from the tampered brakes, that is. So, it's still a mystery on why she would have been driving so fast. I hate mysteries like that, but there's nothing we can do about it."

"Nothing, indeed. So, their expert's name is Josh Day. We don't have an expert to counter it. I say we let his testimony stand. Our expert, Joseph Savolo, agreed that the brakes were tampered with, so there's nothing we can really do with this witness. Do you agree?"

"Of course," Harper said. "So, we won't cross examine their automotive witness. In fact, I think we should go ahead and stipulate that the brakes were tampered with. If we stipulated to the brakes being tampered with, that would mean that there wouldn't be any need to put the expert on the stand."

I shook my head. "They will still have to put the witness on the stand. The jury needs to hear that evidence."

"That's true."

"Okay," I said. "Let me see who else they plan to call for their case in chief." I looked through the witness list. "It looks like the next witness will be Officer O'Reilly, the officer at the scene of the crime. Is there any reason to cross-examine him?"

"Nah, let's skip it. That officer won't prove anything but the fact Shelly was dead," Harper said. "Who's next on the list?"

"Hannah Bailey. She's one of the witnesses who will testify about Shelly's erratic driving. In fact, she's the only witness they have lined up."

Harper looked down at her pad of paper she was writing on and seemed to contemplate what she might want to do with Hannah as a witness.

"So, it has been established Shelly was driving at a high rate of speed when she crossed the median." Harper shook her head. "Again, this witness does nothing for us. Or nothing really against us, either. I say we skip her as well. Let's save our firepower for somebody who matters."

"Somebody like Ara Babyan maybe?" I was looking down at the witness list and saw that the second-in-command in the Gregorian clan was scheduled to testify. "I wonder what his testimony will be?"

"I guess we'll find out. At any rate, he'll be fairly easy to cross-examine, really. Whatever he'll say about what Erik might have told him, we can counter. You can ask questions about his position in the clan, what he does for them and then you can move onto making him look like a climber who wants Erik out of the way so he can take Erik's job." Harper nodded her head. "Nail him on the things his clan does. Ask him about the white slavery, the drug dealing, the prostitution rings and the identity theft. Everything the clan does, ask him about it. You have to soil him up completely so the jury will think they can't believe a word coming out of his mouth."

"Of course," I said, "However, there's a risk to that strategy. Namely, we'll be demonstrating to the jury everything Erik does as well. If we don't put Erik on the stand, the jury might not know the kinds of activities he's involved in. But the jury will come to the conclusion that anything and everything that Ara is involved in, Erik was just as involved."

"Listen," Harper said. "The jury will come to the conclusion that our client isn't a choir boy. They know he's in the Armenian mafia so they can just imagine all the criminal and nefarious acts he commits. Personally, I think we should put Erik on the stand. He hasn't ever told us he killed Shelly, so it wouldn't be suborning perjury to put him up there. I think we should get him in here and prepare him for his testimony. At this point, it really couldn't hurt, and it might actually help."

Of course, it always helped to put the client on the stand. For one, if the client didn't take the stand, the jury would inevitably think there was a reason for it. No matter how many times you instruct the jury they are not to take into account the fact the client doesn't testify, and no matter how many ways you tell the jury that it is your client's right not to testify, the jury would still hold the lack of testimony against him. That was one thing I knew in my bones.

Still, putting Erik up on the stand to be cross-examined about all he did for the Armenian mob was a risky, risky strategy. It could very well blow up in our face. The prosecutor would, no doubt, make Erik look like an Armenian Tony Soprano. That couldn't be a good thing, to say the very least.

But perhaps Harper was right. Perhaps the jury would already have it in their heads that Erik was a very bad guy. Maybe his testimony wouldn't be a net negative and might even be a net positive. It was difficult to tell.

"Okay, so I come at Ara with both barrels about his criminal activities." I nodded. "The next witness on the list was one of Shelly's best friends. Her name is Charlize Allen. She was a sorority sister down at MU and was also somebody who Shelly hung out with here in Kansas City."

"And her testimony will be..."

"I have no clue. Obviously, she can't testify to anything Shelly told her, as that will be hearsay, plain and simple. Perhaps she will just be a character witness."

"And the same thing with Yasin Ahmadi, also on the list" Harper said. "I can't imagine why they would be calling him. Again, he can't testify to anything Shelly might have said, so why will he be called? The great thing is, I can cross-examine him. If they're going to put him on the stand, I say more power to them. Yasin is somebody I think we need to cross-examine by asking questions that might lead the jury to believe he did it. Or his father did it."

I looked at the witness list for the prosecution and saw they hadn't planned on calling any other witness.

"Okay," I said. "So, let's go over our witnesses. We have Yasin on our list as well. We also have Abdullah Ahmadi. We have Wells Armstrong, and Shelly's father, Andrew McMason. As I see it, we can call all of them as hostile witnesses, so we can use leading questions on direct examination. I also have decided to call Irina Kovokosky, who will be none too happy about coming out here in the dead of winter, but it can't be helped. She's a vital witness to tie our theory of the case together."

Harper was sitting across from me and was thinking about something.

"What are you thinking about? You look like you're lost in thought over there."

"Yeah, I am." Harper nodded her head. "I am. What do you think about us calling Sargis himself to the stand? I still wonder if he had something to do with it. I think that perhaps Sargis and Erik weren't exactly on the best of terms. The fact that somebody is lying about whether or not Sargis knew Shelly's story before she was hired tells me all I need to know. Either Erik is trying to drag Sargis under the bus, or vice-versa. Either way, there's a rat there somewhere. I think we need to smoke it out."

"Sure. Let's call Sargis. He's on our witness list, so it's not too late to call him."

We had to get our witness list into the DA's office 10 days before the start of trial. Anybody who wasn't already on our list couldn't be called. It wasn't like in the movies where there's suddenly a surprise witness who shocks everybody in the courtroom, including the other side. Movies like *The Verdict*, actually one of my favorite movies, couldn't happen in real life. In that movie, a surprise witness changes everything. She couldn't be found prior to trial, so the other side didn't have the chance to depose her or find out what her testimony would be. The other side didn't ask for a recess so there could be a motion *in limine* to determine if the testimony should even be allowed. While that dramatic moment when the witness made her statement at the end made the movie incredible, unfortunately, in real life, that moment never could happen.

I didn't really know what would happen when we called Sargis. For that matter, we didn't really know what would happen when we called any of these witnesses. Each witness we called would be questioned about their relationship with Shelly, and the questions would be geared towards showing how each person had a reason to murder her. That was the best strategy Harper and I had at the moment and was the only strategy we could even try.

"Okay, let's go over our *voir dire* questions," Harper said. "How confident do you feel about your jury selecting skills?"

"I feel reasonably confident," I said. "I usually have a good intuition for who might be good for our side and who might not be. I firmly believe that choosing a jury is an art as opposed to a science."

"Well, that's the best way to approach that," Harper said. "Because it truly is an art instead of a science. What questions will we ask on our *voir dire*? Aside from the usual ones, of course – the questions about whether or not they know our client, whether or not they have been the victim of a crime, whether or not any potential members of the jury know the witnesses or any of us. Also, of course, whether they are a member of law enforcement or in the legal profession. Other than the usual questions, what will you ask?"

"I'll ask them if they heard anything about the case or if they knew Shelly at all. Even if they had met her one time, I need to know that. I think I should also ask some questions about whether or not, if they have knowledge our client is a member of the Armenian mob, would that cause them to be prejudiced against him. Maybe ask some questions about what they know about organized crime and the people part of these types of organizations. That's pretty important to note. I need to see if they have any kind of prejudices against our client going in."

"Okay," Harper said. "But I don't know if that's a good idea to go down that road. Bear in mind we might not put Erik on the stand. If we choose not to, the jury might never know our client is in organized crime."

"But they will know because the prosecutor's office is putting Ara Babyan on the stand. He'll testify he's in the Armenian mob and second-in-command to Erik. Then the prosecutor will ask him all these questions about what he does. That's the back-door way that Nick Wright will get all of Erik's activities before the jury. It's clever, really. They know they can't ask Erik about prior bad acts, but they can establish his criminal activity by calling his counterpart to the stand. I think we need to tackle Erik's colorful background head-on. No use pussy-footing about it. It's coming in, so we might as well prepare the jury for it. And we might as well find out what kind of prejudices they have going in."

Harper nodded her head. "Okay, I think you're right about that. Let's ask questions about that. What other questions might you have for them?"

"I think it might be a good idea to ask some questions about how they feel about hackers. Shelly was a computer hacker and used her computer hacking skills for nefarious means. I can ask questions to see who is passionately against that kind of behavior, and that will be the person I'll want. You see, there's psychology at work. If we can't show that somebody else might have done her in, the next best thing would be to subtly show she got what was coming. That way, we have the possibility of some kind of jury nullification."

"Jury nullification," Harper said. "I hope we don't have to rely on that, but I like your way of thinking. That's another risky strategy, blaming the victim, but if that's all we got..."

"No, that's not all we have, of course. I still like the idea about bringing in all those other witnesses who might have wanted her dead. And who knows? There might be something else that might come up. Some other motive that one of them might have had to do

Shelly in. That's the beauty of this strategy, really. I have a list of questions I'll ask all of them."

"And Irina? What questions will you ask her?"

"I need to know why Shelly only wanted to meet men who were well-placed in the pharmaceutical industry. I think she might know more than she is letting on. Perhaps I can get something from her on the stand that will help us figure out who might have further motive to have killed her."

"Well," Harper said. "I think we need to get Erik in here one last time and prep him for the stand. Are there any motions *in limine* we need to bring up in front of the judge?"

Motions *in limine* were motions that requested that certain pieces of evidence might be kept out. For instance, if there was something that was found in an improper search, the attorney would ask the judge to keep out that evidence. The best way to do that would be with a motion *in limine*.

"We could conceivably ask that Ara Babyan not be allowed to take the stand," I said. "After all, there is a good chance his testimony will be more prejudicial than probative." In this case, if I decided that Ara Babyan not be allowed to testify and I filed a motion to keep his testimony out, the judge would ask for him to testify in court without the jury hearing the testimony. The judge could then rule on whether or not Ara's testimony would prejudice the jury while not providing any clear probative value.

"That's good thinking," Harper said. "Excellent thinking. If we can exclude Ara from testifying, then we'll maybe keep the fact that Erik is in the Armenian mob out of the jury's ears. At any rate, even if we can't prevent the jury from realizing that Erik is in the Armenian mob, we can at least lessen the damage of them knowing. We don't want them to know everything Erik is involved in with the Armenian mob, and the best way to do that is to exclude Ara. If they don't call Ara, then perhaps it wouldn't be a good idea to call Erik to the stand, either. We don't want to open the door to the prosecutor asking him about all the dirty deeds he has done for the mob."

I wrote that down on a piece of paper. "Okay, so we'll try for a motion *in limine* on Ara's testimony. Chances are we won't get it, because I have the feeling the DA's office wouldn't be calling Ara unless Ara had something extremely relevant to add to the case. In other words, I think Nick Wright knows better than to call a witness who will simply get up and testify about what he does for the Armenian mob. They know they'll have to tie him to Erik, and they'll have to be tight about doing that. If they aren't tight about doing that, the entire testimony will have to go out the window. So..." I nodded my head. "I have a feeling Ara will testify that perhaps Erik confessed to him about killing Shelly. Or he might have testimony about Erik's relationship with Shelly. Perhaps he witnessed the two of them fighting or having words. Maybe there was tension between the two of them somehow. That's what I think that this Ara will say."

"I think so too," Harper said. "That said, it's worth it to try to exclude him. Go ahead and try the motion *in limine*. That will be useful because it will give us a heads-up on what his testimony will be. We'll be able to prepare better for him when we're in front of the jury if we can hear his testimony ahead of time."

"Is there anybody else we can try to exclude on their list?"

"I don't want to exclude Yasin," Harper said. "I don't know what he can add to their case, but I like that the prosecutor has opened the door to us cross-examining him about his relationship with Shelly. We need to find out if he ever knew about Wells or about Shelly's call girl activities. If he knew about that, we can ascribe motive to him from there."

"What about Charlize Allen?" I asked. "Should we try to have her excluded as well?"

Harper shrugged. "I don't know. I still don't know what she'll add to their case. I suppose we could ask for a motion *in limine* for her testimony as well. If the prosecutor puts her on the stand to testify to things Shelly might have told her, then obviously her testimony won't be allowed. That would be impermissible hearsay unless Shelly testified to something against her own interest. We know that Charlize can't testify about a dying declaration, because nobody was in Shelly's car at the time she crashed it. Nobody could have heard Shelly's dying declaration – she was killed instantly."

The hearsay exception, when the witness was unavailable, which Shelly was, stated that dying declarations and statements against interest are permissible. Everything else the deceased might have said would not be. Therefore, Charlize couldn't tell the jury anything about what Shelly might have said about whether or not she was afraid of Erik or any kind of similar testimony. I imagined this would be what the prosecutor would try to elicit, and I would have to shut that down immediately.

"They're also going to call Lena Williams," Harper said. "She's the editor at *The Star* in charge of Shelly. She gave Shelly the assignment, and she was the person who Shelly was reporting to. She's obviously an indispensable witness to them because she corroborates that Shelly was infiltrating Erik's clan and was getting her story ready for publication."

"How should we cross her?"

"Well, let's see. Without her testimony, it would be difficult for the prosecutor to establish Shelly was ready to publish her story about Erik's operation."

Harper and I went through the case thoroughly that day. We took turns trying to anticipate any holes that might need to be plugged up, and we ran through the witnesses, one by one. We wrote down tentative cross-examination questions and bounced theories off of one another. In the end, we both felt ready to go. We had our strategy, we had our tactics, and we knew where our blind spots would be.

Winning this case would be an uphill battle, especially since the case was so close to Christmas. That was a problem because we knew the jury's minds would not only be elsewhere, but we also knew they would hate us. We were the reason why they had to spend the week before Christmas in a courtroom, as opposed to spending it going shopping or baking or seeing their friends. We would have to somehow counteract that resentment the jury would naturally feel towards us.

I ended up feeling confident in our case, but not completely so. There was still the chance we would be blind-sided by one witness or another. There was always that chance.

We just had to prepare for it as best as we could.

TWENTY-ONE

DECEMBER 18 - FIRST DAY OF TRIAL

I met Erik at the courthouse. I had him in the week before and I prepped him for what he could expect to face. I found that Erik actually made a decent witness. He stuck to his story, even though Harper cross-examined him relentlessly.

I was impressed by Harper's skills. She was a natural – she was aggressive, but not overly so. She knew just what questions to ask to try to break him down. Yet, Erik was steadfast in his testimony. He firmly stated he had nothing to do with tampering with Shelly's brakes and didn't know who did it. He also handled the testimony about his "job description" remarkably well. He matter-of-factly talked about what he did. He believed he was like the CEO of his clan, which meant he wasn't actually doing the dirty work. He wasn't finding the girls for prostitution, nor was he involved in kidnapping people and selling them into white slavery. He wasn't hacking and he wasn't drug dealing. Rather, he was managing the people who were doing all of these things. Like a CEO.

Not that it made it any better that he wasn't getting his hands dirty. The reason why it was so important to emphasize the fact that

Erik didn't micromanage his soldiers was pretty simple – since he wasn't involved in the crimes at the granular level, he couldn't have carried out the hit on Shelly. He envisioned his role as being that of an overseer, and that meant he not only didn't commit crimes, but he didn't order individual crimes to be committed, either. The way his organization worked, as he explained it, was that individual hits were ordered from the intermediaries. Each division of his organization had a boss. That meant his white slavery "division" had a boss, the hacking "division" had a boss, the prostitution "division" had a boss and the drug dealing "division" had a boss. The individual bosses of the individual divisions ordered the hits. The soldiers beneath them carried out the hits.

Erik explained the hierarchy in a different way. "Think of it like the military. You have your generals, you have your sergeants and you have your privates. Right? Well, think of me as the general. I'm not down on the field directing the privates to do anything. That's the job of the sergeants directing their platoons. Now, if a sergeant directs his privates to do something wrong, that's not on the general, right? The general has no idea what is going on. The general's job is to oversee and plan military attacks. And if an individual employee in a large corporation does something wrong, it's not the fault of the CEO. If a team leader in, say, a large bank, directs his team members to do something illegal, that's not the fault of the CEO, either. I have no involvement in hits."

I had to admit, it was a good defense. I had no idea if it would fly. A good cross-examination by the prosecutor could poke holes in his testimony about how he doesn't get his hands dirty. Still, it was better than anything else we had. I would have to use that defense and hope for the best.

As for the motion *in limine*, it failed. Ara Abayan would be allowed to testify because he apparently had something relevant to say. I was happy I tried to get him banned from testifying, however, because I could get a sneak peek on what his testimony would be. He basically would tell the jury that Erik and Shelly were having a love affair, and that Erik was upset with Shelly on the day she died. According to Ara, Erik and Shelly had words in front of him, because Erik had just found out about Yasin and Wells.

When I told Erik what Ara's testimony would be, he laughed out loud. "Oh, I get it, I get it," he said. "That bastard. He's trying to say that me and Shelly were having an affair because that would mean I would have a personal reason for killing her, as opposed to a business reason." He shook his head. "Brilliant."

I knew what Erik was talking about. His defense was that he didn't get his hands dirty, and if somebody in his organization killed Shelly, he had no knowledge of it and didn't order it. But if a more personal motive was established, her murder could be directly tied to Erik himself.

"Is it true?" I asked him. "Were you and Shelly having an affair?"

"No," he said. "It's not true. Listen, Shelly and I were friends, I'm not gonna lie. But I knew she was into Yasin. She talked about him all the time. I didn't know about Wells, though. I may be a lot of things, and I might do a lot of bad things, but I don't fuck with other guy's girls. I draw the line there."

"So, why is this guy going to lie about you?"

"Because he wants my job. Plain and simple. I get sent down and he becomes the boss. It's really as simple as that."

I sighed. "Okay. Well, his testimony has to be tight. If he veers into topics other than what he's going to say about you and Shelly having words, I'll object on the basis of relevance. That means I won't let Nick ask Ara about what he does for the organization. I think we should keep you off the stand. I think that's the best trial strategy. That way, there's the possibility that your job duties of overseeing slavery, drug dealing and hacking won't come in. You get on the stand, however, and all bets are off. The prosecutor will ask you about all of that and you'll have to answer for it."

Harper nodded. "I agree. If you can limit Ara's testimony, then there's no need to put Erik on the stand."

So, that was our decision. Erik would not testify. There wasn't a reason for him to testify, as long as I limited Ara's testimony and made sure Nick stayed within the boundaries of what the judge deemed relevant.

We got to the Jackson County Courthouse and Erik was there, waiting on the steps, smoking a cigarette. His hair was trimmed and his suit pressed. He still looked like he wanted to be anywhere but where he was at that moment.

"Hey," he said when I approached him on the steps. "I hope you and Harper are ready for this."

"We are. We're as ready as we can be, really."

I always felt that was a lie. There was always something else that could be done. Always another witness I could have uncovered. I did the best I could, but I wasn't perfect. Nobody was, of course.

We took the elevator to the sixth floor, and there were hundreds of people standing around the hallway. I knew they were the potential jurors and I felt sorry for all of them. I would never want to serve as a juror. Trials were boring. They were held inside a stuffy courtroom that was old and musty – the Jackson County courthouse was built in the 1920s, and although it was grand, as Art Deco courthouses of that era usually are, it was still old. They had to sit in uncomfortable chairs and try not to fall asleep as people were speaking. That was probably the hardest thing, I thought – staying awake, especially in the afternoon after they had their heavy lunch. I remembered going to depositions and having to sit there while the lead counsel conducted them, and I had a hard time staying awake for that.

It didn't help that the temperature in the courthouse wasn't all that well-regulated. It was inevitably freezing in the summertime, because they always had the air conditioner up too high. You needed a sweater in the courtroom. In the wintertime, the heat was always blasting, so woe to the jurors who showed up wearing a sweater. I, myself, hated trying cases in the dead of winter for just that reason – I couldn't take off my suit jacket and tie so I ended up sweltering. And, since the heat was up high, that probably contributed to the juror's sleepiness.

On top of all that, the jurors got a pittance for their service. Six dollars a day + seven cents a mile. That was a criminally low amount of money to pay the jurors, if you ask me. They have to take off work and come down to the courthouse every day and sit there and die of boredom, all for six bucks a day plus seven cents a mile. I felt really sorry for the people who were hourly workers and selected for jury duty – they didn't get paid time off so they just had to suffer. I tried not to choose them for that reason alone, even though the poor hourly workers were more likely to sympathize with my clients than people well-off. They often got chosen anyhow and I felt bad for them.

I walked through the throngs of people in the hallway, thinking about how each of them were probably plotting and planning about how to get out of serving, and I had to smile. It was really so easy to get off jury duty – you just had to say you couldn't judge the case without prejudice. You would be struck for cause in that case.

Harper, Erik and I took a seat at one of the counsel's tables, and I saw Nick Wright and his second chair, Ally Hughes, were already there. Ally was actually one of my favorite prosecutors. She was starting out in the DA's office when I was a baby lawyer with the Public Defender's Office. I started off doing the grunt work of covering initial appearances – basically, when the accused criminals were arrested, they have to appear before a judge within 24 hours. That first court appearance was called an "Initial Appearance." Some circuits called that first appearance an arraignment, but in Jackson County, the arraignments came after the case already went through the Grand Jury or the Preliminary Hearing stage.

I was assigned the initial appearance dockets, in which 30-40 defendants appear to have their charges read to them and are given an preliminary hearing date. I didn't do much during these appearances except meet with the clients, explain the process and negotiate with the prosecutor about sentencing. Most of the clients ended up pleading out and it was up to me to get the prosecutor to give the best deal possible.

Ally Hughes was the prosecutor I worked with the most during that period of time, and she and I became pretty good friends. We even got drinks after work a time or two. In another life, I would have asked her out, because she was pretty cool. She and Colleen Sutton, my co-worker at the PD's Office, were the women I most fantasized about whenever Sarah and I were on the outs.

Ally saw me, smiled and walked over to our table. "Damien," she said. "I was wondering what had happened to you. I saw you were on the other side of this case and I got pretty excited. How the hell are you?"

I nodded my head. "Good, good," I said, thinking about Amelia. She had her bone marrow transplant and so far, so good. I had been taking her in for her monthly checkups, and, thus far, her body hadn't yet rejected the new bone marrow and was doing what it was supposed to be doing as far as fighting the cancer. We were hopeful she would go into remission soon. Of course, Sarah was still not in the picture. She had never even apologized for giving up on our daughter. She had moved in with John Gibson, the slimy worm with the slicked-back hair, and rarely saw our children. That was okay, however. Good riddance, as far as I was concerned. "And you?"

"Can't complain. By the way, I heard about your medical malpractice case. Congratulations. Guess you drew a pretty good hand there, what with that crazy doctor deliberately killing people and all."

"Yeah, I definitely got lucky." It felt weird to say I had gotten lucky, because Austin was still dead. Nothing would change that. And my client was still sleazy. She was a mother who arranged for the murder of her own son. I still couldn't get over my feeling that that award was tainted.

Yet it wasn't tainted enough I wouldn't want to spend it. I did spend it – I bought a new house in Harper's neighborhood, a fixer-upper. I wanted a house that needed work because I wanted to work on it in my spare time. Working on the house took my mind off Sarah's leaving and Amelia's sickness, and it was something I needed. My house needed a lot of work, too – every weekend, I worked on replacing the floors and repairing the plumbing and electrical. I tore off the roof and replaced it in full. I knocked out walls, rebuilt the staircase and tore up carpet and replaced it with hardwood. I loved working with my hands that way, even though Nate and Amelia always complained about the noise.

Ally was still smiling and nodding. "And Sarah? How is she?"

"I wouldn't know," I said, feeling uncomfortable. "She moved out a few months ago. But it is what it is."

Ally cocked her head and I swore she looked halfway excited when I told her my wife had moved out. "Oh, well, I'm sorry to hear that," she said. "But, hey, maybe when this trial is over, we can grab a drink. I know some awesome places in Midtown."

I chuckled. "Are you asking me for a date?"

"Maybe," she said. "It depends."

"On what?"

"On whether or not you want it to be a date."

I took a deep breath, thinking that Ally was cute, cool and fun. I probably would hit that. "Let's do it."

She smiled again. "Loser buys." And then she went back to her counselor's table and sat down.

I turned to Harper, watching Ally and me with evident amusement. "If only it was always that easy to get a date," she said. "But don't let Ally distract you."

"I won't."

IN THE AFTERNOON, the jury was picked and seated, and we were ready to get going. I had my opening statement prepared and I was anxious to get in front of the jury and plead our case. I had a feeling I knew where our case would go and I hoped it would go right where I wanted it to.

Nick was the first to address the jury with his opening statement. "Ladies and gentlemen of the jury, first of all, I would like to thank each and every one of you for your service. I know that it can't be said enough how much you are appreciated. I understand that it's not easy to leave your family and your jobs to come down here and sit in a stuffy courtroom, listening to us lawyers make our case, all while trying to stay awake."

The jury laughed lightly and a couple of people nodded their heads.

"The reason why you are here, of course, is a very important one. You are here to dispense justice. Justice for Shelly McMason. Shelly was a beautiful young girl who had her entire life ahead of her. Her whole life ahead of her. She was only 23 years old. She was a computer genius and was from a prominent family here in town. Her mother is right over there," he said, pointing to Emma McMason, sitting in the back of the courtroom, Kleenex in her hand. "And her father isn't in the courtroom, as he will be a witness in this case. But if he had the chance to be in this courtroom right now, believe me, he would be."

"Shelly was full of life and dreams and goals. All that was cut short on the morning of October 1 of this year." He paused dramatically. "On October 1 of this year, Shelly was driving to work. She had a job with the Kansas City *Star* and was on a dangerous assignment for them. She was to infiltrate the Armenian Power and write a story about what she had found. That meant she had to work for the Armenian Power, without them knowing she was working on a story for the newspaper."

"She was driving to work, ladies and gentlemen, when she discovered that her car did not have brakes. They were tampered with and she was on the highway when she found this out." He shook his head. "Could you imagine the panic she must have felt when she discovered she didn't have a way to slow down and stop her car? The abject fear? She ended up careening over the median of the highway and hitting a semi truck barreling down the road at 70 miles per hour. She hit that truck head-on, ladies and gentlemen, and there was very little of her to scrape out of her car at that point. Her casket was closed by necessity."

Then Nick pointed dramatically at Erik. "Erik Gregorian tampered with Shelly's brakes, ladies and gentlemen. He had two reasons why he wanted Shelly dead. First, and probably most important, was the fact that he had found out Shelly was working for the Kansas City *Star* and Shelly was ready to publish her expose on him and his organization. Evidence will show this to be true. That would mean that not only would everybody in the city know about his organization and what it does but also that the authorities would be pressured into shutting it down. If the people of Kansas City knew what Erik's organization was up to, the local police and the feds would have no choice but to bust Mr. Gregorian's nefarious operation. Public pressure would demand no less."

"So, Erik Gregorian, the head of the clan that ran most of the East Side, had to shut Shelly up. And that's exactly what he did. But he didn't just have that reason to kill Shelly. It wasn't just Shelly would shine a light on what his organization was up to." He shook his head. "No, it wasn't just that. It was also because Erik and Shelly were having an affair. The problem, ladies and gentlemen, was Shelly also had a fiancé. His name is Yasin Ahmadi, and Mr. Gregorian knew nothing about Yasin. At least, he knew nothing about Yasin until the afternoon of September 30, one day before Shelly was murdered. The evidence will show that Mr. Gregorian and Ms. McMason had heated words about the fact she was engaged and failed to tell Mr. Gregorian this news. So, there you have it. Mr. Gregorian had two reasons why he wanted Ms. McMason dead. One was professional the other was personal. Mr. Gregorian tampered with Ms. McMason's brakes and she was killed as a result. I urge you to send a message to Mr. Gregorian that he might get away with criminal acts in his job but he won't get away with this criminal act. Thank you very much."

I stood up. "I would like a word with opposing counsel at the bench, please," I said.

Judge Clarion nodded and summoned both Nick and me to the bench. "Counselor," he said, looking at me. "What is this about?"

"I would like to ask for a mistrial," I said in a whisper, glaring at Nick. "For slipping into his opening statement that my client has committed criminal acts. My client's prior bad acts are off-limits in this trial and by alluding to them in his opening statement, Mr. Wright has already poisoned the well."

Judge Clarion looked over at Nick. "I'm inclined to agree with Mr. Harrington," he said. "But I would like to hear your side."

"Judge Clarion, I think it can be assumed that since the defendant is working in organized crime, he has committed criminal acts. That's not a spectacular leap of logic for the jury to make. It's like when you buy a bag of almonds and the bag has an allergy warning that the bag contains nuts. I think that can be assumed. Likewise, it can be assumed here as well."

"That's not a good enough argument," I said, trying to keep my voice in a whisper. "Nobody can assume my client has committed criminal acts just because he works for an organized criminal organization. Besides, the fact that the Armenian Power is involved in organized crime won't be spelled out to the jury. I would like for this court to declare a mistrial."

Judge Clarion looked at both Nick and me and then shook his head. "Take it up on appeal, counselor," he said to me. "This is a judgment call, but I will warn Mr. Wright that he is not to go there again. If you so much as breathe a word about anything this defendant has done in the past then I will call a mistrial and I'll do it *sua sponte*. I hope I have made myself perfectly clear."

"But Judge Clarion, with all due respect, that horse has left the barn. You have no choice but to call a mistrial."

He shook his head again. "Take it up with the appellate court. In the meantime, it's time for your opening statement."

Nick took his seat, a smug look on his face. I was infuriated. He knew exactly what he was doing, the little bastard. I looked over at Judge Clarion one last time. *I'll take it up with the appellate court, alright. I have an open and shut case.* This was complete and utter bullshit I would have to continue on even though the jury was surely tainted.

Shake it off.

I walked over to the jury and began. "Ladies and gentlemen of the jury, I also thank you for your service. I know how much time and sacrifice you are giving, and your role in this courtroom is invaluable."

I paced up and down, looking each person in the eye. "You heard the opening statement of the prosecutor, and, with all due respect, I believe his statement shows what a flimsy case he has on his hands. Yes, I agree Shelly's brakes on her car were tampered with. I'll stipulate to that. Somebody killed her. Somebody wanted her dead. I'll agree to that fact all day long. But that somebody wasn't my client." I shook my head. "And nothing that opposing counsel said in his opening statement points to my client. To say the evidence against him is circumstantial is an understatement."

"Now, let's go through what the prosecutor just said. He said Shelly McMason was infiltrating my client's organization and she was about to expose his organization to the world. She was working with the Kansas City *Star* and was about to write a story about what my client's operation was up to. I'll stipulate to this fact. But even if this is the case, so what? So what?" I shrugged my shoulders and stuck out my hands. "What does that show? My client is the head of the organization Ms. McMason was allegedly infiltrating. He is not involved in the day-to-day operations of his clan." I wanted to go further, but I chose not to. This was a strategic choice as I didn't want the jury to necessarily hear that Erik's clan was involved in criminal activities, such as hits.

"My evidence will show something very different. Namely, that there are no less than four individuals who had the motive to kill Shelly, and none of them are named Erik Gregorian. The evidence will show that Ms. McMason was in love with a Muslim man by the name of Yasin Ahmadi. Mr. Ahmadi had the motive to kill Ms. McMason because Ms. McMason was also romantically involved with an individual by the name of Wells Armstrong." I nodded. "Yes, that Wells Armstrong, the CEO of Armstrong Pharmaceuticals, a strong rival for Argyros Pharmaceuticals, the company founded by Ms. McMason's father, Andrew McMason. If Yasin did not kill Ms. McMason, then his father, Abdullah Ahmadi, might have. Abdullah is a very traditional Muslim man, an Iraqi refugee who came to America in the early 1990s before Yasin was even born. He has traditional views, which meant he disapproved of Shelly's relationship with his son. Wells Armstrong himself had reason to kill Shelly. Although Ms. McMason saw her relationship with Wells as strictly business, Wells thought differently. He was kept in the dark about the fact she was engaged to Yasin Ahmadi. Finally, there was her father, Andrew McMason. The evidence will show that her father was enraged about Ms. McMason's relationship with Mr. Ahmadi. In fact, he was so bothered by her relationship with Mr. Ahmadi that he cut Ms. McMason off financially. He was against his daughter dating a Muslim man and was extremely prejudiced against Mr. Ahmadi. Add to that the fact that his daughter was also seeing the CEO of a rival company and you have a recipe for disaster. Maybe even murder."

I decided not to mention Sargis because I had no idea if I would call him or not. While he was on my witness list, therefore I reserved the right to call him to the stand, I wasn't sure if I would actually call him. Therefore, I thought it best I didn't mention him in my opening statement.

"So, you see, ladies and gentlemen," I said. "My client was one of many individuals who might or might not have had the reason to murder Ms. McMason. The prosecutor in this case will try to convince you that Mr. Gregorian was the one. But I'm here to tell you that the evidence against Mr. Gregorian is flimsy at best and that there were several other individuals with even more reason to want Ms. McMason dead." I nodded my head. "Thank you very much, and again, I value your service."

At that, I took a seat next to Erik, who put his arm around me and squeezed. "Good job," he whispered. "I think you got 'em."

I thought differently, but I didn't say as much. "Maybe, maybe not," I said. "At any rate, we gave the jury something to chew on."

EVERYBODY TOOK A BREAK, and then we all came back in. It was 2 PM, and the prosecutor was ready to call his first witnesses. The first person he called was Gregory Barter, their expert on the car and the brakes. He droned on and on about how he could ascertain the brakes were tampered with. I didn't care. I knew Nick had to call this dude on, otherwise the jury might have come to the conclusion Shelly died simply because of a tragic accident.

I didn't object to this testimony nor did I try to cross him. There was no reason to. Our expert also ascertained the brakes were tampered with, so it wasn't like we had a dueling expert. Not only that but our expert, Joseph Savolo, determined there was nothing else wrong with the car.

After he gave his testimony, Judge Clarion asked me if I had any questions for the witness.

"No, your honor," I said, standing up.

"Counselor, you may call your next witness," Judge Clarion said, addressing Nick.

"State calls Officer O'Reilly," he said, continuing the dog and pony show. I had told Nick I was prepared to stipulate Shelly was murdered. I didn't know why Nick had to go through the rigamarole of showing Shelly's death wasn't accidental, but, apparently, he found it necessary.

I doodled on my yellow pad while Officer O'Reilly talked about arriving at the scene and interviewing the witnesses after the accident. He couldn't go into just what the witnesses told him but he could talk about the condition of the body and how the body had to be cut out of the car. Personally, I found his entire testimony to be more prejudicial than probative – Shelly died, she was murdered, nobody disputed that, yet the prosecutor got to show pictures of the death scene. If the person was murdered, pictures of her death shouldn't be deemed relevant, in my opinion. All it did was gross out the jury and make them hate the defendant, whoever the defendant happened to be – in this case, as Nick dramatically got out his death photos, the person the jury was glaring at was Erik.

"Can you tell me how Ms. McMason died?" Nick asked, as I heard an audible sob coming from the back of the room. I looked over and saw Emma McMason, Shelly's mother, crying into a wad of Kleenex, and I had to stifle a roll of the eyes.

"Objection," I said. "I stipulate that Ms. McMason's car crash was a murder. I fail to see how dragging this officer out to emphasize that fact, along with showing these death photos, aids the jury in this case. As I see it, this entire testimony is highly prejudicial and I frankly do not see the relevance in it."

"Sustained," the judge said. "Move along, counselor."

Nick nodded his head. "I have nothing further for this witness."

"Counselor," Judge Clarion said to me. "Do you have anything for this witness?"

"No, your honor," I said, standing up.

"The witness is excused."

Then came Lena Williams. She was the editor for the Kansas City *Star* and was in charge of Shelly's assignment. Her testimony was important because she could establish Shelly was going to publish a story about Erik's operation therefore she could establish Erik's motive for killing Shelly.

I would have to try to break her down.

Nick did a good job with Lena as far as establishing Shelly's work assignment. She testified she had given Shelly the assignment and Shelly had reported back to her on a weekly basis. She ended her direct testimony by stating Shelly was, indeed, about to publish her findings from Erik's organization at the time she was murdered.

I had to admit, she was good.

Still, it was my job to break her down.

I walked up to her, clearing my throat. "Ms. Williams," I said. "Good afternoon."

She nodded her head politely. "Good afternoon."

"Now," I began. "You just testified on direct examination you are an editor at the Kansas City *Star*. Is that correct?'

"Yes."

"And you are, in fact, the editor in charge of Ms. McMason's expose of my client's activities, is that also correct?"

"Yes." She wouldn't give me an inch. She would just answer my questions with a "yes" or "no" answer and that was that. I would have to draw her out a bit more.

I turned to the jury and then turned to face her again. "Isn't it true that the story was not going to be published in the Kansas City *Star* for another six months after Ms. McMason was killed?"

"Well, yes," she said. "Any story has to go through a process of editing, fact-finding and verification. That's true with any story."

"So, then, it's not true what the prosecutor said when he claimed to the jury Shelly McMason was close to publishing her findings at the time of her death."

She straightened up her back. "Yes, but you have to understand. She was getting to the end of her assignment when she was killed. The story wouldn't break until we went through all the proper channels. But that doesn't mean Shelly wasn't in danger at that time because she obviously was."

I paced around. "Did Shelly tell you she was at all nervous about publishing her findings?"

She shook her head. "No. She never told me that."

"So she never thought somebody in the Gregorian clan might want to kill her?"

"No, she never told me that."

"So it is safe to say Shelly wasn't even aware that somebody in the Gregorian clan might have found out about her?"

"I believe that's true. All I know is Shelly never said a word to me about anybody finding out about what she was really doing for the Gregorian clan."

I started to pace, thinking I might be getting somewhere. "So Shelly wasn't aware that somebody might be trying to kill her and her articles about the Gregorian clan were not due to be published for an additional six months. Is that what you're saying?"

"That's what I'm saying."

"And, in all actuality, the story wasn't killed in the end. Is that right?"

"I beg your pardon?"

"You're still going to run the story. Correct?"

"Of course. Just because Shelly was killed doesn't mean the story was also killed."

I grinned. I had her on the run, only she didn't quite know it yet. "Just because Shelly was killed doesn't mean the story was also killed. So, Shelly's death didn't make a difference in whether the story ran or not, is that right?"

"Yes, that's correct," she said, nodding. "We have her notes and the rough draft for her feature. Now the story is in the hands of the fact-finders and the researchers. The people who double-check all of her sources and meticulously ensure that nothing that is printed is false or slanderous in any way."

"And, really, the fact Shelly died in a such a spectacular way is a actually a boon to the newspaper, is that right?"

"I'm sorry?"

"Shelly's death and the publicity surrounding it will get more eyes on the story, isn't that right?" I felt as if I was getting into my groove, and considering this was my first trial in quite a long time, it felt wonderful.

"I suppose so," she said.

"And your paper will play up the fact Shelly died getting the story, isn't that right?"

"In what way?"

"You're going to contact the local media about this story when it breaks, and you're going to tell the media Shelly died getting the story. Shelly, a pretty blonde sorority girl, died getting the story. That's a pretty big deal. I would imagine that will be a selling point for your newspaper."

"I don't like to think of it that way."

"Oh but you do have to think of that way, isn't that correct? You're working for a business. A business that runs on publicity. Shelly's death has been gold for your business, am I right about that?"

"Well..."

I went over to my newspaper clippings on Shelly's death. "I would like for you to review what has been marked as Defendant's Exhibit A," I said. "Are these newspaper headlines that your paper has run about Shelly's death?"

She looked at them closely. "Yes, yes they are."

"And there are five different headlines about her death, am I correct?"

She looked at all the headlines and counted. "Yes. Five different headlines."

"And these headlines are all in the front section of the newspaper, is that correct? Not the Metro Section, not the Entertainment Section, not the Sports Section, but the front section. Isn't that right?"

She nodded her head. "It would seem so."

"So, five different times, your paper has run a screaming headline about Shelly's death. Is that safe to say?"

"I wouldn't call them screaming headlines, no."

"You don't call one-inch letters above the fold, all caps, to be screaming?"

"No." She crossed her arms. I could tell she was getting defensive, but I didn't care. I would press on. That was my job.

"I would say that it looks to me, as a lay person, that your paper is really milking Shelly's death along for ratings. Or the newspaper equivalent of ratings."

"Objection," Nick said, standing up. "Counselor is using prejudicial language. Nobody is saying the newspaper is milking Shelly's death but Mr. Harrington."

"Overruled," Judge Clarion said. "You may proceed, counselor."

I cleared my throat. "So, your newspaper has run five different articles, all of them with headlines in large capital letters above the fold, about Shelly's death. Is it safe to say that, when you publish Shelly's expose of the Gregorian clan, you're going to revisit how Shelly died?"

"Are you accusing us of having her killed?" she asked, her arms folded in front of her. "To sensationalize her articles about the Gregorian clan?"

Truth be told, I hadn't even thought about that. But she opened the door to this line of inquiry, so.... "Did you have her killed?" I asked.

"Of course not. Shelly was one of our most respected reporters."

"Most respected reporters? She was brand-new. She was hired in January and was assigned this investigation in May of this year. Five months she worked for your paper before you gave her this dangerous assignment. Isn't it true that, at the time Shelly was working on her assignment, she was one of your most junior members?"

She visibly squirmed in her chair. "Yes," she said. "That is true."

"And why would you have assigned such an important story to somebody just hired onto your staff? Why assign such a dangerous story to a 23-year-old new graduate from journalism school? She hadn't interned for your paper previously. Why would you give her this assignment?"

She spoke directly into the microphone. "Her father asked us to give her an important assignment," she said. "And her father is one of the paper's largest benefactors."

Now I'm getting somewhere. "Oh, her father intervened, is that correct?"

"Yes," Lena said, nodding. "Her father intervened."

"And did her father directly tell you that he wanted his daughter to work on this assignment?"

"Yes," she said. "He did."

"So you were actually in contact with Andrew McMason, is that what you're saying?"

She nodded.

"Please answer verbally," I said. "The court reporter can't transcribe head nodding."

"Yes," she said. "That's what I am saying."

"And you told Mr. McMason, then, what Shelly would be doing? What assignment she would be completing?"

"Yes. I explained it all."

"And he encouraged it."

"He did."

"Did he explain to you, at any time, that he was not on speaking terms with his daughter?"

She shook her head. "No."

"Oh, so he never came out and told you he had cut Shelly off because he didn't approve of the man who she was dating. Is that your testimony?"

"I was unaware he had a problem with Shelly."

I was getting evidence I could tie into my theory of the case, and that was what I was aiming for. "So, he's a father who not only called you to ask you to give Shelly a dangerous assignment but he also didn't care the assignment you gave Shelly brought with it a high risk of death?"

"I didn't see her as having a high risk of death," Lena said. "Not if she was trained correctly."

"But she wasn't trained correctly, was she? You just threw her into this assignment, sink or swim, didn't you?"

"No," she said indignantly.

"No? Let me ask you this, Ms. Williams. Did Shelly have any kind of experience doing this type of thing? Infiltrating dangerous organizations in order to get a story. Had she ever done anything like that before?"

She shook her head. "No."

"No. She had never infiltrated an organization in order to get a story before. That is your testimony, correct?"

"Correct."

I took a deep breath. "And, in fact, Shelly had never done any kind of dangerous assignment before this. Isn't that right?"

"Right," she said into her microphone.

"Her prior experience, before coming to work for you, consisted of working for *The Maneater,* covering college bands and events around Columbia, Missouri, for her college newspaper. Isn't that right?"

"That's correct."

"So prior to working for the Kansas City *Star,* Shelly worked for the school newspaper, and, to your knowledge, she never covered any kind of dangerous topics in Columbia, isn't that right?"

"Right."

I turned back to her. "So, it's your testimony that the only reason why you put Shelly, a neophyte, on this major dangerous assignment is because her father asked you to. Right?"

She nodded her head. "Right."

"Not because she had the experience, not because she was prepared and not because she was right for the job. But only because her father wanted her on this assignment. Correct?"

"Well, she had hacking skills," she said. "Which set her apart from everybody else on the newspaper staff. We needed somebody for this job with the right skills for that organization. So that was the main reason why we sent her over to Erik's organization."

"Without the proper training," I said. "Right?"

"Well..."

"Well, what?"

"That's not true. She went through training."

"What did her training consist of?"

"We gave her a background review of the Gregorian clan and gave her a list of things she should never do or say."

I laughed out loud. "A review and a list. Seriously? That's the training she got from her bosses at the newspaper? That's what you're telling me?"

"We didn't want her to seem too rehearsed."

I shook my head and opened my mouth and shut it, several times. "I can't..." I shook my head, hoping the jury would see how exasperated I was with this woman. Then I looked over at Nick. "Your witness."

Nick got to his feet as he obviously wanted to redirect Lena. "Ms. Williams," he said, smoothly. "Why did you give Shelly this dangerous assignment?"

"Because I believed in her. I was impressed with her. She had excellent grades in college, and, most importantly, she had hacking skills. I needed somebody with skills that would be valuable in that organization. Nobody else at the newspaper had these skills, just Shelly. That was why I assigned her to the Gregorian clan."

"And you didn't give her that assignment just because her father asked you to, isn't that right?"

"Right."

"I have nothing further."

I was going to stand up and do a re-cross examination, but I thought better about it. As far as I was concerned, I drew blood on my original cross-examination of Lena. No need to beat a dead dog.

"Counselor?" Judge Clarion asked, looking right at me.

"I have nothing further for this witness," I said.

"Ms. Williams, you are excused," Judge Clarion said, looking at her.

She stepped down.

"Mr. Wright, call your next witness," Judge Clarion said.

"The state calls Ara Abayan."

I turned around and saw a slight young man ambling towards the witness stand. He was around 5'6" and probably didn't weigh much more than 120 lbs. His hair was black and curly, his eyes were just as black and his skin was olive. He was dressed down in blue jeans and a light-blue button down shirt, with sneakers on his feet.

He glanced at me when he passed by the table and stared hard at Erik. I caught him trying to intimidate Erik with his glare, so I stared right back at him. He glanced at me again and then went to the witness stand and sat down.

"What was that?" I asked Erik.

"What was what?"

"That stare-down he just gave you as he passed by you just now. You didn't catch that?"

Erik shrugged. "Ara hates me, of course. He wants to be the boss. He wants me out of the way. I told you that."

I shook my head and glanced over at Harper. Her gaze was fixated on Ara so she didn't even notice me trying to get her attention.

"Okay," I finally said to Erik. "I hope that's all it is. If I find out something new on the stand, something you didn't tell me, I won't be happy." It was bad enough I found out Ara would testify that Erik and Shelly had a lover's quarrel right in front of him. It was worse that Erik didn't seem all that surprised about this when I told him about it.

If was I blindsided by yet something else, I would have to take my client to the woodshed.

Ara was sworn in and the prosecutor asked him the preliminary questions about his name and whether he swore to tell the truth. He affirmed the oath and then stared more daggers at Erik. I looked at Erik and saw he was giving Ara the exact same look Ara was giving him, and I was irritated.

If you know something, you better goddamned tell me, I wrote on a piece of paper.

Erik said nothing but just shook his head and continued to stare.

As for me, I had to concentrate on what was being said, so I turned my attention away from Erik and towards the weasel at the witness stand.

"And how do you know the defendant?" Nick was asking him.

"He's my brother," he said. "My half-brother."

I bit my lower lip and shook my head. *Half-brother. And you didn't think this was a piece of information we needed to know?*

I stood up. "Your honor, I would like to request a short recess to confer with my client."

Judge Clarion looked over at Nick, who was looking at me like the cat that ate the canary. "Mr. Wright, do you have any objections?"

"None."

"Okay, then," Judge Clarion said. "I think we all need a break anyway and this witness hasn't been testifying long." He looked at the clock. "I'll dismiss the jury for a short recess, and let's all meet back here at 2:30." It was currently 2:10.

The Judge got off the bench and disappeared into his chambers.

As for me, I tapped Erik on the shoulder. "Come with me," I said. "We need to go into the witness room and talk."

Harper and I got up and Erik followed along behind.

We got to a witness room at the far end of the hall. There was nothing in that room but a long table and several chairs. Like all witness rooms in this courthouse, the paint was a putrid beige with peeling paint and the legs of the table were metal. This was definitely a no-frills room, designed for one purpose – to kill one's client. It was a place where you could take your client to the proverbial woodshed, as I was planning on doing right at that moment.

I sat down and gestured to Erik to do the same. He quietly obeyed.

"Okay." I took a deep breath. "Why didn't you think to tell me that Ara Abayan was your half-brother?"

Erik shrugged. "I didn't think it was relevant."

"It might be relevant. It might not be. That's not the point. The point is that it's a fact you didn't disclose. I'm just wondering what other facts you haven't disclosed."

Erik glared at me. "No. Why do you keep asking me these questions?"

"Because you keep lying to me, that's why."

"I'm not lying to you. I just haven't told you certain things. That's not really lying."

"That's a distinction without a difference," Harper chimed in. "And you're smart enough to know that. Now, this is strike two, as far as I'm concerned."

"What was strike one?"

"Strike one is that Ara will testify you were having an affair with Shelly and you and Shelly were having a lover's quarrel right in front of him." Harper took a breath. "Now cross-examining Ara will be more difficult than it would be before."

"What do you mean? Why is cross examining going to be more difficult than before?"

"Because," I said. "I would make him look bad because it would be difficult to believe you and Shelly would have a lover's quarrel in front of one of your colleagues. But he's not just a colleague. He's your brother. People have fights all the time in front of their family members. Not so much in front of their co-workers. I'm still going to cross-examine him on that same point but it will lose its punch."

"Not only that," Harper said, "but we'll have a hard time convincing the jury that your own brother would lie about you on the stand. Unless we have the time to draw some kind of Cain and Abel analogy, that is."

I stood up. "The thing is, we didn't prepare for this witness as if he was your brother. We prepared for him as if he was some kind of unrelated witness. Unrelated to you, that is. Why didn't you tell us? I don't understand that. Why?"

Erik shifted uncomfortably in his seat. "I didn't tell you because nobody is supposed to know. He wasn't supposed to say anything about that, either. Our father will be extremely angry with him. Hopefully he won't be as angry with me."

"I don't understand?" I was confused, and getting moreso with every word he spoke. "Why does Sargis care if people know that guy out there is your half brother?"

Erik crossed his arms and glared. "Because my mother doesn't know about it. That's why. My mother doesn't know my father had a kid with another woman while he was married to her. My mother and father are still together. They've been married since they were 18 years old." He shook his head. "My father will cut him off at the knees. The guy below him will become the boss at this rate. My father will just go on down the line until he finds somebody loyal to him. Ara obviously isn't that person."

"Who is the person below Ara on the hierarchy?" I asked Erik.

"His name is Narek Bedrossian," Erik said. "My father wants him in charge, anyhow. He would rather have Narek in charge than me."

"Why is that?"

Erik opened his mouth, but the bailiff poked his head into the witness room. "Time's up," he said. "The jury has been seated again and Ara is already on the stand."

I groaned and rolled my eyes. I hated being blind-sided by clients, and, once again, I was being blind-sided. This little worm Erik wasn't the first guy to snow me and wouldn't be the last.

I still had that question in my mind, however. *Why does Sargis want Narek Bedrossian in charge of the clan instead of Erik and, apparently, Ara?* This was the first I was hearing of this particular angle and I felt like killing Erik. Before the trial began, I impressed upon him the importance of not only being thorough, but of being honest. I didn't really expect this kid to be honest, although I wanted him to be. I hoped he would be thorough. That would mean not lying and not omitting, period. So far, he seemed to be doing both, especially omitting.

The three of us hustled to our seats. I caught the eye of some of the jurors and saw they looked annoyed. Since they would decide Erik's fate, I would rather they not be annoyed. But it couldn't be helped.

Ara was on the stand smirking at his half-brother. Erik was staring daggers at Ara. I wondered about these two. They were half-brothers, but was there some kind of drama between them? There often was in these cases – a kid born out of wedlock, the wife of the kid's father having no clue her husband had been fooling around. That caused all kinds of drama and strife in my experience.

Ara had reason to bring Erik down – he wanted Erik's job. But did he also have his own personal reasons for bringing Erik down?

I guess I would soon find that out.

TWENTY-TWO

Nick resumed his direct-examination of Ara, peppering him with questions, and I was ready to object if he started to get into anything Ara did for the organization. Any kind of criminality questions could not be asked, according to the judge, because the jury could reasonably infer that any kind of criminal activity Ara did would be the same kind of criminal activity Erik did. After all, Ara was, temporarily, in Erik's position at the clan.

"Now," Nick said, and I concentrated on every word he said. After his sneakiness in the opening statement, telling the jury casually that Erik was involved in crime, I didn't trust him any further than I could throw him. "You are the half-brother of the defendant, is that correct?"

"Yes," Ara said, nodding his head. "I am."

"And, at the moment, your position with the Armenian Power network, the division located on the East Side, is?"

"My position is that of leader of the Gregorian clan," he said. "The Kansas City Division of the Gregorian clan."

"So you have repeated exposure to the defendant, correct?"

"Yes," he said. "That's right."

"And you've been around the defendant and the deceased, Ms. McMason, right?"

"Yeah," he said, nodding his head. "I've been around them separately and together."

"When you've been around them together, how do they act?"

"They act like two people doing each other," he said. "But I wouldn't say they were in love or nothing like that. Just sex."

I looked over at Erik and he was shaking his head. He looked up at the ceiling and then back at Ara and shook his head again.

"Did you get the feeling it was just sex for both Erik and Shelly? Or did you get the impression that perhaps either Shelly wanted more out of the relationship or that Erik wanted more?"

"Objection," I said, standing up. "The way this question is worded calls for speculation."

"Sustained," Judge Clarion said. "Counselor, please rephrase the question."

"Thank you, your honor," Nick said. "I will do just that." Then he turned back to Ara. "Did Erik Gregorian say anything to you that would indicate he wanted more out of the relationship than did Shelly?"

"Yes," Ara said.

"And what did he say to you about that?"

"He told me he wanted Shelly to be his girlfriend."

"And was she just as interested in that?"

"No. She wasn't."

"Did Erik tell you she wasn't interested?"

"Yes. Erik said he had found out Shelly was living with this Muslim dude named Yasin Ahmadi."

"Yasin Ahmadi," Nick said, as if he had never heard that name before. "So, Erik told you Shelly was engaged to a person named Yasin Ahmadi. Did you see the two of them argue about this issue?"

"Yes. I did."

"When did you see them argue about Shelly's relationship with Yasin?"

"When I was over at Erik's house, September 30, the day before Shelly was killed. I was paying Erik a visit when Shelly came over unannounced. They went on Erik's porch but I could hear what they were saying to each other and I could hear they were arguing about Shelly being engaged to Yasin."

"Was this the only time you heard them argue?"

"About this topic, yeah, but I head them argue about many things over the past few months. Ever since Shelly came to work for the Armenian Power, they've been arguing."

"You say the two have been arguing ever since Shelly came to work for the Armenian Power. That implies that Erik and Shelly knew one another before she came to work for the Power. Would that be fair to say?"

"Yes. That would definitely be fair to say."

I hung my head and sighed. *What next? What will I find out next? What else has Erik neglected to tell me?* I suddenly understood just how Shelly came to work for the Gregorian clan. He blamed it on an associate named Vardan Dorian but I suddenly knew that Vardan Dorian wasn't the person who brought Shelly into the clan. It wasn't Sargis, either.

It was Erik himself.

And I was about to find out just how Erik and Shelly really met.

TWENTY-THREE

I sat there and silently steamed while Ara was on the stand. I was used to being blindsided. It was difficult to find out everything there is to know about people and their relationships, even for experienced investigators such as Tom Garrett. Garrett apparently didn't find the link between Erik and Ara and he didn't figure out that Erik and Shelly knew one another before Shelly came to work for Erik. That was fine. I would have to have a talk with him about sharpening up his investigation skills a bit but he wasn't the person I was really angry with.

The person I wanted to kill, right at that moment, was Erik himself. He was digging his own grave, really, by not telling me these important bits of information. Who knows? Maybe that was all a part of his plan somehow. Blind-side me every which way, put me in the blender and see what shakes out.

I would have to focus, however. Focus and try to figure out how to approach this guy. I had a feeling Erik wasn't telling the truth about his relationship with Shelly, either. He insisted they were just friends. Yet, he had been lying all along. What was stopping him from lying now?

Nothing. That was what was stopping him from lying now. Nothing at all. The kid lied with impunity. Hell, he probably did kill Shelly. It sure was looking that way.

"Now, tell me how long Erik and Shelly knew one another."

"They go back several years. When Shelly was in college, she met Erik. He was down in Columbia for a football game and the two of them met in a bar. Harpo's Bar in Columbia, Missouri. As far as I know, though, they were only friends from that point on. Then, when Shelly moved to Kansas City, Erik invited her to work for the organization. He knew she was a computer hacker and he needed her skills."

"I see. So, the two of them met in Columbia several years ago. And do you know when they began a romantic relationship?"

"I believe their relationship became romantic when Shelly moved to Kansas City last January."

"And Erik never knew about Yasin, is that correct?"

"Yeah, that's right. He never knew Yasin existed. Yasin was never around, anyhow. He's in medical school, studying to be a doctor, so he was never around."

Nick paced back and forth while he interrogated Ara. "And did Erik ever tell you anything about a baby?"

"Yes," he said.

My heart started to pound as I remembered Shelly's stricken face in front of her video camera. The bruise on her eye, the reference to the unnamed person who hit her, and her nightmares about "the baby."

I drew a breath, waiting for the next shoe to drop.

Which it did.

"And what did Erik tell you about a baby?"

"He told me he got Shelly pregnant and he forced her to have an abortion."

TWENTY-FOUR

I put my thumb and forefinger and pinched the bridge of my upper nose as I stared down at the defense table. I couldn't take much more of this. This testimony just kept getting worse and worse. And worse. Erik, for his part, was sitting there next to me, as still as a statue. He wasn't writing me outraged notes, which was what I expected he would do if he were innocent and this Ara was lying through his teeth. I had the distinct feeling, as I looked at him staring at the ceiling, that Ara *wasn't* lying through his teeth. On the contrary, I had the feeling Ara was telling the truth and my idiot client had been lying to Harper and me all this time.

I wrote a note to Erik. *Is that true? About the baby?*

No. He shook his head. *It wasn't like that. She didn't know if I was the father or Yasin was so she aborted the baby. She didn't want to deal with that.*

I sighed. I would have to cross-examine this guy but I felt completely defeated. I had clients who lied to me before, of course. That's what criminals do. They lie. This was nothing new. But I was outraged all the same. I looked over at Harper, and I could read, in her body language, she was just as annoyed. She was sitting very rigidly in her chair, she kept closing her eyes and she was taking deep breaths. Like she was trying to calm down.

Her body cues were very subtle, however, too subtle for the jury to pick up. That was one thing we were always trained to do – never let the jury see us sweat. As defense attorneys, we could never give away how we were feeling especially when things went south. As this trial was, second by second.

"So," Nick said, seeing that he had triumphantly drawn blood with this witness. "Erik forced Shelly to get an abortion. Do you believe Erik killed Shelly?"

"Objection," I said, standing up. "Calls for a conclusion."

"Sustained."

"I have nothing further, your honor." Nick smiled at me smugly as he sat down.

I got to my feet and went over to Ara. "Mr. Abayan," I began. "You just told the court you heard my client and Ms. McMason arguing on occasion. Is that right?"

"Yes, that's right."

"Is it fair to say that people have disagreements with one another from time to time. Not just Ms. McMason and my client, but people in general. They have arguments and heated words. Is that fair to say?"

"Of course. People argue with each other all the time."

"And is it fair to say that, even though people in general might have heated words with one another, those same people don't usually go out and kill that other person?"

"I guess."

"You guess. You mean, you don't know? Do you believe that most people who have heated words with each other end up killing that other person?"

"Well, no."

"And you said you saw them arguing, but you never said my client actually made any verbal threats against Ms. McMason. I would imagine that is because there weren't any verbal threats made against her. Isn't that right?"

"Yes, that's right."

"In fact, there wasn't anything about their arguments out of the ordinary, isn't that right? There wasn't anything physical between them – no punching, no kicking, no shoving, none of that. Isn't that right?"

"Yes. That's right."

"And you knew Ms. McMason personally. I didn't know her, but I know her personality, and she had never struck me as the kind of woman who wouldn't call the police if she felt threatened in any way. Wouldn't that be fair to say?"

"Yes. That's fair to say. If Shelly had felt threatened by Erik, she would have called the police."

"And she never called the police on Erik. Isn't that right?"

"Yes, that's right." He nodded but then glared at Erik.

I paced a bit in front of the stand. "So, she never called the police on Erik. The fights you describe between my client and Ms. McMason were not violent and you never heard any threats. Does that sum up your testimony correctly?"

"That's right, but-"

"And isn't it also true that Ms. McMason was engaged to Yasin Ahmadi at the same time she allegedly was having sexual relations with my client?"

"Yes."

"And would it be fair to say that Ms. McMason actually didn't know who fathered her unborn child and that was why she had an abortion, not because my client forced her into it?"

"Objection," Nick said, on his feet. "Calls for speculation."

"Sustained. Please rephrase your question, counselor."

"Did Shelly ever tell you she didn't know who fathered her unborn child?"

"Objection, hearsay," Nick said.

"Statement against interest, your honor," I said. "If she told Ara she didn't know who fathered her child, that would besmirch her own reputation. That makes it a statement against interest."

Judge Clarion nodded his head. "I'll allow it. Please answer that question, Mr. Abayan."

"Yes. She told she didn't know who fathered her child."

"So, then, she actually had an abortion because she didn't know who the father was of the child, and she didn't want to admit that fact to her fiancé, Yasin. Isn't that fair to say?" I knew I wouldn't get away with him answering that question, but I didn't care. It was out there, and that was all that mattered.

"Objection, calls for speculation."

"Sustained."

"I have nothing further."

I sat down, and Erik wrote a note. *Good job,* it said.

You're an asshole, I wrote back. *A lying asshole.*

Charlize Allen was next on the stand. She didn't add much as it turned out. I figured she was on the stand to humanize Shelly some more. I didn't object to her testimony, nor did I cross her. She was insignificant.

Not so insignificant was Yasin Ahmadi. I knew that he, too, was brought to the stand to be more of a character witness than anything else, but I wanted to cross-examine him, anyhow.

He was just as I pictured him. He was a handsome guy with long curly hair worn in a man-bun. He was dressed in a blue button-down with a white t-shirt underneath, blue jeans and work boots. His skin was caramel-colored and his teeth were perfectly straight. His eyes was large, brown and expressive. I could see the appeal of the man.

He sat down and I realized that he looked weary. As if he was working too much and was dealing with too much stress. Which he probably was. Between being a first-year medical student and dealing with the death of his fiancé, I knew Yasin had much on his plate.

The bailiff swore him in and Nick had him state his name for the record, and then he started asking him questions. It turned out that Yasin, like Charlize, was called because Nick wanted to humanize

Shelly a bit more. Make the jury see her as three-dimensional and make her death seem that much more tragic. If I wanted to, I could have objected to Yasin taking the stand, because his testimony wasn't really relevant to the proceedings, but I didn't object. I wanted to cross-examine him because I wanted the jury to believe there was the chance that Yasin murdered Shelly.

I got my chance after Nick rested with his questions.

"Mr. Ahmadi," I said, approaching him. "You testified on direct examination you and Shelly were very much in love, isn't that correct?"

"Yes," he said, nodding his head. "That is correct."

"Were you aware of how her father felt about you?"

"Yes. He hated me. He hated me because of how I look and what I believe. I'm not Christian and I'm not white, so I wasn't good enough for his daughter." He stated this matter-of-factly, with little emotion. Yet, he had to have been angry. Anybody would have been angry under these circumstances.

"He hated you." I nodded my head. "And did you happen to know Shelly was seeing men behind your back? Not just Wells Armstrong, but also my client, Erik. Did you find out about this before she was killed?"

"No," he said, looking down at the stand. "I didn't know that. I didn't know that until after she died and I started seeing articles in the paper about her life."

"And you also weren't aware she was pregnant and didn't know if you or my client was the father? You didn't find out about that?"

"I did not." He looked down at the stand again. "I thought I knew her but it turns out I really didn't."

"Now, you loved her and she was sleeping around behind your back. You say you didn't know about that, but if you did, would that have made you angry?"

"Of course. I would have definitely been angry about that. Who wouldn't be angry to find that out?"

"Who, indeed?" I crossed my arms in front of me. "Maybe it would have made you angry enough to kill her."

He glared at me and shook his head. "No. I would have never been angry enough to kill her. I loved her. I still do. She was the love of my life. Her father despised us together and so did mine. They did everything in their power to keep us apart but we stayed together. We fought for each other."

"You were fighting for her but she was sleeping around." I nodded.

"Yes," he said softly, tears coming to his eyes. "That's right."

"I have nothing further."

I felt terrible for Yasin. He was a broken man who had lost his fiancé and now was looking, to the jury, like somebody who might have killed her. At least, if I did my job right, the jury was thinking that.

I still felt sympathy for him as he dragged himself off the stand, his shoulders slumped as he walked out the courtroom doors.

The judge looked at the clock. "Okay," he said. "It is now 4:30. We will adjourn for the day, and everybody must be back here tomorrow right at 9 for day two. I thank all of you again for your service, and I'll see all of you back here tomorrow." He banged the gavel, and the members of the jury all stood up and filed out of the courtroom.

I stood up and, without a word, left the courtroom as well.

I wouldn't deal with Erik right at that moment. Fuck him.

TWENTY-FIVE

Harper followed me out the door and waited with me for the elevator. The slimy worm Erik was still in the courtroom. I guessed he didn't want to hear the lecture from me. That was smart, because I was tempted to give him a piece of my mind right in front of the jury. Several of the jury members were standing in the hallway with us, waiting for the elevator, too, and I would have given them a show. I had a hard time controlling my temper with guys like Erik, and I just didn't want to deal with him.

"You going somewhere tonight?" Harper asked.

I nodded. "My daughter Amelia is in the hospital with the flu." I still hadn't told Harper about Amelia's battle with lymphoma. I didn't know why I didn't let Harper into my world. I guessed it was because I was always so closed-off. Being in prison for five years did that to me, in a way. It made me guarded. In prison, if you let people know too much about your life, they would inevitably use it against you.

"In the hospital with the flu?" Harper said incredulously. "Wow, that must be some flu."

I bit my lower lip and watched for the elevator to appear on my floor. I took a deep breath. "You going anywhere this evening?"

"No. I don't have any plans."

"How about you come to the hospital with me? She's only going to be in there overnight for observation. I know she wants some company and I would love for you to meet her."

"Okay." Harper nodded her head. "I'll call my nanny, Sophia, to make sure my girls are fed and they take their baths and do their homework. I'll be glad to go to the hospital with you."

"Good. I need to get away from this place and we need to talk about our strategy. Things obviously changed today," I whispered, as I didn't want any of the jury members to hear me. "And we need to maybe rethink things."

She nodded. "I was just thinking that myself."

The elevator finally arrived and we rode it down. We got to the ground floor and went out the door. It was only 4:30, but the sky was dark and it was cold. It felt like snow and the weatherman was calling for it. Everything was lit up for Christmas – the trees had lights in them, and many of the downtown buildings did as well. That was one thing I loved about Kansas City – Christmas felt like Christmas around here. Feeling the Christmas season was something I didn't have in prison nor did I have it growing up with my single mom. I was grateful I still had Amelia this Christmas. A year ago this time, I didn't think she would have lived to see another. Yet she was getting better and stronger all the time. This latest hiccup not-withstanding.

"She's in Children's Mercy," I said. "Room 505. You can meet me there if you like."

"I'll be there."

I walked to my car, wondering if I was doing the right thing. I would obviously have to tell Harper the truth about my daughter. She would have to know my daughter was in the oncology ward. I didn't know if I was ready for Harper to find out about Amelia. I didn't want her to give me the sympathy eyes all the time and I didn't want to have to constantly answer well-meaning questions about Amelia. I didn't want Harper to think she had to treat me differently. I didn't want things to change. Unfortunately, once people knew your child was sick with cancer, things usually did change.

I GOT TO THE HOSPITAL, and Harper was already waiting for me in the lobby. She saw me and she linked arms with mine.

I closed my eyes. *She knows. She's already giving me the sympathy eyes and the sympathy gestures.* "Why didn't you tell me about Amelia?" she asked.

"Because I didn't want you to feel sorry for me," I said. "I hate pity. Things are fine with Amelia. She's a little sick with the flu, which can be very dangerous for her right now. They're pumping her with fluids and giving her Tamiflu and there's not a reason to get bent out of shape about it."

She nodded. "I understand."

We got to the elevator and rode it to the fifth floor. I found Amelia's room and we walked in.

She was sitting up in bed, playing with her iPad, when we walked in. Since she was no longer in danger of dying from an infection, she was allowed to have non-sterile items, such as iPads, with her. That delighted her beyond measure.

"Daddy," she said, excitedly. "I was dying to find out how your trial is going. I've been thinking about that all day."

I chuckled. "You're six years old and obsessing about my trial." I shook my head. "You're a freak, kitten."

She looked over at Harper quizzically and then looked down at her iPad. "Who is that?"

"This is Harper. She's my boss."

Harper beamed at Amelia but Amelia looked away. I think I knew why Amelia was so cold to Harper – she could tell Harper was taking pity on her. Amelia was like me – to her, pity was the absolute worst emotion you could express. Amelia would take rage, jealousy, vengeance or any other ugly emotion over pity and would take it gladly. I knew Harper meant well, but I also knew she wouldn't be scoring any points with my daughter.

"Daddy," she said, ignoring Harper. "When am I getting out of here?"

"Tomorrow," I said. "I talked to your charge nurse and she assured me you will be blowing this place tomorrow."

"Good," she said, smiling. "Does that mean I can make Rosalind bring me to see you in your trial? Everybody's talking about it today. It's even shown up on my iPad under Yahoo! News. You're famous, Daddy."

I sighed. "Kitten, no. This is an adult trial. In fact, all my trials are adult trials. Maybe when you get older, you can come."

"You mean *if* I get older." She looked down again at the iPad and her words struck me like daggers.

"*When* you get older," I corrected her.

"Whatever. I want to see you try this case," she said. "That girl, Shelly, she seemed like she was nice. And your client seems like –"

"Not so nice," I said. "I know."

"I would say he sounds like a douchebag, but okay."

I felt embarrassed to hear my six-year-old daughter saying that word, but I felt that words were just words – they didn't hurt anybody, so I didn't feel like correcting her for saying things she shouldn't. Still, I felt I should probably correct her in front of Harper.

"Amelia, we don't say those words," I said.

"I say that word all the time. It could be worse."

Harper laughed and I shook my head. "Anyway, Kitten, you need your rest. I wanted to drop in and tell you I love you, as usual. I'll be by tomorrow after my trial to get you out of this place."

"Whatevs," she said.

I kissed her forehead and Harper and I left.

"She's very intelligent," Harper said. "Not that that's a surprise, considering you're her father."

"Yeah. She's 6 years old, going on 26. It is what it is, though."

"I hate to pry," she said. "But what kind of cancer does she have?"

"Lymphoma. Non-Hodgkin's. But she's beating it. She just had a bone marrow transplant, and, so far, so good."

"And your son? How is he handling it?"

"As well as can be expected. I try very hard to not neglect him. That was one thing my therapist told me – don't neglect him. I got a family therapist for all of us after Amelia got sick and her mother ran off. It was hard to cope for awhile. But we've all turned a corner."

Harper smiled. "I was raped when I was in college," she said. "I figured that since you're opening up a bit to me, I should do the same with you. My rape is why I became a drunk." Then she shook her head. "That's not true. I was a drunk long before then, but it made me into even more of a drunk. And I white-knuckle my sobriety every day of my life."

I nodded, feeling that Harper and I had turned a corner. We were maybe trusting one another just a bit. Finally. "Well, I would say let's get a drink, but it sounds like that wouldn't be appropriate."

She laughed. "I can go to a bar now and not want to drink. I just got back on the wagon, though, so that was very difficult for me for a long time. But I'm okay again. Let's go. We need to talk about Erik's case, anyhow."

"Erik. That bastard."

"Yes," Harper said. "He's a bastard for sure. But nothing we can't handle. And we will handle it. We have to. Not just because of Sargis' threats, but also because he's our client. They threw us a curve-ball today, but we can throw it right back at them. We can and we will. Bank on it."

Harper and I arranged to meet at a bar so we could talk more about Erik's case.

It was an uphill battle and was only getting worse.

But we would get through it.

TWENTY-SIX

The next day, the prosecutor called several more witnesses, none of whom were terribly consequential. Then it was our turn.

The show was about to begin.

"Counselor," Judge Clarion said, addressing me. "Call your first witness."

Harper and I had decided the best witnesses we could call would be Wells Armstrong and Andrew McMason. I felt they would be better bets, as far as alternative suspects, than would Yasin and his father.

Wells would be good for us because I knew he would make Shelly seem less sympathetic. He would confirm to the jury Shelly was less than pristine and sullying her up could only be good for our side.

"The defense calls Wells Armstrong."

Wells came to the stand. He was around 50 years old with a full head of dark hair. He walked with a straight back, his head held high. He was dressed casually, at least more casually than a CEO of a company would usually dress – he was wearing khaki pants and a yellow button-down, open at the collar.

The bailiff swore him in and he sat down.

I asked him his name and he answered. And something seemed off to me.

His voice was high-pitched and he had a slight Southern twang.

That was when I realized that my gaydar was pinging with this guy. It was just in the way he walked and was also in his voice. I blinked. Was this really Shelly's other man? Besides my client and Yasin, supposedly this was the other man causing so many problems in Shelly's life and in her relationship. But what if we were totally off base about this?

Irina was also on my witness list. Maybe she could provide the jury better insight.

"Um, Mr. Armstrong," I began, suddenly wanting to ask pinpointed questions to find out his sexuality. Garrett had indicated Wells was married to a woman named Naomi but he got the impression it was a marriage of convenience. *A marriage of convenience.* My wheels started to spin. "Do you understand why I've called you to testify today?"

"Yes," he said. "I think."

"I wanted to ask you some questions about your relationship with the deceased, Shelly McMason. It's my understanding you met Ms. McMason last summer, is that right?"

"Yes. That's right."

"And you met her through an escort service, is that right?"

He shifted uncomfortably in his seat. "I needed a date," he said defensively. "To a white-tie event in Santa Barbara, California. I hired an escort because I didn't want to appear at this big event without a woman. That was why I hired her. No other reason than that."

"Be that as it may, you did hire her, isn't that right?"

"Yes, but it was strictly platonic. She accompanied me to this event and that was that."

"But that wasn't that, was it? You actually continued to see her long after that event. Isn't that right?"

"Yes," he said. "But it's not what you think. Shelly became a friend of mine, a confidant. And she and I were working on a very important project."

"An important project. What was that project?"

He took a deep breath. "Shelly was in need of some information from me, or should I say, she was in possession of some very important information for me. It was a mutual thing. A quid pro quo, you might say."

"A quid pro quo?" I asked him. I was suddenly intrigued. "What do you mean by that?"

"I mean I provided her with a comfortable living and she provided me with some information I needed for my business. In the end, it backfired spectacularly, but I always land on my feet."

"And what was the information she was providing for you?"

He cocked his head. "I believe I will have to plead the Fifth on that. I'm very sorry."

He was pleading the Fifth? He was afraid that he would self-incriminate? Seriously?

"Okay," I said, suddenly realizing this guy was probably far more of an intriguing witness than I thought he would be. I figured he would tell me about his sexual relationship with Shelly and would tell us something that would lead the jury to believe that maybe Yasin had reason to kill Shelly – if this guy and Shelly were hooking up behind Yasin's back, that would have driven Yasin to kill her. "You are not going to provide me the information you were getting from Shelly because that information would self-incriminate you. Is that what you're saying?"

"That's exactly what I'm saying. I consulted my attorney before I was called to testify and he informed me I have a right not to say anything that would self-incriminate me. So, I cannot tell you the information Shelly provided me because if I did, I would incriminate myself."

I closed my eyes. I suddenly felt I was at a standstill with this witness. He was more mysterious than I had thought he would be. It didn't appear Shelly and he had a sexual relationship after all. I felt he was probably gay and, if anything, Shelly was his beard. But I no longer thought his relationship with Shelly would have bothered Yasin enough to kill her. This was a harmless gay man. Yasin, from all accounts, was a liberated and modern man. I couldn't see him killing Shelly because she had a gay friend.

"I have nothing further for this witness," I said. I suddenly knew I would have to piece together Wells' issue by calling Irina to the stand. Maybe she could provide more insight to me about what was going on. I had spoken with her before, of course, and she emphasized Shelly wanted to meet men who were highly placed in the pharmaceutical industry. She didn't exactly say why that was. Perhaps she could elaborate now. She would be placed under oath, so she couldn't weasel out like she did before. She would have to answer my questions. If she failed to, I would treat her as hostile and make her answer.

I would get to the bottom of what Wells was hiding if it was the last thing I did.

"Counselor," Judge Clarion said to Nick. "Do you have any questions for this witness?"

"No, your honor," he said, smirking at me. I knew what he was thinking. He was thinking that my calling Wells to the stand just blew up in my face. He figured he would give me enough rope to hang myself, and nothing more.

No matter. I would figure this puzzle out or die trying.

"Mr. Harrington," Judge Clarion said. "Please call your next witness."

"The defense calls Irina Kavokosky."

The bailiff went out into the hallway and retrieved Irina.

She was wearing a suit with a fur collar and tall leopard print heels. Her hair was bleached white and she was wearing a little fur hat on her head. Her skirt was about two sizes too tight and she was almost spilling out of her jacket. Her lips were bright red and she was wearing heavy eye-shadow. She walked rapidly to the stand, sat down, and glared at me.

I knew what she was thinking. She was thinking about how her tits were freezing in this weather. How she wanted to get back to the warm weather of LA as soon as possible. No matter, she was here now. And she would answer some serious questions.

She was sworn in and stated her name, and I got right to it.

"Ms. Kavokosky, I would like to ask you a few questions about Shelly McMason and Wells Armstrong. You are responsible for the two getting together, are you not?"

"Yes," she said, in her thick accent. "I am."

"Now, as I understand it, you run an escort service in Los Angeles. Is that correct?"

"Yes," she said. "I do."

"And was it through this escort service you introduced Ms. McMason to Mr. Armstrong?"

"Yes. That's correct."

"What was it about Shelly that convinced you she would be a good match for Mr. Armstrong?"

"Shelly was a beautiful and charming young girl," she said. "And very intelligent and witty. Well educated, good breeding, knew her etiquette. She wouldn't have embarrassed Mr. Armstrong."

"When you hired Shelly, did she tell you about the men she was interested in meeting?"

"Yes. She said she wanted to meet men well-placed in the pharmaceutical industry. CEOs and high-level executive officers in the pharmaceutical industry."

"And were you aware Shelly's father was in the pharmaceutical industry?"

"Yes. Of course."

"What was your understanding as to why Shelly wanted to only meet men high up in the pharmaceutical industry?"

She shook her head. "I don't really know."

"You don't know? She never said anything to you about why she wanted to meet men from the pharmaceutical industry?" If I elicited the answer I thought I might, it would be another statement against interest, and hopefully Shelly's answer wouldn't be stricken as hearsay.

"No. I don't know."

"Were you aware that Mr. Wells Armstrong was gay?"

She sighed. "Yes. I was aware of that. That was why he needed an escort. He had a wife but she was tired of pretending, so he needed girls to show up with him at these functions. This may be the 21st Century, but people still talk."

So she was lying to me before when she told me Shelly and Wells hit it off romantically. I wondered what else she had been lying about previously.

"So, it's safe to say Shelly and Wells had a relationship not based upon sex?"

"Yes, I guess so."

"What was their relationship based upon, then? To your understanding, what was Shelly and Wells' relationship based upon?"

Irina's back got a bit straighter. "It was my understanding Shelly's relationship with Wells was one of convenience. And information."

"Yes," I said. "Information. Wells was on the stand earlier, and he, too, intimated Shelly had information for him. And that he, in return, paid her handsomely. But what information was she trading with him?"

"How am I to know the answer to that question?"

"Because she told you. She must have told you. Is it your testimony Shelly was very specific about who she wanted to meet and you didn't ask her any questions about she had such specific tastes in men? You didn't ask her why she didn't want to meet bankers or tech CEOs or oil company execs or anybody like that? You weren't curious as to why she only was interested in men working in the pharmaceutical industry?"

She shook her head. "Daddy issues. She was working through daddy issues."

"Daddy issues," I said. "And what does that mean to you?"

"She was having issues with her father. She and her father were estranged. She was working through that."

"In what way was she working through that?"

"By finding men who were like her father. Getting to know them. That's all."

I shook my head. "No, that's not all. You just said Shelly and Wells had a relationship based upon information given and money received. That would imply there wasn't a psychological void being fulfilled, but, rather, there was something else bonding the two people together. And I think you know what that thing is."

Nick stood up. "Objection. Defense counsel is badgering his own witness."

"Sustained. Counselor, please either request to treat this witness as hostile or stay within the boundaries of direct questioning."

I nodded my head. "Permission to treat this witness as hostile," I said.

"Permission is granted," Judge Clarion said. "You may proceed."

"Now," I said to Irina. "Isn't it true you knew Shelly was not signing up with your escort service because she wanted to meet men for a sexual relationship?"

"No, that's not true. I didn't know that about her."

"Oh, but you did. You did. You knew Shelly was looking for men because she specifically wanted to provide information for them about her father and his business. Isn't that right?"

"No. That's not right."

It was all coming together. I now knew just where I wanted to go with this case. I suddenly knew I would have to go with a different theory of the case than the one I started with.

"I have nothing further for this witness," I said. I was suddenly anxious to get to my next witness, because I knew smy next witness would be the key to the case.

I was about to call Andrew McMason.

And I would break that bastard down.

TWENTY-SEVEN

I called Andrew McMason, and, when I got a look at him, I felt enraged. With his slicked-back hair, perfectly-tailored suit and smug look on his face, he reminded me of that rat-bastard John Gibson. While I didn't blame John Gibson for the break-down of my marriage – that was 100% on Sarah – I still associated Gibson with that painful part of my life. Gibson was a bastard and this guy looked like a bastard, too.

Of course he was a bastard. He was the one who was so prejudiced against Yasin Ahmadi that he cut his own daughter off for dating the guy. By all accounts, Yasin was a decent guy. He seemed that way on the stand, too. I still lightly suspected Yasin of being involved in Shelly's death, but the evidence, so far, was pointing away from him.

The witnesses who spoke to Garrett all said Yasin was an amazing person. Yet this rat-bastard only saw the fact that Yasin was brown and Muslim. That was apparently enough for him to cut off Shelly.

I took a deep breath as I approached Andrew. I always had to shake off my personal feelings in these cases. I needed to calmly and methodically take this guy apart. Bit by bit, piece by piece, he would end up mine.

He was sworn in and he calmly stated his name.

And the questioning began.

"Mr. McMason, I called you here to testify in this case. Are you aware of why I called you?"

"Because I'm Shelly's father. I was Shelly's father, that is."

"You were Shelly's father." I nodded my head. "Were. Shelly's father. You no longer consider yourself to be her father, then?"

"Of course not," he said, in clipped tones. "She's deceased. Therefore, I'm no longer her father."

I nodded. "See, most parents who have lost a child would still consider themselves to be that child's mother or father, so your answer doesn't ring true to me."

"Objection," Nick said. "Counsel is editorializing and I didn't hear a question."

"Sustained," Judge Clarion said, glaring at me. "You know better than that. Please limit your inquiries to questions and not statements."

"Withdrawn," I said. "And, Mr. McMason, when your daughter was alive, did you consider her to be your daughter? And did you consider yourself to be her father?"

"Of course," he said, his voice still clipped and short. "She was my daughter and I was her father. Of course."

"Oh? You mean, you didn't cut her off financially and emotionally because she was dating a Muslim man?"

He blinked, and his look unnerved me. He had light eyes, like Erik, but they were dead. There was nothing behind them. No warmth, no mirth, certainly no love. Just.dead. "No," he said. "I didn't."

I turned to the judge. "Permission to treat witness as hostile," I said.

"Sustained." Judge Clarion nodded his head. "Go ahead, counselor."

"I'll remind you you are under oath, and I'll remind you I have Yasin Ahmadi ready to go as a witness," I said to Andrew. I was prepared to re-call Yasin to the stand as a rebuttal witness if I had to. "So, you're saying it's not true you stopped speaking to your daughter two years ago because she was dating Yasin Ahmadi, and you cut her off financially around that same time?"

"No, that's not true."

I went over to my files. "I would like to show you what I've marked as Exhibit C," I said. "This is a copy of Shelly's Free Application for Federal Student Aid, commonly called FAFSA. It shows Shelly McMason applied for financial aid starting in her junior year in college, and she stated on this form that the reason why she required financial aid was because her parents cut her off financially. Do you see this form? Do you see Shelly signed it?"

Andrew examined the form. He had to have known he was caught in a lie, although his face didn't show as much. "Yes," he said. "That is my daughter's signature. But I didn't cut her off. She told me she didn't want financial assistance from me anymore. She wanted to pay for her own college. My daughter was an independent sort."

"Oh," I said, pacing. "So, you're saying your daughter wanted to go into debt to the government, as opposed to asking her billionaire father to finance her education. Is that what you are expecting the jury to believe?"

"Yes. That is how it happened."

"Mr. McMason, did you approve of your daughter dating Yasin Ahmadi?"

"No. I did not."

"And why didn't you approve of your daughter dating Yasin Ahmadi?"

"'Because I raised Shelly as a Christian and I expected my grandchildren would also be Christians."

"You mean you expected your grandchildren to be white, don't you?"

"There's nothing wrong with that," he said. "There's nothing wrong with wanting to keep one's bloodlines pure."

"And marrying a brown man, such as Yasin Ahmadi, would not only mean that your future grandchildren would be non-white, but they would also probably be raised Muslim. That wasn't acceptable, was it, Mr. McMason?"

"Again, I do not see anything wrong with that. I do not see anything wrong with wanting my grandchildren to be Christian."

"Christian and white," I said. "Don't forget that last part. It was very important to you that your grandchildren would be Christian and white."

"Yes." He nodded. "There is nothing wrong with wanting that."

"Oh, but you didn't just want that. You demanded that, didn't you? You demanded that from your daughter, and when she refused, you cut her off financially and emotionally. Isn't that what happened?"

He sat up straighter in his chair and apparently decided just to own his bigotry. "If your child does not accede to your wishes, then it is time to use every effort to force her to accede. So, yes, I told her she was to receive no more money from me as long as she persisted in her desires to marry Mr. Ahmadi. I have nothing against Mr. Ahmadi personally, you understand. I just did not want him in my family bloodline. That is all. Nothing more and nothing less."

"Oh, I see. So, you were lying earlier when you told the court you didn't cut Shelly off financially. Is that right?"

"No, I wasn't lying. I will admit, Shelly and I had words. But it was her choice to walk away from my largesse."

"You mean you told her she had to break up with Yasin or else you would cut her off. She refused to break up with Yasin, so that meant, in your eyes, she voluntarily walked away from your finances. Isn't that what you mean?"

"I guess so, yes."

"So if somebody kidnapped your child for ransom, and you

refused the ransom, and the kidnapper killed your child, it would be your fault for not paying the ransom. Is that what you're saying?"

"No, of course not."

"Then what is the difference, here? You tried to blackmail your child, she refused the blackmail, and you blamed her for refusing. How is that different than the kidnapper blaming you for refusing the ransom?"

"I guess it's not." He straightened up his spine and looked me square in the eyes. He would try to intimidate me, because he was a bully, but I wouldn't allow that.

I turned my back and looked at the jury while I asked my next question. I had a theory on what happened and I wanted to see what he said about it. "Mr. McMason, were you aware that your child, Shelly, was working with your rival, Wells Armstrong, and feeding him confidential information about your business?"

I turned back around and saw his face. His dead eyes were focused on me and he looked like he wanted to kill me. I was bluffing him but he didn't know that. He didn't know I didn't actually have any information backing up this question. If he lied, I couldn't prove it.

At the same time, I knew I was onto something. I knew Shelly was communicating with Wells and Wells was paying her richly because she had inside information about her father's business. She was a hacker, and it would have been not difficult, at all, for her to get into her father's confidential files. It wouldn't have been hard for her to give Wells confidential drug formulas, or information about Argyros' Pharmaceuticals' financials, or anything else. She was the ultimate corporate spy for Wells Armstrong.

I had a strong hunch about that and I also had a strong hunch that Andrew McMason was behind the downfall of Armstrong Pharmaceuticals. Armstrong Pharmaceuticals had seen its stock price crash because of the media fallout behind a drug failure, specifically the fact that some of its chemotherapy drugs were tainted with chemicals that made the drugs less effective. But what really did the company in was the media fallout. It was the screaming headlines, day after day, about the tainted chemo drugs. The newspaper made this look like a huge scandal, when, in all actuality, it was simply a mistake. I did my research on the chemotherapy "scandal" and it was caused by lax oversight by one of the regulators within the company. It could happen to any company, really, and nobody actually died from these tainted drugs. People who received these drugs just had to increase their dosage to get the same effectiveness as before.

Andrew McMason had clout with the newspaper. That was demonstrated with Lena Williams' testimony – she stated she sent Shelly on that dangerous assignment because Andrew McMason, Shelly's father, wanted her to. That also looked suspicious.

No, it didn't just look suspicious.

It looked like vengeance.

Andrew was still staring at me, still looking like he wanted to crush me like a particularly vile and loathsome bug. But he wasn't saying a word.

"I plead the Fifth," he finally said.

"Your honor, I would ask you to direct this witness to answer this question. Whether or not somebody else was working with his daughter to undermine his business will not self-incriminate him."

Wells had a reason to plead the Fifth on this particular question, because he was open to liability for corporate espionage. But Andrew would have been the victim in this scheme, not the perpetrator. I couldn't see where self-incrimination would lie in this particular scenario for Andrew.

"Counselor is correct," Judge Clarion said. "I fail to see how you being a victim of something like corporate espionage, not the perpetrator, would involve self-incrimination. Please answer the question."

He shifted uncomfortably in his seat. "Yes." That was all he said.

"Yes, you knew that your daughter was working with your chief rival, Wells Armstrong, to undermine you with confidential information she obtained about your business?"

"Yes. I knew that. I never gave her information about our business. She hacked into my business' database and stole highly valuable blueprints for some upcoming drugs we were going to submit to the FDA early next year. She gave him information about the chemical compounds, interactions and the uses for these drugs." He glared at me. "But I took care of that. I tamped that down."

"You took care of that," I said. "You mean, you manipulated the Kansas City *Star* into running article after article about an allegedly tainted chemotherapy drug that Armstrong Pharmaceutical was producing. Isn't that how you took care of Armstrong? You made sure that the stock tanked because the public was fooled into being afraid of taking their drugs, which, in turn, forced Wells out of his position? Isn't that how you deal with your rivals? By bullying them into submission?"

He crossed his arms in front of him. "That wasn't bullying, that was telling the truth. His company actually *was* producing tainted chemotherapy drugs, and I felt the public should know."

"The public should know? Mr. McMason, is your company, Argyros Pharmaceuticals, pristine?"

"Yes."

"You mean your company has never produced a drug that turned out to have harmful side-effects? Or a drug that had to be pulled from the market?" I knew the answer to that question. Argyros Pharmaceuticals had actually produced a drug several years back that had to be pulled from the market after it was discovered it caused cardiac arrest in many of the people who took it. It was supposed to be a cure for depression, but it caused death. Argyros was forced to recall the drug, but, since Argyros had an excellent crisis manager, they survived. The *Star* didn't run continuous front-page articles about this incident like they did for Armstrong, and that made all the difference.

"Yes," he said, his teeth gritted. "Of course, our company made some mistakes. Every company does. No company is perfect."

"Yet you made sure the one mistake that Armstrong made, and it wasn't all that serious of a mistake, was blown up in the media, didn't you? You got your revenge on Wells for undermining your company, for stealing your trade secrets, didn't you?"

"No. I had nothing to do with that."

"You didn't? Are you telling the court you didn't have a thing to do with the front page stories that ran about that tainted drug, day after day, in the *Star?*"

"That's right. I don't have influence like that."

"You don't? Then why did Lena Williams, a prominent editor for *The Star,* testify in court you had profound influence over the paper? She testified she sent your daughter on a dangerous assignment because you asked her to. Sounds like you have influence to me."

"I did ask Shelly take that assignment, but that doesn't mean I have editorial influence over at the paper."

"Oh, so you did ask Lena to make sure Shelly took a dangerous assignment. With a dangerous clan. Isn't it true you specifically asked for that because you wanted there to be a fall guy for when you killed Shelly?"

He narrowed his eyes and crossed his arms. "I resent your insinuation I would do that to my own daughter."

"Oh, so it's a coincidence Shelly was killed, and my client, Erik Gregorian, was charged with her murder? You arranged for Shelly to work for Erik because you wanted Erik to take the fall for killing her. That's pretty brilliant chess-playing right there, but it wasn't brilliant enough, was it?"

"I didn't kill her."

"Mr. McMason, what did Shelly call you?"

"Dad or father."

"She didn't call you Andrew? I'll remind you you are under oath, and I have witnesses lined up who were around the two of you."

He looked out the window and then looked back at me, daggers in his eyes. "Yes. She called me Andrew."

"Yet she called her mother, Emma, 'Mom,' isn't that right?"

"She was closer with her mother than she was with me."

"Wasn't she closer to her mother because her mother never judged her?"

"Emma was always too lenient with our daughter. That was why she grew up as spoiled as she was."

"By lenient you mean your wife allowed Shelly to love who she wanted to love, right?"

"Yes. Emma approved of Yasin. I didn't. I told you why and I feel I had a good reason to stop that relationship."

"And leniency also meant that Emma didn't actually want to have Shelly killed, isn't that right?"

"Of course she didn't want to have Shelly killed." He shook his head. "Emma loved our daughter, as did I."

"Did you know Shelly was pregnant with a baby? It was either the child of Yasin Ahmadi, or possibly my client Erik, but, either way, that baby would be half-brown and had a fifty-fifty chance of being the child of a Muslim. I'll bet that really chapped your hide, didn't it? Didn't it?"

He looked away again and I knew he knew all about the baby. And I suddenly knew the real reason why Shelly got an abortion. "Yes, I knew she was pregnant with a filthy child," he spat.

I had to suppress a smile. He was becoming unhinged as white supremacists often do. They can only hide behind their "purity" excuse for so long until they have to come right out and say what's on their minds.

"And you actually forced her to have an abortion, didn't you? You beat her up and you forced her to kill her own child, didn't you? Didn't you?"

"She wouldn't soil our bloodline with a child that belonged to either Yasin or Erik." He crossed his arms in front of him. "Again, you wouldn't understand, but the McMason blood line has been pure all the way down the line. It will remain that way."

"You know, that's funny," I said. "Your name is McMason. That's Irish, isn't it?"

"Yes. Yes, it is."

"Do you know that, around the turn of the last century, the Irish were considered filthy?"

"Objection," Nick said. "I fail to see the relevance of this particular question."

"Withdrawn," I said. "I have nothing further for this filthy witness." I glared at him and sat down.

I looked at the judge, who was shaking his head at my "filthy" comment, but he didn't move to sanction me. Something told me he found Mr. McMason just as abhorrent as I did.

I was quite sure the jury felt the same way. I could see it in their faces. They were disgusted with this man. And they knew he was more than capable of murdering his own daughter.

I did my job.

TWENTY-EIGHT

I called several more witnesses, none of whom as consequential as Andrew McMason.

Then it was finally time for closing arguments.

Nick went first.

"Ladies and gentlemen of the jury," he began. "You heard the evidence in this case. You heard it. Now, I'll admit the attorneys for the defendant did an excellent job of putting up smokescreens. That's what defense attorneys do. They muddy the water with this suspect or that, so you, the jury, do not know what to believe. Who to believe. Well, I'm here to tell you you have to believe one thing, and that is that Erik Gregorian murdered Shelly McMason in cold blood. In cold blood."

"Now, you heard the evidence. You heard it. You heard that not only was Shelly about to uncover the evil doings of his organization, the Gregorian clan, which is a part of a larger organization out in Los Angeles called the Armenian Power, but that Erik was in love with Shelly and she did not return his affection. She was in love with Yasin Ahmadi, not Erik Gregorian, and Mr. Gregorian couldn't stand that. He couldn't stand that. That alone would give him motive to kill

Shelly, but when he found out she was about to expose him and his men to public scrutiny..." He shook his head. "That meant it was time to get Shelly out of the way. It was time to make sure she was permanently silenced. Because one thing is for sure – if she would have lived to publish the stories she was working on about the clan, public outcry would have necessitated that the clan would have to be stopped in any way possible. Any way possible."

He paced around. "Now, the defense counsel would have you believe that maybe Wells Armstrong killed Shelly because who knows why, or perhaps Yasin might have killed her when he found out Shelly was seeing Wells Armstrong and Erik Gregorian behind his back. Or, God forbid, Andrew McMason would kill his own daughter. His own daughter, ladies and gentlemen. His own flesh and blood. He gave Shelly life, and defense counsel would like for you to believe that he would take it away. Now, I know Mr. McMason wasn't the most attractive soul in the world. He wouldn't win father of the year. Yes, you could even say he is a white supremacist. I know that's what you're thinking, so I'll just say it for you. Andrew McMason wouldn't win father of the year, and he wouldn't win man of the year, either. He's distasteful and disrespectful and is not anybody's idea of a good person."

"But a killer? Seriously? Just because the man doesn't like people who aren't members of his own race doesn't mean he's a killer. And it certainly doesn't mean he would kill his own flesh and blood."

"As for the other men who might have been suspects in Ms. McMason's murder, according to the defense counsel, they are even more implausible than Mr. McMason. Wells Armstrong held no animus for Shelly, nor did he have a reason to kill her. He had a business relationship with her, nothing more and nothing less. And Yasin Ahmadi loved Shelly. You saw him on the stand. He was a broken man about Shelly's death. A broken man." Nick shook his head. "He didn't kill her."

"No, ladies and gentlemen, the killer is sitting right here in this courtroom. His name is Erik Gregorian, and he had not one but two reasons to kill Shelly McMason. I urge you to find Mr. Gregorian guilty of murder in the first degree. Thank you very much for your time and service." He put his fingers to his lips. "Justice for Shelly. Justice for Shelly."

And he sat down.

I stood up and approached the jury. "Ladies and gentlemen, I'm not going to bore you with a long recitation of what the evidence in this trial showed. You saw the witnesses with your own eyes. You did. Yes, my client isn't an angel. He is the head of an organization that is less than legal and less than ethical. You know that. But I'll tell you one thing – the prosecutor in this case has the burden of proof. The burden of proof was on him to show you that my client killed Shelly. And he didn't meet that burden in any way, shape or form."

"Think about it. He didn't produce any eyewitness to say my client wanted Shelly dead. There were no fingerprints on the brake line in Shelly's car. He did produce a guy who said Shelly and my client fought a lot, but who doesn't fight? Seriously. Their fights weren't physical, nobody got hurt and Erik never openly threatened Shelly. So what? They fought." I shrugged. "So what?"

"Now, I will admit Shelly was about to run an exposé in the newspaper about what she found out about Erik's clan. But you heard the testimony of Lena. That expose will still run in the paper. It's running in the spring. So Erik literally had nothing to gain by killing Shelly. The damage was done, so to speak. She had her notes and the story will go ahead as planned. So, if you think about it, my client didn't have a real motive to kill Shelly."

"Now, Andrew McMason...." I shook my head. "He's another story, ladies and gentlemen. He had ample reason to want Shelly dead. Number one, she apparently had a taste for the wrong kinds of people. At least, in his book. By that, I mean Shelly liked members of a different race. Her fiancé, Yasin Ahmadi, is an Iraqi man, the son of Iraqi refugees, and Muslim. He's modern and you met him on the stand. A very upstanding man. Studying to be a doctor. Handsome, mannerly, intelligent and loved Shelly. Yet, he is not the right color for Mr. McMason and not the right religion. Then there is my client."

I gestured to Erik. "As you can see, he's also not the right color for Mr. McMason. His skin is also too dark. He's not Muslim, but he's not exactly Caucasian, and his last name is too foreign. So, as far as Andrew McMason is concerned, Shelly was 0-2 in the man department. And she was determined to one day marry Yasin. That would never do in Andrew's world. No, Shelly must never marry a man like Yasin. She must never soil his bloodline like that. You heard him. He referred to Shelly's unborn child as 'filthy.' Filthy. That's the word Hitler used to describe the Jews. Filthy. Filthy."

"So, yes, ladies and gentlemen. Shelly was going to marry a man who would father, with Shelly, a half-brown baby who would no-doubt be raised Muslim. Andrew McMason's worst nightmare. There's motive number one for killing Shelly. Motive number two? Shelly was conducting corporate espionage on Andrew's company, in favor of his rival, Armstrong Pharmaceuticals. That made her danger-ous. She was a hacker which meant she had access to Argyros' data-base. That also meant she had access to all of Argyros' trade secrets. She was selling these secrets to Wells Armstrong, but this might have just been the beginning. Wells Armstrong was possibly just the first person who Shelly was willing to deal with in an effort to undermine her hated father's company. She was very dangerous to Argyros' bottom line. Extremely dangerous."

"So, you have a daughter who is a hacker willing to use those hacking skills to undermine her father's business. Who knows? She might have eventually brought her father's business down with her hacking skills. That's what hackers do. They target companies and steal their secrets and put worms in their computers and do all kinds of nefarious things. If they don't like you, you better watch out. Shelly didn't like Argyros. She didn't like that company because she absolutely hated the CEO. Her father forced her to have an abortion and tried to force her to stop seeing Yasin. She hated her father and would do whatever it took to bring him down. And he wouldn't let her do that. So, he killed her. Simple as that."

I clapped my hands together, as if I was getting rid of something vile. "Simple as that. Two birds, one stone. Shelly no longer has the ability to undermine Argyros and she no longer has the ability to produce a brown baby. A filthy brown baby who would soil the McMason bloodline." My voice was dripping with sarcasm. I nodded. "The prosecutor would have you believe that my client killed Shelly. That he had the most motive to have done it. But I submit to you that the only one who had motive to kill Shelly was her father. Andrew McMason. He had motive to kill Shelly and he is the one who did it."

"Therefore, you must acquit. There's enough reasonable doubt to drive a truck through. Seriously. There's not just reasonable doubt here, there's no proof that my client did anything wrong. No proof at all, except for the weakest of circumstantial evidence. And you know the law. You cannot convict on conjecture and circumstantial evidence. You must have proof beyond a reasonable doubt. The prosecutor didn't supply that. It's that simple. You must acquit."

I bowed my head. "Thank you very much."

At that, I sat down. The judge gave the jury instructions, and they filed out.

And the waiting began.

Although I had the feeling we wouldn't be waiting long.

TWO HOURS LATER, I knew that my hunch was correct.

The jury was back with a verdict.

"Has the jury reached its verdict?" Judge Clarion asked.

"We have, your honor."

"Would the defendant please rise?"

I stood up with Erik next to me, and Harper on the other side of Erik.

"In the case of State v. Erik Gregorian, on the charge of murder in the first degree, how does the jury find?"

"The jury finds the defendant not guilty, your honor," the foreman said.

"Is this the unanimous verdict of the jury?"

"It is, your honor."

Judge Clarion nodded his head. "The defendant is free to go. Thank you for your service. You perform perhaps the most valuable service in the judicial system. I understand your sacrifice, and I am humbled by it."

At that, the jury started to file back out of the courtroom.

I glanced over at Ally, who was smiling at me. She came over.

"Looks like I'm buying," she said.

"Let's go out tomorrow. Tonight, I have to get my daughter out of the hospital." I shook my head when I saw Ally's concerned look. "Don't ask." I looked over at Harper, gathering her things. I put my hand on her arm. "Looks like you will live another day. And so will your girls."

"I know. I didn't think Sargis would have made good on his threats after all. I don't know. He and I have a weird connection." She shook her head rapidly. "And I somehow think I haven't heard the last of him. But I guess I'm happy Erik was acquitted. It's bittersweet, though, knowing you got our scum client off of one charge but you know he'll catch another case in a month or two. Maybe even sooner."

"Ah, but them's the breaks. We just deal with the case in front of us. That's what we do. Anyhow, Ally and I will get a much-needed libation tomorrow evening. You want to come with?"

"And horn in on a first date?" Harper said with a snort. "I wouldn't think of it, but thanks."

"It's not a date," I protested. "We made a bet."

Harper laughed. "Okay." Then she whispered. "I've seen the way that girl looks at you. Talk about undressing you with her eyes."

I shook my head. "I'll see you tomorrow in the office."

At that, Harper and I walked out of the courtroom.

We didn't say a single word to Erik before we left.

ALLY and I had a great time on our date, and we made plans to do it again. She was a lot of fun, and we spent the entire evening catching up on each other's lives and having a lot of laughs. It had been so long since I laughed, I had forgotten what it felt like.

Things were coming together in my life. Finally.

And professionally, things were also going well.

I picked up a new murder case and it would be a doozy. The accused's name was Gina DeGrazio, and she was accused of murdering her husband, Vittorio DeGrazio. Vittorio was a notorious mobster perennially standing accused of every crime in the book.

"I didn't do it," she said, in a voice heavily tinged in a Brooklyn accent. "I was busy fucking his brother Enzo at the time that rat was choking on his own last stinking breaths." She shook her head. "Vittorio deserved so much worse than what he got."

"I'm sorry? What does that mean?"

"That means that bastard died good and easy. Not painful and hard like he should have died."

"I take it you and Mr. DeGrazio were in love and in a good marriage," I said sarcastically as I made notes.

She snorted. "What do you think? I would have burned him alive in a car if I had my way. That's how you know I didn't do it."

I had to smile.

This would be an interesting case.

WANT to find out what happens next? Pick up *The Alibi* today! https://amzn.to/3ykjnZL

The Alibi:

The wife of a gangster is accused of offing him. Damien soon finds that nobody is who they seem - quite

literally. But to defend his client, he must break every ethical rule.

Damien Harrington is fresh off his come from behind victory when he's thrust into yet another harrowing scenario. Gina Degrazio, wife to Vittorio Degrazio, notorious gangster, stands accused of Vittorio's murder. Gina's a tough-talking native New Yorker transplanted to Kansas City. She swears she didn't do it. She was with her boyfriend, Enzo Degrazio, Vittorio's twin brother, at the time of the murder. Or so she says. However, bit by bit, her story falls apart. Damien doubts that Gina was anywhere near Enzo at the time of the murder, yet he must use that alibi excuse if he is to win Gina's case.

In the meantime, Damien and Harper together work several wrongful death suits that were the result of toxic mold in various homes on the East Side. The plaintiffs are all poor and minority, the landlords are all slumlords and scummy, and Damien works these cases with a passion that he has not felt for the law in many years.

With all the hairpin curves and twists you've come to expect from a Rachel Sinclair legal thriller, this first installment featuring Damien Harrington in the lead is not to be missed! https://amzn.to/3ykjnZL

FOR INFORMATION **about upcoming titles in the *Harper Ross Legal Thriller* series, sign up for my mailing list!** You'll be the first to know about new releases and you'll be the first to know about any promotions!!!! https://mailchi.mp/2e2dda532e99/rachel-sinclair-legal-thrillers

9 798223 561644